*UN*PLANNED PARTY

MEL A ROWE

Also by MEL A ROWE

Winter's Walk

The Football Whisperer

Avoiding the Pity Party

Unplanned Party

The Australian Bestselling

ELSIE CREEK SERIES:

The ART of DUST

DIAMOND in the DUST

CAKED in DUST

XMAS DUST

Visit MelAROWE.com for more

Copyright

***Caveat: As a courtesy, there may be some sparse language choices in this story that may represent an obstacle for the reader and I am offering this warning. Please note this language is purely for fictional purposes only and not designed to offend any individual persons, culture, or religions implied.*

The Following Is Written In Australian English

For those who have ever had a planned birthday party that just … sucked.

ONE

Happy Birthday—*not.*

Emma slammed her van door shut and sighed at her silhouette darkening its white panel. She was reminded of Fiona from Shrek—the ogre Fiona, and nothing like the birthday girl she was supposed to be. She'd rather be back in bed ignoring the whole damned day. But couldn't. With her mother's shiny red sports car parked beside her, she was well aware her family and friends were waiting for her.

'Delivery vans park in the laneway, it's easier to unload back there,' called out the man, exhaling cigarette smoke as he strolled along the pathway from the beach side of the small cove.

Typical, still being treated like staff. 'Sorry, I'm not delivering today. I'm here for lunch at Neptune's.'

'Oh, my bad. Just saw the van.'

How could anyone miss her work-van? It was big and white with *Parte'* written in pink champagne bubbles spilling from a bottle. It stood out like a clown parked amongst the luxury cars, while their equally sleek owners indulged in Sunday lunch.

'Hey, I've heard of your business. You did the Mad Hatter's dinner party for my sister-in-law. It was brilliant.'

'Thanks, it's a popular theme.' Emma smiled, she loved theme parties. She used to love that one too, but it had been overused by the masses like a song saturated on the radio. Kind of like her kettle, still hanging on for grim life, straining to boil her that perfect cup of coffee in the morning.

'I'm Neptune's owner. Please, allow me to walk you over.' He ditched his smoke in the bushes and popped a mint.

'Sure.' She recognised the look. *Here comes the pitch, to push a party his way.* Emma didn't mind, she loved her job and was always searching for the perfect party venue.

Sneaking in through the kitchen with the manager, she listened to his pitch as he made her a complimentary drink at the bar. The packed restaurant had a glistening view of calm azure seas to one side, with assorted luxury yachts moored on the other. It was a gloriously warm day outside, yet she was inside, talking shop, staring out at a million-dollar view.

She frowned, spying her older sister, Helen, seated beside their mother, Irene, at a table across the room. Her friend, Victoria, sat opposite, wearing dark sunglasses, with her hair styled between an up-do and her I-just-got-out-of-bed look that she still made chic. Beside Victoria was Emma's immaculately dressed assistant, Benjamin.

Emma narrowed her eyes at the table, it held a neat posy nestled amongst the cutlery and glasses set for service. There were no garish presents wrapped in ribbons. No streamers. No party hats. Nothing to show it was her birthday lunch. *Thank God.*

She eyed the exit to her *Parte'* van which had an even better view of the beach. Could she run away with her van and not face her own party?

Emma sighed, and with drink in hand, she made her way through the restaurant towards her table, praying they didn't sing and pop confetti bombs in her face.

She approached the table as their voices greeted her, and she politely waited for them to notice her. She was well-trained to never interrupt guests.

'I hope Emma hasn't forgotten,' said Victoria, pushing up her dark sunglasses and sipping on a Bloody Mary.

'No,' said Benjamin. 'I reminded Emma last night when she dropped me home. Even though she kept saying, *don't remind me, don't remind me.* I reminded her.'

'Emma has always hated her birthdays,' said Irene.

'How come?' Benjamin asked.

'When Emma started school, we threw her a party,' said Irene. 'Silly me, I'd accidentally written the wrong date on the invitations so no one came. Emma never wanted another party after that.'

'And now the babe makes a living throwing fabulous parties,' said Victoria.

'I love my birthday. I throw a big party every year and tell people what presents I want. Which reminds me, no one got any gifts involving a gym membership, or some gym equipment-workout-thingy, did we?' Benjamin arched his eyebrow, waiting for their responses.

'God no.' They shook their heads.

Irene tucked her sleek silver bob behind her ear. 'Good, otherwise Emma will think we're all picking on her.'

Trying to catch the light on her ring, Helen tilted her head so far over, her gold dangle-earring rested on her shoulder. 'Well, we are talking about the butterball.'

'Don't say that about your sister,' said Irene, frowning at

Helen beside her.

'It's true. The other day I was finishing my scrapbooking project about me as a child, and in every photo, there's Emma as this big, blobby butterball.'

'Emma hasn't been gifted with the figure we have. She's your grandmother all over.'

'Figure-shmigure. If Emma didn't shove a chocolate bar in her mouth or swig on a beer all the time, she'd never have a problem. You know, Emma was always eating, she never played sport or went anywhere. She'd just sit there, eating Mum's butter biscuits, doing all her craft-crap in the kitchen,' said Helen, talking to the rock on her finger.

Benjamin and Victoria rolled eyes at each other and snatched up their drinks. 'Emma,' they chorused.

Damn. She'd been busted trying to escape. After overhearing that crap, she wanted to be as far away from them as possible. Had she blended in so much like a staff member that no one had noticed her sooner?

Emma took a deep breath—it was time to sprinkle some glitter onto her freak flag and smile.

'Hi, everyone.' Emma kissed her mother's cheek. She then air-kissed Helen, leaving enough room for a drone to do cartwheels in the space between them. Benjamin bounced to his feet and hugged her. Then, taking her seat, Emma draped an arm around her best friend's shoulders, inhaling Victoria's signature fragrance, Chanel No 5. 'Hello, beautiful.'

Victoria peeked over the rim of her sunglasses and crinkled up her nose. 'And that's why you're my friend.'

'Hungover?' Emma asked Victoria, resembling Holly

Golightly in a Breakfast at Tiffany's re-make.

Victoria raised her spiked tomato juice in one hand and her unlit cigarette in the other. 'Not anymore. Glad you could make it, babe. Otherwise, I was about to discover what a Bloody Mary could do for your sister's complexion.'

'Why waste a fine spirit on the soulless?' Emma mumbled to herself. 'Are you ready for your tour of South America, Mum?'

'Why can't I go on a holiday with my toy-boy paying for it all?' Whined Benjamin.

'Because your perfect partner is a man who's too busy keeping politicians in line to take a holiday this time of year,' said Emma. 'Do you need me to water your plants while you're away, Mum?'

Her mother nodded. 'Yes, please. You can stay there, you know?'

'And give up my luxurious getaway in the treetops?'

'You live in a shed,' spat out Helen with her nose screwed up.

'It's a classy shed,' Benjamin said with raised chin.

'Must be, for Benjamin to grace the peasants with his presence,' said Emma.

Benjamin wagged the tip of his finger at Emma like it was a dancing worm. 'See—did I ever tell you I have the best job, working for the best boss in the world!'

'You know I pay you to say that, right?'

'You don't work,' scoffed Helen, inspecting the prawn poised on the end of her fork.

'Don't.' Emma patted Victoria's hand to reduce her

friend's bitchy comeback to a mutter.

'Waiter, I need another one.' Victoria held up her near-empty glass and turned to Emma. 'Are you drinking?'

'No, I'm driving, and I promise to not throw any wild parties while you're away, Mum.'

'Talking about holiday preparations,' said Irene, 'I had my first Brazilian the other day and now Mitchell won't leave me alone.'

'MUM.' Helen cringed, and Emma slapped her palms over her ears.

'Look.' Helen displayed her perfectly manicured finger bearing a shiny ruby and diamond ring. 'My darling husband gave me an eternity ring. Isn't William adorable.'

'Haven't you already got an eternity ring?' Emma remembered, because Helen had shoved it under Emma's nose every chance she got.

'I can have more than one, can't I?' Helen arched a perfectly plucked eyebrow. 'Jealous much?'

'It's nice.' Emma tried to smile, instead she sneered at the glamorous, stay-at-home mother, whose job was to get in your way in the supermarket whenever you were in a rush. Not in suburbia, but in millionaire-alley. Helen's rug in the laundry was worth more than Emma's *Parte'* van.

Helen made Cinderella's stepsisters look positively angelic.

'*Uh, I forgot*—I've got a new ring too.' Victoria held out her left hand that displayed a large diamond solitaire.

'You're engaged!' Emma squealed, and the other diners stopped and stared.

'Ooh, lemme see,' said Benjamin, eyeing the ring.

'No, let me.' Helen reached across the table.

'Ow. Helen, the ring is attached to my hand that's attached to my arm, you know.'

'Wait, for it. I'm sure she was a jeweller in a past life,' said Emma, grinning at Benjamin over Victoria's back.

Helen crouched in for a close-up of the ring. 'Great cut, clarity, setting. It's a keeper.'

'I'm wearing it, aren't I?' Victoria tugged her hand free and resumed her seat.

'Have you decided on a wedding theme or anything?' Benjamin asked. 'Simon and I are still working out ours. I want over the top, yet Simon wants conservative, so some of his co-workers can attend.'

'Why would you want a politician to go to your wedding?' Victoria asked.

Benjamin rolled his eyes as he smoothed over his brown hair. 'For the gifts, duh.'

Emma grinned at him. 'Are you going to dress as Tina? You've got the legs for it.'

'No.' Benjamin sighed as his shoulders sagged like a deflating balloon. 'My days of drag-queening-cabaret are over. I'm practically a married man.'

'I'll never get married again,' Irene said.

'I'm happily married, thank you,' said Helen, polishing her new ring on the napkin.

'I'm...'—*the only single person sitting at the table.* Emma snatched up her water and drank it dry. What she really wanted to do, was slink low into her chair and disappear under the table.

'Well I'm not married, yet. I haven't thought about the wedding or anything, except ...' Victoria sat straighter and pointed her unlit cigarette at Emma. 'Babe, I'm locking you in to do my hen's night. I'm thinking boat, booze, and boys.'

'Oh yeah, we're on board for that.' Emma grinned, the ideas already starting to formulate.

'What about the wedding?' Helen asked.

'Oh, yeah, that too. I'd love your help with the wedding,' said Victoria, taking a drag of her unlit cigarette.

'Emma doesn't do weddings,' said Benjamin.

Emma refused to look at her family as she said, 'Brides, and dealing with the mother of the bride, it's all too emotional. I deal in fun, not horror-movie-memories.'

Helen cleared her throat, turning away from her mother. Irene wiped the tip of her nose, refolded her napkin, and clasped her hands on the table. Neither of them looked at Emma.

'But...' Victoria pouted.

'I do love hen's nights. We'll get your name in the paper for that one, shall we?' Emma winked at Benjamin who'd leaned forward nodding. She loved her ever-eager party-hard offsider who was perfect in their party planning world.

'When is the wedding?' Helen asked.

Victoria plonked her elbow on the table, and lowered her sunglasses. 'Listen, Helen, does being a fake-blonde interfere with your hearing? I just said, we only got engaged last night.'

'How did Paul propose?' Emma asked.

'Babe, I'm so-so sorry I didn't call you and blab all, but...' Victoria paused to puff on her unlit cigarette. 'I got home, annoyed about working on a Saturday, while Paul's laid out on the couch watching football, with a beer in hand, and his crap everywhere. It's his one annoying habit. He'll come home, take off his tie and jacket and throw them over the dining-chairs. By the end of the week they're everywhere. I refuse to put them away now, and they build up until he has none left in the closet and starts using the lounge as his dressing room.' Victoria paused again to sip her cocktail.

'And?' Benjamin asked with wide eyes.

As the Queen of her own court, Victoria put down her glass and her lips curled into a sly smile. 'That's when I lost it. I grabbed all the clothes he'd left lying around and dumped them all over him. He was lying on the couch laughing at me from beneath this pile of clothes, when this jewellery box fell out of his suit jacket and onto the floor. So Paul, still lying on the couch, picks up the box and asks me if I wanted to lower my standards to his depth, and join him in a low-life partnership—'

'No candlelight dinner?' Helen asked with her face screwed up. 'No flowers? No fancy proposal?'

'Paul was planning to take me out to dinner, but I didn't want to go out. I've been out every night this week for work.'

Helen winced even more as if sucking her way through a thousand lemons. 'How rude! Where's the effort?'

'He didn't need to,' replied Victoria. 'If Paul puts up with me and my many over-demanding moods, I can put up with his lazy habit of not putting his clothes away. Why not make it official and claim my right to the title of nagging wife?'

'He called you a nagging wife?' screeched Helen, who'd forgotten to add the sweet to the sourness in her expression.

'All the time, and long before Paul moved in four years

ago. But he did get on one knee, considering he was halfway there already, and proposed as colourfully as a word-playing journalist can. Then we made our own special night…if you get my drift.' Victoria grinned from behind her cocktail glass.

'So, you humped like rabbits on the couch,' Irene said. 'I like couch sex. Although, give me a good rocking recliner any day.'

'MUM!' Helen and Emma cried out.

The waitress collected their dishes, scraping assorted shells into one bowl as she made her way around the table. With shaky hands, she balanced the finger bowls onto the mountain of discarded seafood.

'We'll have our dessert now,' Irene said to the waitress.

'Certainly.' The waitress leaned forward to collect Emma's plate, when a customer bumped her from behind. '*Oh no*,' she cried out as the large bowl full of assorted seafood shells, fishy finger-water, prawn heads, oyster shells, squeezed lemon rinds, and parsley garnish fell all over Emma.

'*Shiiit!*' Emma sat frigidly still as cold liquid trickled through her scalp, dribbled down her neck and back, with the large metal bowl landing in her lap—*empty*.

Liquid oozed into her cleavage. In front of her face, tangled prawn heads swung from her hair. Limp parsley hung off her ears, and a wedge of lemon landed in her cleavage. Her lap resembled the leftovers of a buffet table used as ammunition after a food fight.

'I'm so sorry. I'm so-so sorry,' sobbed the waitress, picking off oyster shells clinging to Emma's shoulders.

'DON'T—*touch me!*' Emma clenched her teeth, in fear of

thumping the waitress. She didn't want to breakdown before a live studio audience where all eyes were on her. Many gasped in shock, mirrored by her mother. Others were as horrified as Benjamin and Victoria in their silent-horror-movie poses. While some were on the verge of laughter, led by Helen—of course.

But Emma never made a fuss. Ever.

'Excuse me.' She stood up, creating a tsunami slide of prawn juice, fish scales, and crab shells that spilled across the floor. With wet dress held outwards and pink prawn heads swinging from her hair, Emma walked past the room full of people. Refusing to cry, she cast her eyes downwards and raced for the loo like an over-garnished sea-hag.

At the row of sinks, Emma rinsed herself off. The harsh lighting only highlighted her mess in the wall of mirrors.

The door swung back hard against the tiled wall as Victoria stormed inside. 'That waitress should be fired.'

'It was an accident,' Emma said, tossing more paper-towel into the bin. 'I'm not having someone fired over this. Not over me.'

'But it's your birthday and look at what she's done.'

'I'll live.' Was misery missing her company today? *Oh, wait, did rock-bottom leave a message too?*

'The Manager is giving you a free meal for the future.'

'I'm not coming back here in a hurry.' Facing the mirror, Emma wiped off her makeup, exposing her pale skin that highlighted her washed-out mop of hair. Her dull, over-sized eyes stared back, as she chewed on her fat bottom lip. She hated her birthday. 'I'm going home to shower before I start attracting flies. Tell everyone I'll catch up later.' Emma headed for the nearest exit as Victoria followed.

'But we have cake and presents.'

'Save it for next year.' *Or never.*

'I'll call you later?'

'Sure.' Emma paused at the front doors. 'Hey honey, congratulations on your engagement. Give Paul a hug for me too.'

'I will.' Victoria shared a sulky pout and limp wristed wave.

Emma tried to act as dignified as possible, pretending it was perfectly normal to walk down the road with wet-patches in her hair and clothes on a sunny Sunday afternoon.

She rummaged in her bag for her car keys as she approached her parking spot.

Instead, she stood in a vacant space turning full circle.

It wasn't a tow away zone, and her mother's sports car was still in the same spot.

'Where's my van?'

In the Marina's car park, there was an assortment of luxury cars, motorbikes, SUV's, and four-wheel drives that suited the yachts moored behind them. But no white work-van.

'Sweetie, why are you still here?' Benjamin called out, bouncing beside Irene.

'I think my van's been stolen?' Emma held her keys in hand ready to unlock the door.

'Oh, snap. I'll call the police.' Benjamin, being the ever-efficient offsider, whipped out his mobile phone.

'It isn't your day, is it, honey,' said Irene.

'Mum, it's meant to be my birthday. *The day.*' But it was

all turning to crap. Okay, her kettle didn't die this morning, which was a bonus. But it was still a crappy day. She was covered in sticky prawn grit that smelled, and as an added bonus, she was starting to itch. 'Am I allergic to seafood today? Because I don't think this new oceanic perfume is agreeing with my skin.'

'Who would want to steal a van?' Irene asked.

'Who knows,' replied Benjamin, 'but the police are on their way.'

'So much for my fast getaway.' Emma spied the wine bottle in Benjamin's hand and reached for it. 'Thanks. I'll take that drink, now I'm not driving anymore.' She sat on the curb at the end of the vacant car lot where her van had once stood, cracked open the bottle, and took a deep drink of the white wine. No glass, no savouring, and no pinkie in the air, but at least it was cold, wet, and alcoholic.

'You can't sit there and drink,' scoffed Irene.

'Unless you've got glasses in the car, Mum, I believe I have the right to celebrate my birthday any way I please. Want some?' Emma held out the bottle.

Irene shook her head. 'I'm driving.'

'I'll indulge. Who knows how long it'll be before the police arrive?' Benjamin bounced to sit beside Emma on the gutter. He took a sip from the bottle, then wiped his mouth with the back of his hand. 'Hey, does this make us a couple of winos?'

'Gutter tramps, maybe?' Emma and Benjamin snickered at each other.

'What are you doing?' Helen's jaw dropped as she raised her sunglasses with Victoria standing beside her.

'Am I missing something?' Victoria waved her unlit cigarette at them like a wand.

'Emma's van's been stolen, and we're commiserating,' said Benjamin.

'No, I'm celebrating *and* commiserating.' Emma took another mouthful of wine. 'Keep frowning like that, Sis, and you'll get lines on your forehead that even Botox won't fix.'

'Well, you can't have a *carpark party* without presents. Here's mine.' Victoria exchanged a red envelope for Emma's wine bottle and sat beside her on the kerb.

'I didn't want gifts, just lunch—that I'm wearing.' Emma giggled, it was either laugh or cry.

Emma opened her card that held a voucher to a beauty parlour. 'Thanks Victoria, but, unless you want to smell like Neptune's after-party, don't get offended if I don't hug you.'

'Here's mine.' Benjamin handed her the same coloured red envelope. It was another voucher from the same beauty salon for a manicure and pedicure.

'Nice.' Emma grinned.

'My turn.' Irene's red card was for a facial, and Helen's was for a haircut.

'Wow, thanks, everyone, I love it. At this point,'—Emma glanced at her ruined dress—'I could do with a full makeover.'

'Don't I know it. Right, I'm going home now. Bye.' Without a backward glance and with head held high, Helen toddled off in her heels.

'I'll go fetch more wine,' said Benjamin as he crossed the road.

'Ask if they'll share some glasses,' called out Irene.

'Don't bother, it's a gutter party,' said Emma. 'Brown paper bags are optional.'

Victoria swallowed another swig of wine. 'Sorry about your birthday, babe.'

'Hey, it's not all bad. I get to have that drink with you.'

'True. Mind you, it's usually done the other way around. First you get drunk, then you sit in the gutter. Preferably not in daylight.'

'You should get out more.' Emma grinned, sharing the bottle between them. They were the only people outside enjoying the water views, even if it was from the car park.

'Police are here,' called out Benjamin, carrying another bottle of wine while waving at the police car. 'I hope they're cute. Gotta love a man in uniform.'

The police car parked before the vacant spot Emma's van had once occupied. Two uniformed men got out and spoke with Benjamin and Irene.

'He's cute,' said Victoria, passing the bottle to Emma.

'Which one?' Emma asked, taking a mouthful of wine.

'The one with the stripes on his shoulders.'

'The one frowning at me?'

'Miss Toplin?' The officer approached, removing his sunglasses.

'Emma, please.' She arched her neck right back, he was so tall, and Victoria was right, he was handsome. *Ugh* — rephrase — *he was smoking.* His short brown hair resembled the mixed shades of toasted malts of an Indian Pale Ale through to the Imperial Stout. It matched the stony stare of his chartreuse eyes, a liquor the French monks perfected, now worn by the man of her sinful thoughts.

Her heart pounded. Her tongue was too big for her mouth, and she cupped her jaw to stop drooling, all while staring up at the god of her gutter party. 'Who are you?' *Adonis?*

'Officer Ryan Lewis. There's a law against drinking in public without a permit.'

Emma knew all about those permits and carried heaps of them in her van. Now stolen. 'Fine, give me a ticket. It'll totally top my day off.' *At least the view had improved.*

'Care to confirm the make and model of your stolen van? And I'd like to see your driver's licence.'

'It's a white van that has two front seats and a steering wheel, along with an exceptionally high-quality stereo inside. Sorry, I know nothing about cars, except to drive—when it's here to drive.' Emma grabbed her purse, then paused to stare at the asphalt where her van once stood. *I have no van!* She had clients to meet tomorrow, a function in the morning to set-up, and party equipment she'd hired out to collect this afternoon. How was she going to do all this now without her trusty van?

'Anything else that makes it uniquely yours?' Ryan asked.

'There's my logo with a large champagne bottle and the words *Parte'* written in pink bubbles on the sides. Here's my licence, and business card with the same design.' Grateful her hand remained steady while her tummy twirled its own glitter parade as she stared up at the guy. Aware how close their fingers were when passing him her cards, if he touched her, she'd faint.

Ryan read her driver's licence. 'I see it's your birthday.'

'Please don't say happy birthday. I was meant to just eat lunch, but courtesy of the waitress, she spilled this lovely fly-attracting prawn-ponging perfume all over me. And no, I don't normally sit in the gutter and drink straight from a wine bottle. My mother taught me manners, that I seem to have forgotten since my van's vanishing act. And because I can't drive anymore, I'll drink instead. So, if you want to give me a ticket, by all means, make my day.' Yes, let's kill all forms of profit margins she'd been counting on from this month, because she'd have to a hire a taxi now. *Was there a nearby hire company open on a Sunday afternoon?*

'How are you getting home?' Ryan asked.

'Um...' She glanced down at her ruined appearance. 'I don't think a taxi will accept me in this condition.' Pulling a prawn head out from behind her ear she burst out laughing. *Could it get any worse?*

Ryan's smile was dynamite. Thank god she was already seated or she would've buckled to the pavement.

'Sorry, I'm not normally like this.' A heated prickly irritation spread across her skin.

'Understandable,' he replied in deep silky tones that sent goose bumps shimmying down her spine. 'I hope your day improves.'

'Can't get any lower than this, can I, Officer?' She gave him a slight shrug from her position in the gutter.

'Maybe I should give you that ticket to top your day off?' He said straight-faced, flicking the cover shut on his notebook as her smile dropped. 'But I won't. Happy birthday, Emma.' He had the smile of a movie star, and she had the opening night tickets to sit front and centre.

'Thank you,' Emma squeaked. Dry in the throat she

swigged more wine and watched his swagger.

Victoria whispered, 'nice arse.'

'Ah-huh.' Their heads leaned sideways, admiring his walk from their gutter view until the police car pulled away.

'I think he was flirting with you, babe.'

'Doubt it.' Men who looked like Ryan never bothered with girls like her.

'Come on, I'll take you home, if you don't mind playing sardines.' Irene put the top down on her nifty sports car. Benjamin climbed into the back seat with Victoria beside him. Knees to their chests, they shared the wine bottle between them.

With the other bottle of wine in hand, in the front passenger seat, Emma stared at the vacant car park where her van should've been. What sort of adventures was her van having on its day out with the thief? Was it better than her day?

Happy birthday—*not*.

TWO

Inside the common white work-van, with the *Parte'* logo on its sides, Jae drove away from the Marina. He steered with the stereo cranked loud and lit a joint while Bob Marley crooned, *No Woman no Cry*, over the speakers.

'Sorry, just can't, Bob. That's too much for me right now. A woman's tears are the worst tears.'

Jae sighed as he tapped the tablet he'd found on the seat, and the next song played through the speakers. The van's amazing stereo was the best surprise; with an empty back, it had full surround sound and a tablet full of music.

Another Bob Marley classic came through the speakers. 'I might know this one? *Old pirates, yes, no,* aaand I have no idea what to sing...' He toked deep, as he sang the wrong words to the right song for the occasion.

This was a new artform, learning to drive with windows open and music playing. Music itself was new to Jae, it'd never been allowed in his world. Yet, it sang to him like an old friend, putting its arms around his shoulders and saying in a Rastafarian voice, 'there, there, man, let the music look after ya.'

Jae pushed up his glasses and squinted through the smoky haze of the lenses for a sign. Clueless as to where he was, there was no GPS in the van, the tablet had no Wi-Fi access, and he'd lost his phone. But he did find a simple roadmap in the centre console that he tried to read through his smudged glasses.

Distracted, he ploughed through an intersection and into the path of another car. Tyres screamed and smoke poured from beneath a gold utility that slid sideways, heading for Jae's passenger side.

'*Oh-no.*' Jae braced himself. A car horn blared as Jae planted both feet on the brake. His hand dug for a handbrake that he finally found on the side and yanked—hard. The van slid in short squeaks, then slammed to a rocking stop as if in its own earthquake. Then it stalled.

'Damn.' Jae peered over his glasses as he leaned down to the steering column and tried to restart the van. He winced at the smell of burnt rubber and fuels as he crossed the wires together and the engine whined over.

'Ya bloody idiot, didn't you see the stop sign?' The driver slammed the door of his modified gold ute and stormed towards the stalled van in the middle of the intersection.

'Excuse me, weren't my mixed signals clear enough for you?' Jae peeked out the window and couldn't see any stop sign. He did spot another beefy guy getting out of the gold ute's passenger side. 'Are you on drugs too, or is that part of your technique?' Jae asked the ute's driver.

'What did you say, you woggy little prick?'

'Now, there's no need to bring race into this, mate.' Jae sat up and pushed his spectacles higher along his nose. 'I'm sorry, my van stalled, okay? Please, let's not turn this into an international racist incident where you'll wave your yobbo flag that matches your ute. Although, you're missing the mullet as part of the brand.' Jae shrugged at the driver and resumed his position below the steering wheel to start the van.

'What did you say you, little cocksucker?'

'So now I'm gay, huh?' Jae touched the two wires that sparked, but the engine didn't start. *'Oh, come on.'* He slammed his hand against the steering wheel. Had he flooded it?

The ute's driver tore open Jae's door. 'Oi, you little immigrant mongrel.'

'Excuse me, I was born here. Hooray in your observations to notice I'm already behind in this height game.' Jae knew he was skinny, and standing a mere five-four, he was always picked on. Normally he shut-up or ran away—but not today.

'Hey, aren't you some famous rugby player?' Jae asked the ute's driver with his thick neck and wide shoulders as big as a raging water buffalo. He pushed his glasses higher up his nose and looked closer at the guy. Jae had never seen a game of rugby before, so why did this guy look so familiar?

'Yeah, and I'm gonna play footy with your head in a minute, mate.' He grabbed Jae by the shirt front.

'I get it, I've offended you without even trying, because there's no rest for the stupid.' Jae knew he was in for a face-full of pain and reached behind for his day-pack resting on the passenger seat. Among his sketch pad and a copy of *The Architecture of Glen Marcotte*, his desperate fingers slid around the cold steel barrel until they gripped the handle tight. 'Leave me alone, or I'll blow your bloody head off, *mate*.' He aimed the heavy handgun at the bully's chest. It was so big and broad he couldn't miss.

'Uh, easy there...' The driver stepped backward with

hands raised in surrender.

'Not so tough now, are you?' Jae sat taller, but his hand trembled from the gun's weight. 'You should be nicer to other drivers in the future.'

'I'm sorry, man.'

'And I'm sorry I stalled the van. I've lost my keys, I'm late for work, and you're not helping the situation by shouting at me.' Jae put the revolver in his lap, crossed the wires, and the engine kicked over. Then it hit him. He had no job—not anymore.

He frowned with the hate burning in his chest like lava ready to spill over. He glared at the man who'd picked on him. Another bully in his face.

But this was the first one Jae had dared to stand up against.

'Consider this payback for bullying me.' Jae pointed the gun through the open passenger window toward the fancy gold ute where its passenger waited. Jae tugged hard on the heavy trigger, twice. One bullet pierced through the bonnet, followed by a loud hiss as steam poured through the grill. The second bullet shattered the front and rear windows, as the ute's driver and passenger cowered onto the road with hands covering their heads.

'Wow, this thing kicks banana-butts.' Jae grinned at the smoking gun in his hand. He had no idea what type of firearm it was, but it sure made a mess, and the noise had his ears ringing from the shots. He dropped the firearm onto the passenger seat, where it slid to rest beside the boxes of bullets.

He couldn't stop grinning, savouring the destruction and

personal win. He smiled wider at the ute's driver, who was face down on the road. 'Have a nice day, butt-wipe.'

He re-lit the joint as the music came back online, and steered down a side street. He was just meant to borrow this van to get him back to his room. But he didn't want to go back.

Why should he go back?

All he had was his best mate, Stu, and nothing else to look forward to.

But now he felt like celebrating. He rolled his skinny shoulders that felt lighter, free from the shackles he'd been made to live under all his life. He was on his own path, refusing to look at the past and wasn't looking for tomorrow. Not now he'd begun a journey he couldn't come back from — he didn't want to. He was done serving his life sentence.

* * *

Ryan flicked shut his notebook and walked away from the ambulance that was surrounded by police cars and a fire truck, cordoning off the intersection. The shot-up gold ute rested on the rear tray of the tow truck. The ute's driver and his passenger were in the ambulance when the doors closed and drove them away to get checked out for shock.

'Whoever heard of road rage on a Sunday,' said the shabby, plain-clothes detective, David Warcroft, to Ryan. 'How long ago was this van reported stolen?'

'I spoke with the owner only an hour ago at the Bay carpark. Poor woman, she'd gone to lunch and the waitress spilled all that fingerbowl seafood muck all over her.'

'That'd suck.' David chuckled. With squinty eyes he scanned the scene where firemen swept the glass from the road. 'Now, statistics state most stolen cars are found within a ten-kilometre radius of the starting point.'

'The Marina's carpark is only five k away,' Ryan said.

'But it's rare for a car to be stolen in the middle of a Sunday in an open carpark area. They'll do late afternoon or evenings, mostly at the humble home garage.'

'Does that make this guy a joyrider?'

David shrugged, tugging on his loose tie that hung crookedly, it matched his crinkled suit. 'Probably. Almost seventy percent of stolen cars are used for short term transport. Now, the driver told the victim he was late for work, but where? A light commercial van would be used for many types of work, but what kind of work? Criminal work? Did the owner say there was anything distinctive about this van?'

'Here's her business card. Emma said it's the same logo on the van.' Ryan handed the card to the Senior Detective. 'What's the average on a car being found in this region?'

'Thirty three percent are recovered in twenty-four hours. Seventy eight percent within fourteen to thirty days. After that it's chop shop material. It's a classy logo for party planning. What did this Emma Toplin look like?'

Ryan gave a sly grin he tried to wipe away. 'Cute. Considering she was plucking prawn heads out of her hair, drinking straight out of a bottle of wine, sitting in the gutter, with her mother shaking her head.'

David snorted a laugh, then frowned. 'Don't ever get involved with a victim.'

Ryan remained emotionless while internally kicking himself for saying Emma was cute.

'Unless, you think the van's owner had anything to do with this? Could be an insurance scam?'

'She's got no priors, not even a traffic ticket.' Ryan also remembered Emma's amazing smile.

'Can you call the van's owner and ask if she has a photo of her van we can use. I'm sure she'd have one for her business, or on her website.'

'Why?'

'Aren't you starting with us tomorrow, Detective?'

'Yeah.' Ryan nodded, trying to stop the school-kid smile as his chest expanded like a proud sea eagle. Today was his last shift in General Duties and he couldn't wait to start in his newly promoted position.

'With your skillset, you took a long time to come around to becoming a Detective, didn't you?'

Long way, all right, like right around the country and overseas. But he was back now like a boomerang, hoping for a fresh start. 'Any idea who my new partner is?'

'Yep. Me. As your senior, I don't mind answering questions. So, feel free to ask away.'

Relief loosened Ryan's shoulders. David was a well-respected detective which made the job a whole lot better. It'd been a long time since he'd had a partner, set rosters, a desk, and a routine, and he was looking forward to it. 'Thank you.'

'Don't thank me, just be there at eight o'clock. Suit and tie. Ironing is optional. Don't be late.' David handed back the business card to Ryan. 'And, don't forget to call this Emma

Toplin. That's if she isn't too drunk in that gutter.' David chuckled, heading to his unmarked police car.

Ryan wouldn't forget to ring Emma with her big eyes that reflected the sky, and wide smile. She saw the good in her day, no matter how bad it was—and that was a rare thing in his job.

But he couldn't afford to think of her like that.

He was on the job. Finally, back where he wanted to be.

It'd taken him years to get back here, and he was not going to stuff it up over a woman—again. He had to prove to himself he deserved to be here too. Perhaps he could do that in one swift move by finding Emma's van

But, if the statistics were right, how soon before they could recover this *Parte'* van before it disappeared for good?

THREE

It was a lot of hassle getting her van stolen. Not only dealing with police, but the insurance company. For hours Emma had tangoed with them over the phone trying to make her claim.

So far, she'd shouted at a computer-generated voice, then got put on hold for thirty minutes before she got through to a real live person—in the *wrong* department. So, again, the merry-ring-around-game began.

Must have been a big weekend for the insurance company.

The rest of her Monday, so far, was spent cancelling client bookings, with no van to attend—she'd lost money on future work. Her credibility of showing up on time to collect her own hired gear from yesterday was now ruined. And lots of precious time wasted that she could be using to work on other things, but no—her world had come to a screeching halt because her van got stolen.

Although, it took longer for her kettle to boil than to speak to someone live at the Insurance company, at least it boiled and didn't die today—so that was one good thing for her Monday morning.

Grateful for the small miracle, she exited the elevator and

stepped into the Police Station's corridor. Another unscheduled, but necessary appointment she had to make. The sooner they found her van, the sooner her life could get back on track.

Like the words of a cheesy cop movie playing in her mind, *she had the right to remain forgotten. Anything she was bound to say was due to her case of Monday morning blues, caused by her hangover.* So cruising the corridors of a cop-shop certainly made day one interesting in her post-birthday survival plan.

Did her van survive too?

'Can I help you?' The young woman asked from behind the reception desk.

Emma read from her scribbled note. 'Hi, I'm looking for a Detective Lewis?'

'He's here.' The receptionist's eyes widened with her smile. 'Take a seat and I'll get him for you.' Emma watched the woman's hips swing on the slender figure. The short skirt showed off great legs, complimented by a set of stylish stilettos.

Emma stared at her boring black flats. She couldn't do heels, her hand to feet co-ordination was a life-long grapple with gravity. Her pencil skirt's hem went below her knees. Her long-sleeved blouse covered everything, while the chunky necklace had disappeared into her cleavage. After rescuing her necklace, she adjusted her buttons, afraid to show too much cleavage, but why bother? No one would be checking her out. Not in a police station.

If she didn't have to do this, and then lunch with Victoria, she'd still be hiding in bed and not be dressed like a prudish old school ma'am from the 50's.

Emma sucked in her stomach at the receptionist's return.

As if she could compete with the young slender clerk who was all legs and boobs. Emma gave up, releasing a posture deflating sigh. She wasn't here for a fashion parade.

'Detective Lewis is coming. He's new.' The receptionist's laugh twittered like a star-struck teenager.

'Great, thanks,' Emma mumbled, hoping the new guy knew what he was doing.

From her bag she retrieved her stack of insurance papers. Having filled in most of the blanks, she needed the contact details of the Police Officer in charge. Was it normal for stolen vans to get a Detective in charge of the case?

'Emma?'

'Yes,' she replied to the man in a dark navy suit and tie, approaching her from the sea of desks.

The receptionist sat taller, pulling her shirt lower. She then beamed up at him as he walked past. He didn't notice.

How could he miss that?

The receptionist wasn't worried, chewing the end of her pen with tilted head, watching the officer's rear end.

'Thanks for coming.' He held out his hand as Emma tried to register where she knew him from. He was gorgeous.

Oh no—it's Adonis.

Boom! Off went the glitter canon in her tummy that swirled its storm of magical colour.

Emma managed to shake his hand while trying to find her voice. 'Detective Lewis? Aren't you the officer from yesterday?' *How was that possible?*

'Yes. Please, call me Ryan. This way to the interview room.' He guided her down the corridor.

'Interview room, why?' Emma hesitated at the door, peering at him over her shoulder. His cologne was divine. It reminded her of toasted cardamom and nutmeg, with the edginess of mint, so exotic and yet warmly sophisticated. It matched his warm roasted mix-malted hair and chartreuse eyes. He was the perfectly branded specialised liquor she could drink all day long. Hangover, phhft—she'd happily stay drunk on whatever his package was selling.

'I need you to go over your statement. Please, take a seat. My partner will be joining us shortly.'

She sat hard before she fell, arching her eyebrow at the one-way mirror showing off his amazing backside. No wonder the receptionist had leaning-neck-syndrome.

The pretty receptionist—and the old maid.

Huh? Well, that thought woke her up. Ryan was here to do a job and she was here hoping he'd found her van.

* * *

'Is this where you interview criminals?' Emma pointed with an unsteady hand at the electrical equipment, camera, microphone, a table and four chairs. Chewing on her bottom lip, her big slate-blue eyes darted around the room like a wild quoll about to jump ten metres in the air for being trapped in a corner.

Ryan had a sudden urge to take her to a nicer room, perhaps a café to put her at ease. Were the chairs clean enough for this lady to sit on?

'Emma, please don't panic. We bring lots of people in here.' Mostly hardened criminals who never smelt like tropical tangerine and frangipani from the exotic hinterlands of New Guinea.

'Sorry.' She shrugged with stiff shoulders. 'Stupid, huh? Not like I've done anything wrong to get arrested.'

Words he'd heard thousands of times, but this was the first time he actually believed it. 'Is this your first time at a police station?'

'Am I that obvious?'

Ryan chuckled, and she shared her smile. It was like the brilliance of dawn stretching across the outback desert.

'Ah good. Thanks for coming in today, Emma,' said David, bustling through the door in his wrinkled grey suit. His collar loosened and yellow tie crooked, he carried a battered manila folder under his arm. 'I'm Senior Detective David Warcroft.' He shook Emma's hand and sat beside Ryan. 'Do you have your registration papers with you?'

'Yes.' Emma pulled a pristine plastic folder from her bag and passed over her papers to David. 'Have you found my van?'

'Not yet.' Although, Ryan was hopeful, it'd make him look good to the new bosses.

'I'll just get a copy of these,' said David, walking out to the photocopier.

Ryan slid the statement across the table for Emma to read. Still trying to settle into his new desk, waiting for sign-on codes from the IT department, the least he could do was this bit of paperwork. 'Here are the details of what you told me yesterday. Please read the statement and if it's all true and correct, sign at the bottom.'

'Sure.' Her big eyes shifted as she read the paperwork,

chewing the corner edge of her plump bottom lip. Her hair, the colour of powdered shortbread, sat in a loose bun with wisps dangling over a well-defined angular jaw that offset her oval face. Her seated posture was stiff with straight shoulders. So different from the girl in the gutter he saw yesterday who was much more relaxed. Today she was timid. Yet, she was beautiful both days.

Not good!

'All good?' Ryan cleared his throat, sniffing her perfume as he waited. She was a *Victim of Crime*, not someone to perv on.

'Sure, where do I sign?'

'There.' He handed her a pen and pointed to the bottom of the page. He glanced over his shoulder to find David fighting with the photocopier and the receptionist trying to help with some paper jam. They both wrestled with paper, opening doors, drawers, and sides of the big machine.

Ryan blurted out the first thing that came to mind, to keep Emma pre-occupied from her nerves. 'So, you're a party planner?' *Lame.* This was an interview room not a bar.

'Yes.' She signed with the ease of someone who'd signed many cheques, then pushed the pen and paper back to Ryan.

'What sort of parties?' Not like he hadn't checked it out on her card, her website, her Instagram account, and Facebook page as part of his cyberstalking—err, research for the job. Yet, he'd found no photos of Emma anywhere, just lots of reviews from satisfied customers.

'All sorts. Children's birthdays, wedding anniversaries, corporate functions, advertising launches and assorted government gatherings. I create parties for everything. Except weddings.'

'Why don't you do weddings?'

'I just don't.' She shook her head, frowning.

'Isn't that what party planners do?' Not that Ryan had a clue. Parties were things he rarely showed up to, although he'd broken up plenty while on the job. The few he did attend, were normally at some house with booze, music, a few balloons, and a barbecue out the back. That was it. He'd have a drink, scout the room, grab a feed, then look for the nearest exit.

'They can hire my equipment, but I'm not a wedding planner.' Emma shuffled in her seat, again frowning, but only for a moment. 'I haven't got the patience for it. Or the sensitivity to put up with over-precious brides and embarrassing mother's-of-the-bride.'

'You'd need danger money and riot gear to want to deal with some brides, huh?' He shared a slight smile, hoping to put her at ease. Why was he talking weddings? It was his least favourite subject.

Ryan glanced over to the copy machine that now had three detectives standing around scratching their heads. David, Mannis and Bercher, the other team members he shared office space with, were watching the receptionist bend over in her short skirt, while balancing on the tallest of heels. It was like watching circus clowns walking on stilts. *How did women do that?*

Emma's twinkling laugh got his attention. Her wide smile almost outshone her big eyes as the overhead light highlighted her hair like a crown of sunlight. She was so beautiful. A fragile, beautiful rainbow who shone in his black and white world of monsters.

'I'd rather hang with the clowns entertaining a bunch of screaming kids high on sugar, dancing to a really bad Elvis impersonator, than do a wedding. I do fun—not funerals.' She gasped with wide eyes, then cringed. 'Sorry, I didn't mean to blurt that out.' Her fine skin reddened across her cheeks as she chewed on that plump lip, staring at her hands in her lap.

Ryan chuckled; her open honesty was surprising. 'Don't be, that's the best description I've heard in a while. You must have a busy social life with all these parties to attend.'

'Not really. I'm part of the staff that sets up and leaves before the guests arrive. My motto is, *it's better to blend than attend, and never stick around for the end.*'

No way she could blend, he'd spot her anywhere.

David returned and handed Emma her papers and took his seat. 'Sorry 'bout that, it seems I've failed photocopying 101. Thanks for giving Ryan the information on the van last night. We've shared the photo from your email to all the patrol groups.'

'Wow, that's efficient for a stolen van.' Emma then leaned over and stage-whispered to Ryan, 'Sorry if that conversation made little sense last night on the phone.' She winced as she said, 'I think I swore. Sorry.'

'The wine must've been good.' Ryan chuckled. Her smile was magnificent. His heart valves gasped in wonder and breathed easier.

'We'd moved onto shooters at that stage.' Still smiling, the blush highlighted her cheeks.

David cleared his throat.

Crap! What was he doing? Ryan shuffled in his seat. He could justify himself, because he was only trying to keep their

VOC comfortable so she wouldn't scamper out the door like an endangered Bilby.

He sat straighter, tugged on his tie that was like rope around his neck and focused on the job.

A job that had taken a long time to get here and he wasn't going to stuff up again—no matter how cute the VOC was.

* * *

'Emma. Did anyone witness you in your van before it was stolen?' David asked.

What a strange question. 'Um, yes. I waved to Mr Brunswick who lives in the corner shed of my street when I went to lunch. And, there's the manager of Neptune's restaurant.'

'The owner of the restaurant where you had lunch?' Ryan asked with a new formality to his tone, giving her a sexy, steely stare.

What happened to the guy who'd been laughing with her before? Had she done something wrong?

'The lunch I wore, you mean.' Emma hiccupped a laugh from the nerves churning her stomach like she was on some hot-air balloon ride from hell. 'Here's his card, he'll remember me. We spoke this morning.' Neptune's manager couldn't be sorry enough, delivering a basket of wine and assorted delicacies as an apology. Emma could relate, having done damage control for her own staff before and could laugh about it now, but not while she was stuck in this interview room. When could she leave?

'I'm glad you're taking it so well, Emma.' David gave a gravelly chuckle as he wrote down the details and returned the card to Emma. He then put down his pen, rested his forearms on the table, and clasped his hands together. 'Besides getting you in here to sign your statement, we thought it fair to explain to you that your van was used in a few altercations last night.'

'What sort of altercations?' She asked David, besides the fact it'd been nicked.

'An hour after you'd reported your van stolen, a young male driver shot up a gold ute.'

'Like a gangsta drive-by? In my van? Surely not. My van has pink champagne bubbles on the side. It'd clash.'

'Then,' David said, 'a few hours later the same suspect held up a bottle shop at gunpoint.'

She clutched her throat, squeaking out the words, 'And used my van as a getaway car? It's not built for speed.'

'I'd say your van is now full of numerous boxes of alcohol, cigarettes and money.'

'Enough for a party,' Emma mumbled, shrinking into her seat. It was ruining her professional reputation as a party planner.

'And then…'

'What, there's more?' Her eyes widened at the Senior Detective, while Ryan remained silent, but she read sympathy in his eyes for her predicament. How bad was it?

'Early this morning,' said David, 'it was spotted ripping up the University campus sports oval.'

'Not my van, that's impossible?' She slapped a cold palm against her hot cheek.

'Traffic cameras have picked it up in various areas for speed and running red lights,' said Ryan. 'Should you get a speeding ticket, check the dates so you're not caught out. They're known to take months before they're sent out to the registered owner.'

'I've never had a speeding ticket,' she said to Ryan.

'I know, and you shouldn't have to pay for someone else's crime.'

'I already am.' Should she start a list on her losses?

David flipped open the folder, and shuffled through the paperwork. 'Witnesses claim the suspect is between twelve and twenty years old, of Mediterranean-Indian-Afghanistan descent.'

'Huh?'

David read aloud from his report, 'Some said Lebanese too. But they all agreed he had black hair, black eyes, and a dark olive complexion. He wears round-rimmed glasses like Harry Potter, or the late John Lennon, dependent upon your era.'

'I know who John Lennon is.' What era did that put her in? She had his songs on her playlist and Harry Potter on Blu Ray, plus a dozen costumes for both.

'He's five feet tall, skinny, and they all agreed he was very well-spoken. Here's the best picture we got from the CCTV security footage of the bottle shop.' David shuffled the photos out from his folder like large tarot cards about to give her a scary fortune-telling of her future.

Emma leaned closer to stare at the grainy footage. Round reading glasses, short, and well-spoken were not the stereotypical traits of a car thief. Not that she'd know any.

'Witnesses claim there was a passenger in the van at the University. Now, there's little description, except it's a tanned,

Caucasian male, wearing a baseball cap and sunglasses.' David placed another photo onto the table before Emma. 'Do you know this person?'

'No. They both look so young.' But then everyone appeared younger, having just celebrated her birthday.

'Are you sure?' David asked.

'No, I've never seen them before. Are these the guys who stole my van?' She knew it sounded dumb to ask—but had to. This world was so surreal to her.

'We can't confirm it at this stage,' replied David, 'except that your van is connected to three crimes, driven by the guy with the glasses.'

'Are they running around on some crime spree, literally partying with a van full of stolen booze? In my stolen van?'

'It looks that way,' said David. 'Now, we'll be releasing the details to the media shortly, which means we'll be sharing information about your van and your business logo. We're hoping someone in the community will recognise it and call it in.'

'Consider it free publicity for your business,' Ryan said.

'I don't want or need that kind of publicity.' It would ruin her. Emma rested her elbow on the table, covering her mouth, she stared at the images of her stolen van connected to a crime spree. 'My poor van, led astray and hanging out with the wrong crowd.'

'Try not to worry about it too much,' Ryan said in a deep soothing tone, sharing an understanding nod.

'I'll try.' Was this a *Pink Floyd, Dark Side of the Moon* moment, where the extended play version would carry her through the five stages of grief?

David scooped the photos back into the file and asked, 'Emma, did you plan the Police Commissioner's retirement party a few months ago?'

'The roaring twenties Bonnie and Clyde bash.' She smiled at the memory of all the officers dressed like Al Capone's henchmen carrying Tommy Guns.

'It was a ripper of a party, had the station talking about it for months afterwards. Not that Ryan would know, he's just transferred in from the AFP programme. Do you do anniversaries?'

'What kind of anniversary?' *What was the AFP?*

'My parents are having their fiftieth wedding anniversary soon.'

'Absolutely, I adore wedding anniversaries that make it past ten years.' She just didn't do weddings and couldn't believe she'd blurted it all out to Ryan like that. He was right though; riot gear and danger money should be mandatory safety requirements for a wedding planner's uniform.

'You-beaut,' said David. 'I'll pass your details onto my wife. She's been pulling her hair ever since she volunteered.'

'See, you're already getting free advertising out of this, Emma.' Ryan shared a slight smile, she had to smile with him.

Ryan was right again. It was how she scored most of her business, being in the right place at the right time with a can-do attitude. No matter what crap was going on in her private life, Emma loved her job. 'Here's another business card, David, to pass onto your wife. I'll offer her a good deal because you've been so helpful.' She rummaged through her bag and put another business card on the table.

David scratched at his two-day bearded chin. 'You don't have to.'

'I know, but I want to, and it's not a bribe.' *Yay for foot-in-mouth.* 'Fiftieth wedding anniversaries are rare and deserve something special. So, with all this happening and my van still out there, how does this affect my insurance claim?'

David slipped her business card into his crinkled suit pocket. 'Do you own the van or have a loan?'

'No, I own it, I don't do car yards.' She half-shrugged at Ryan who arched his eyebrow at her. 'I borrowed a van from the mechanics down the road for the immediate interim, and it's costing me a carton of beer a day—that's if it lasts.' Covered in dirt, it stank of diesel and coughed and spluttered oily smoke, she had to use a towel to cover the seat before she climbed inside. Maybe she wasn't hung-over from last night and just sick from the borrowed van's fumes. 'I may have to hire another van, if I can't get mine back soon enough.' A clean one, with air-conditioning and a radio. She missed driving with her music that had several playlists worth bragging about.

'That's not a bad idea about hiring a van,' David said.

'Why?' How long does it take to catch a big white van and return it to their owner? Or did she have to pay a fine like dog owners did when collecting their errant pets from the city pound?

'Once we've recovered your van,' said David, 'it'll be impounded as evidence, and that'll take time.'

'Really?'

'Ryan, care to explain the statistics?'

'Um...' Ryan shuffled in his seat, cleared his throat. 'Seventy percent of stolen vehicles are recovered. Those used for short term use are found within an average of thirty days. Then there's the forensic testing, and the gathering of evidence needed for court, that may take the longest.' Ryan looked at David who gave a nod, like he'd passed some unwritten test.

But it didn't sound good to Emma.

David flicked back to his folder. 'One last question. Your licence shows your business premises. What is your residential address?'

'I live on the premises,' replied Emma.

'Isn't that a shed?'

She caught their unsure look. It was expected being a shed-dweller. It's not like it was some abandoned house that children ran past screaming on a daily basis, she saved that sport for weekends. 'I have an apartment upstairs.'

'It's an industrial area isn't it?' Ryan asked, and Emma nodded her reply. 'Got a security dog?'

'No, just a stray cat that stayed. The neighbours have two rottweilers who let me know if anything's wrong.'

'Well, that's all we have for you today, thanks for coming. Ryan will show you out and keep you posted.' David stopped at the door and turned around. 'One more thing, Emma?'

'Yes?'

'If you do hire another van, make sure it's not the same as your stolen van. You might wanna leave the logo off for a while or we'll be chasing you all around town.'

'Point taken. Thanks, David.' *I think?* She picked-up her bag and spied her paperwork. 'Ryan, could I bother you with the contact details for the insurance company? This claim I have to make is the size of a phone book.'

'Sure, I'll also get you a copy of your statement, that might help quicken the process with your insurance company.' Ryan filled out the details and headed for the photocopier.

'Thank you.' Emma then hung around by the open doorway and watched his path to the machine, just like the receptionist did from behind her desk. Ryan was tall with straight solid shoulders as the perfect base of an inverted triangle that drew down to a great arse you could balance a round of alcoholic shots off. Ryan looked even better today, now that she was sober.

But he was just a nice guy, doing his job. Nothing more.

Ryan soon returned, passing her the paperwork. 'Thanks again for coming in, Emma. Here's my business card, in case you need anything.'

'Thank you, and I'm sorry for being a little out of sorts yesterday.' Now embarrassed with her whole attitude, and for her errant lust for someone she could never have. Why waste her energy.

'I hope you had a better birthday after I saw you?'

'Oh yeah, we dressed up, did a bit of shed-dancing while singing all these eighties songs on my karaoke machine.'

'Sounds like it was fun.'

'Impromptu parties are the best ones.' She smiled so wide her cheeks ached as she headed for the freedom of the outside world. No doubt the guy thought she was an alcoholic shed dweller. He was just a cop, doing his job for the greater good — trying to find her van that was doing so much wrong.

FOUR

'*Oi, you lot.* This is private property,' called out a man, banging his fists on the side of the *Parte'* van. Jae lay on the van's floor between empty beer cans, bottles of bourbon, and scotch. 'Augh.' He groaned at the intrusion, covering his eyes with his arm. 'Excuse me, but this shop is closed.'

'I can't get out, ya bloody moron.' The man reefed open the van's side door, and with hands on hips he glared at Jae lying on his back. 'Oi arsehole, move ya piece of junk, today.'

Jae blinked at daylight. 'Where am I, and who are you to abuse me?'

'Listen 'ere ya boat-floatin'-illegal immigrant—'

'Excuuuuse me?' Jae sat up, swaying in his half-drunken drug-haze, unsure if he was awake or dreaming.

'No excuses, maggot. Get up and get gone, so I can go. Are ya hearin' me? You speak-a-da-English?' Against the side of the van he slapped his palms like he was rapping on a drum.

Jae winced. This wasn't right, whatever this was.

'Sorry, I…' Jae reached for the lump digging into his side, and his eyes widened at the pistol he'd pulled out. The cold hard steel in hand was like opium to his veins. He was done playing the part of the victim, and pointed it at the stranger. '*Excuse me!*

But who are you calling an immigrant? I was born in this country, *mate.*' His mother would be so proud of his use of manners.

'Woah, woah, woah,' said the stranger with wide eyes, backing away with his hands in the air. 'I want no trouble.'

'No trouble? *No trouble!*' Jae kicked aside the empty spirit bottle, and while clumsily holding up the heavy pistol, he reached for his glasses tangled in his hair.

'Come on, mate, I didn't mean it,' said the stranger, still backing away from the van with hands raised.

Jae stumbled out the door and winced through the smudged lenses at the small alley, where daylight was barley pink in the sky. 'You certainly had no trouble waking me up and abusing the crap out of me,' Jae said in a low scratchy tone, he didn't even recognise himself. 'Where is the sign that says, *do not park here in case of angry trolls slamming the side of a van*, huh?' He waved the gun around the alley like a heavy laser-pointer. 'I don't see a *no parking zone* sign either. Do you?'

'Sorry mate.' The middle-aged man, with his back to the wall, cowered behind his large hands.

'I should shoot you for waking me up. Whatever happened to asking me civilly to please move the vehicle blocking your lane? I wouldn't be so pissed-off at you if you'd done that.' Huh—he swore. Jae never swore. He glanced to the early morning sky waiting for lightning to strike him dead.

'Look, mate, I said I'm sorry.' The man whined, with trembling hairy legs, and knees knocking in his long shorts and sturdy work boots.

'Don't suck up. You were screaming in my face and now

you expect me to hug-it-out with a stranger and make you my Facebook Friend? I'm not even on Facebook, so we can't be frenemies, so I'll shoot you just for waking me up in the most *uncivilised manner imaginable*.' Jae squeezed the trigger. The noise was deafening, bouncing off brick buildings, the sound spearing into his head. He swore his ears were going to bleed.

The bully clutched his chest. Blood trickled through his puffy fingers and he fell to the asphalt.

'Oi, why are you making all that noise, Jae?' Stu, Jae's best friend, poked his head out the front of the van where he'd been sleeping. 'Did you shoot him?'

'I think so.' Jae jammed his finger-tip into his ear, trying to get rid of the gunfire's echo. 'Who knew guns could be so noisy in alleys this time of the morning?'

'Why?'

'Perhaps, it's the way they're made. It didn't come with a silencer.'

'No,' said Stu, 'why did you shoot the guy?'

'He was rude. And we all know I'm a rather testy prick when I'm woken up.'

'True-dat.' Stu opened the driver's door, staggered to the far wall of the alley and threw up.

The retching sound made Jae wince. 'What are you doing, Stu?'

'I'm crook.' Crouched over, with hands on his knees, Stu spat out bile.

'Because I shot some guy?' Jae blinked a few times, as his brain fought the fuzz. 'I shot a guy.' Jae gripped the gun like it was a sword, standing before his slain dragon that was rolling on the asphalt. 'I beat the bully. Me.'

Twice he'd done that now.

Confidence flooded him, making Jae stand taller with his skinny shoulders back and chin raised. He inhaled deep the sweet, warm, baking bread aroma that mingled with cold brick and sunrise.

'What bully are you talking about?' With his palm pressed against the wall, Stu held himself up while scratching his head.

'Want to borrow my glasses to see?' Jae pointed the pistol at the moaning white-whale in the alley. 'Although, my glasses could do with a clean.' Removing his spectacles, he breathed on the lens and used the cotton lining of his baggy jean's front pockets to clean them. All while the other driver groaned on the alley floor.

'Nah, man, I'm crook from all that grog we had last night, or I'm still drunk. I need water.' Stu half staggered to a nearby tap, washed his face and took a long drink. Using his t-shirt, he wiped his face dry. 'Why did you do that?' He stood beside Jae and stared down at the middle-aged man on his back, bleeding.

'I don't understand why, I just did.' He'd broken every rule and organised plan he'd ever been forced to live by. Everything changed the second he broke the *Parte'* van's lock and heard its music over the speakers. Jae didn't want the party to stop now.

'Is he dead?' Stu asked Jae.

'No, he's groaning like a ghost, listen.' Both stood still to hear the stranger's whimper. 'See, he's not dead.'

'I can live with that.' Stu swayed on his feet as if he was still drunk and stoned. 'Where are we?'

'Another good question.' Jae adjusted his cleaned glasses and peered around the grimy alleyway. A small truck was parked behind them, as the aromas of baking bread lingered like heavy mist in the air. 'I'm hungry now, smelling that bread baking.'

'Me too, let's go find food.'

'You're not going to throw up in the van again?'

'Nah, I'm good.' Stu walked to the van's open door and swept out all the empty beer cans that rolled toward the large man moaning on the ground. 'You could've stolen some soft drinks to mix with all these spirits.' Stu cracked open a beer can and took a deep mouthful. Then rummaged for a cigarette from the flattened packet in his shirt pocket, that he lit it in one well-practised move.

'We'll get some shortly.' Tapping the hot barrel of the pistol against his denim thigh, Jae tilted his head at the beefy bully he'd shot. 'I've never shot anyone.' How was he meant to react? It was as if the drug-fuelled fog in his brain was filtering his emotions.

Stu sipped his early morning beer and leaned back against the van, puffing on his cigarette. 'So whatchya gonna do about this bloke then?'

The stranger groaned louder, as blood seeped into his short-sleeved, collared work-shirt.

Jae crouched in front of the guy who'd terrorised him at dawn—the tough-guy that was now cowering from him. 'Now that you're no longer playing the part of the bully, what should I do with you, sir?' The roles were reversed. Had he freed himself from the stereotypical chains he'd suffered under all his life? If so, who was he becoming?

'Stop playin' with the fella,' called out Stu.

'It seems my friend has spoken in your favour,' Jae said to the wounded beast.

'Gettin' ya geek on or what.' Stu chuckled from behind him.

Normally Jae was the geek. The short, scrawny, pimply-faced kid, bullies aimed for daily.

But not today.

'Do you have your phone handy, sir?' Jae asked the wounded bully.

The stranger moaned, and his eyes shunted in the direction of the open truck, while sausage-sized fingers clutched his bloodied stomach and chest.

Jae collected the mobile from the truck's dash and returned to the injured man. 'You can call the ambulance to come collect you. Of course, I'll understand being a bullet wound the police will be involved. But, sir...' Jae crouched in front of his silenced tyrant. 'You did push me by being a bully, and I'm done with that. I won't be a victim to bullying anymore. You know, all you had to do was knock, then ask me politely. Instead you went off on some racially-politically-incorrect rant. Manners are not a sign of weakness. They're simple, free, and universal.'

'Stop lecturing the poor bloke, will ya.' Stu flicked his cigarette butt out and closed the door of the van. 'Hey, I like this *Parte'* on the side of this van. It looks classy the way the party types are written in the pink bubbles from the champagne bottle. It's sparkly.' He wiped at the side. 'It's glitter.' He showed Jae his sparkling fingertips.

'That van sang to me.' Jae grinned at the fun he'd had ever since he'd started this road trip. 'I like the music, but I'm not too sure on the liquor yet. I think I'm still drunk.' He'd never tried alcohol, cigarettes, or weed, until this week, but he was catching up fast.

'Come on, let's get some food. That baking-bread smell has got me starving.'

'Coming.' Jae dropped the phone far enough away for the stranger to crawl for it, allowing them time to get away. 'Have a nice day, butt-wad.'

In the van, Jae twisted the screwdriver in place of a key. No more tapping wires to worry about. Through the side mirror, he watched the great lump laying on the asphalt reach for the phone with bloodied fingers.

'Can we go get food now?' Stu asked from the passenger seat.

'Can't have my privileged passenger faint from starvation now, can I?'

'Bin a helluva party since I jumped in, beats sitting in classes all day. I like the music on this tablet, its got all sorts. There's gotta be more music in this than a radio station. Must be music for all their parties, huh?' Stu used the tablet to lay out the tobacco papers, spreading dry mull in the centre. With his tongue poking out the side of his mouth, he rolled the paper ends together. Twisted the top. Lit the papery tip. Swiped the tablet for music, and passed the joint to Jae. 'Hey, I reckon we find food and females to really rock this day?'

'Me and females, huh?' That was a combination that never happened. But then again, this was the trip of a lifetime. 'Sounds like the perfect plan for this unplanned day.' Jae turned up the stereo and took a gulp from the half empty bottle of bourbon resting in the cupholder. He slid on his seatbelt. Flicked on the indicators, and smiled over the steering wheel.

He was his own champion now, making his own rules to validate and violate.

In only a few hours his world had completely flipped the script from his well-planned micro-controlled lifestyle, he was looking forward to the carefree chaos ahead of him. Wearing a smile, Jae steered into the traffic's stream, just as the bleeding man in the alley finally reached his phone.

FIVE

It sucks you can't smoke in restaurants anymore. Especially after such a fabulous feed.' Victoria pushed her plate forward, rested her elbows on the table, and balanced an unlit cigarette between her fingertips. 'Stop the lecture,' she said to Emma seated opposite.

Emma rested her cutlery across her plate, dabbed her mouth with the napkin that she folded over and put it to the side. 'What lecture, when I said nothing.'

'The lecture about quitting that you're giving me with your eyes.'

'Paranoid much? You'll quit when you're ready.'

'I try. Every day I say, *that's it, today I'm a non-smoker*. Then before I know it, I've poured my coffee and lit a cig while my brain's still trying to switch its lights on. I don't smoke in my apartment anymore, only on the balcony, or while walking The Prime Minister.'

'Have the owners stopped giving you grief for stealing their dog?'

Victoria shuffled in her seat, straightening her shoulders, she swapped her unlit cigarette into the other hand. 'I didn't steal The Prime Minister. I paid them handsomely for babysitting him until I was ready to bring him home.'

Emma burst out laughing. 'You house-sat their puppy and kept him.'

'How could I not? They called him *Precious*—like that ugly rodent from the Hobbit. The Prime Minister might not be pretty, but he has a certain class of character that deserves respect. Which reminds me, are you doing that Pampered Pooch Party?' Victoria asked.

'Yes, and I'd like to use The Prime Minister as a model.'

'Babe, The Prime Minister doesn't have a model figure. He's more of a squelchy paunchy mound of fur.'

'He's perfect for the party, and he's adorable, even if The Prime Minister slobbers everywhere.' The Prime Minister was a fat, waddling, squat British bulldog who drank. He even had his own little ice bag he'd wear on his head just like Victoria, where they'd lie in bed, side by side and waste the day away.

'It's all part of his smile and all over belly-laugh. By the way, he made the top of his class in Puppy School.' Victoria smiled, as proud as any parent.

'Congratulations. You and Paul must be so proud of your progeny.'

'We were, so we celebrated.'

'Hey, I want your dog sober and not hung-over for the Pampered Pooch Parade, okay?'

'You don't call a political leader a dog. He's The Prime Minister. And my fearless escort for public functions.'

'Where you love being treated like a Queen. I'm surprised you haven't got him smoking cigars.'

'Why would I do that, when I'm finding it so hard to quit myself? Now I'm too scared to try, I don't want to get fat before the wedding.' Victoria waved her unlit coffin-nail in the air. 'Will you please, please, please, reconsider being in my wedding? I need you there. Just you, no wedding planning.'

Emma didn't want to do any weddings, ever. Yet, it was the first time she'd been asked to be in someone's wedding party. 'Can I consider it?' She didn't want to disappoint Victoria. But Emma's track record for weddings had her in top position for the Darwin awards, where other wedding planners still whispered her name in ballroom hallways everywhere.

'No rush, we haven't told our parents yet,' said Victoria, 'which will mean an engagement party. We're thinking of a luncheon.'

'I can get you a great discount with water views at the Riverside. No seafood buffet but it's nice on the lawns for privacy. It's quite romantic with the manmade lake and swans.'

'I'll talk to Paul. He'd be happy with a barbecue in the backyard.'

'I know a great place on a beach up the coast for that.'

Victoria sucked back on her unlit cigarette and exhaled air as she leaned in closer, narrowing her eyes at Emma. 'You can do all that over lunch in the blink of an eye, but won't do my wedding?'

Emma cringed. 'I…'

'It's okay, babe, I don't want you to run the thing, I just need you to be with me, so I keep my shiz together and make it to the end of the aisle.' She gave Emma a slight squeeze of the hand to comfort her, but Emma recognised the nervousness in her friend's eyes.

'I'm honoured.'

'Good. I'll take that as a yes.'

'But—'

'We have time.'

Emma hoped for a long engagement then.

Victoria leaned back in her chair and asked, 'What's happening with the whole stolen van situation?'

Emma wrinkled up her nose. 'I went to the police this morning, before I dropped off my pile of insurance papers that was the size of a phonebook. Hey, you know that hot-cop from yesterday?' Hot one second then cold when his partner came into the room.

'The one you called Adonis?'

'Did I say that out loud?'

'Shooters loosen everyone's tongue.'

'Well, he's the Detective looking after the case of my stolen van. Did I sound like a narrator from a Hitchcock movie?' Emma tapped her chin. 'I haven't done a murder theme-party in a while.'

Veronica picked up her butter knife and tapped the side of her glass like a ringside bell at a prize fight, quietening everyone around them. 'Can we please return to the case of your missing van, Miss Mars. What did Detective Adonis say, did he find it?'

'No. They said it could be months before I get it back. *If* I get it back. The police want to broadcast it with my logo on the news for the public's help.'

'Wow, free advertising.' Victoria arched her manicured eyebrow.

'I don't want that sort of front-page news headlines, not

when these young guys are committing armed robberies with my van.'

Victoria leaned forward using her cancer-stick as a pointer. 'Think about it, babe. You're getting the best form of free advertising that carries the public's pity for your predicament.'

'I don't need the pity.' She didn't even want the attention. Emma just wanted to do her job.

'I've always admired your quiet skill-set of just doing and never complaining. Unlike me who'll tell the world if there's a colour crisis with my latest campaign.'

'And don't they run to the beckoning cry of Queen Victoria.'

'Darling, we all know it's for show.' Victoria sipped her drink and then sucked on her unlit cigarette and exhaled empty air. 'So, what are you using for transport?'

'I borrowed a van from down the road. I might hire one. Except the insurance company will only cover certain expenses but not until the claim is finalised. They told me it's a minimum of at least thirty days. So, I'm now out of pocket and vanless for a month. What do I pay premiums for, when they're claiming it was all in the fine print of the policy? I don't read policies, do you?'

'Policies? Ha. I rarely read my future-husband's articles. Come on, it's just the insurance companies' angle to sell fear. We both know this from working in insurance. It's the same spin, same story, just a different decade's dance.'

'I was only the mail clerk, and you were the front receptionist back when you were called Vicki.' It was a place where they fed their soggy sandwiches to seagulls in the company carpark for lunch. It'd been a crappy job that was the start of a beautiful friendship.

'Hey, you should buy another car. We've just been tasked to create an advertising campaign for these new fancy vehicles. Normally, I won't touch soccer-mom-cars, but this one is perfect for you.'

'I need a van to transport gear bigger than soccer balls.'

'But it's a six-seater that folds away to all of this mega space like a van would, with all the benefits of a luxury car and it's reasonably priced.'

'Are you a secret car salesman too?'

'We both know you're allergic to car yards like you're allergic to weddings.'

'Am not.'

'Yes, you are. You never went car shopping with me and refuse to do any car yard's promotional parties when they're launching new vehicles. Don't say you don't know, when I've lined up dozens for you in the past. Just last month I had a car yard luxury vehicle launch, which you knocked back.'

'I was busy. Besides, I don't think I'm qualified to run a car launch, when I know nothing about cars except how to turn a key, put on some tunes, and drive. I'll add fuel occasionally when the light comes on.' It's what her van did, it used to cruise so well with her music that was made to move.

'Babe, you said so yourself that your business is growing so much you're hiring extra staff who use the van more. You were already thinking of getting another one.'

'Forgot I'd said that.' Too distracted with her work, and now disrupted by the saga of her stolen van as her birthday present.

'Wouldn't this be the right time to shout yourself something upmarket?' Victoria asked.

'I suppose so. I might call Mitchell for his opinion?'

'Is Mitchell your accountant?'

'Sort of. He gives me free advice because he's sleeping with my mother.'

'Talking about your family, isn't that your sister's husband, Willy.' Victoria pointed with her unlit cigarette. She smiled slyly, both aware how much Helen hated her husband's name shortened.

William wore his dazzling businessman's smile, with his hair shaved close to the scalp. In his tailored suit and good looks, he stood out amongst the older group of men waiting at the restaurant's bar.

'Mum was telling me that Helen is trying to talk William into getting hair plugs,' Emma said.

'Hope not, they look like crap. I was in charge of their last advertising campaign. It's so hard to sell crap, but I relish the challenge.' Victoria sucked on her cancer-stick and exhaled, squinting her eyes through the imaginary smoke. 'William's put on a bit of weight recently.'

'Helen must suffer from heart palpitations over her husband's weight increase. Mind you, it suits him. He looks healthy.'

Victoria tapped her unlit cigarette against the spare glass as if it was an ashtray. 'I agree. How does he do that, get better in his looks as he ages?'

Emma wasn't answering that when she was still suffering

with her own aging-post-birthday blues.

A leggy blonde entered the restaurant and bee-lined for William, kissing him on the cheek. With their backs to Emma and Victoria, her hand rubbed slow circles on William's lower back.

'Wow, she's got some serious rocks on her fingers.' Emma watched the woman rub her brother-in-law's back. 'Isn't that a little low for the businessperson's professional touch zone?'

Victoria's dark eyes narrowed. 'Mm, looks a little too comfortable for a client.'

William turned around, he smiled and waved at Emma as the other woman's hand fell away.

'Emma,' called out William as he approached their table. 'Happy birthday for yesterday.' He gave her a brotherly peck on the cheek. 'How are you?'

'Good, William. Do you remember Victoria?'

'Of course, I do.' He shook Victoria's hand.

'I like your hair like that, William.' Emma smiled up at her poor brother-in-law who had to put up with a lot being married to Helen.

'Do you?' He slid his palm over his clipped hair. 'Helen wants me to do plugs.'

'No, I like it that way, it suits you.'

'Me too,' said Victoria. 'We were both just admiring it, while you were standing beside that clingy blonde at the bar.' Victoria pointed her unlit cigarette at the blonde talking to the other men.

Emma kicked Victoria under the table to stop stirring.

William shook his head as he grabbed a chair from the

neighbouring vacant table and sat down. 'Hey Em, I heard you had your van stolen. Is that true?'

Emma sighed, slumping her shoulders. 'Yeah.'

'The police are going to start advertising it on the news,' Victoria said to William.

'Why?'

'There's these young guys doing armed robberies, turning my poor van into a getaway car for gangsters,' said Emma. 'How is that possible? It has pink bubbles on it, and it sparkles.'

William patted Emma's hand. 'That's not good, Em.'

'Babe, I told you, it's free advertising.'

'That's true,' said William, 'you could work an angle to promote your business. You'll get the pity vote from the public.'

'I don't want to be pitied.' Emma preferred to blend and not be the centre of attention. She was paid to promote others so they shone under the spotlight—never herself.

Victoria said to William, 'I'm trying to convince Emma into getting another van.'

'Good idea.' William nodded. 'It'll be a sound business move to increase your asset base by buying another car for yourself. You deserve it after all your hard work.'

'You think so?' The man-made money for those who already had money. Not that Emma had much, but any tip from the guy was gold.

'I would. Sorry, I have to go do this business lunch. Call me if you need anything, anytime. I'll even help you check out some cars because I know how much you hate car yards.' He winked at her because it was William who taught her how to drive.

'Told you so,' mumbled Victoria, sipping her drink.

Emma shrugged, reaching for her glass. 'It's not like I have some phobia towards car yards like people suffer with clown-phobia.'

'If you did fear clowns, you'd scare yourself daily in your line of work.' William chuckled, returning his chair to the neighbouring table. 'Good to see you've recovered from your gutter party yesterday.'

'It was great, the Police were our witnesses for authenticity,' said Emma. 'Next time we'll do the brown paper bags for Victoria.'

'To hide my head from the daylight. Thank god for the creation of the Bloody Mary,' said Victoria, raising her cocktail.

'Reminds me of what I used to get up to before I became a married man. Good to see you've got your spirits up. Take care, Em.' He gave her a brotherly peck on the cheek. 'You always had fun no matter the situation, not like your sister.'

They watched William return to his group at their table where he sat two places away from the clingy blonde.

'That was nice of William.' William was always offering to help Emma out, but she never took up his offer.

'Sure it was, not that I haven't offered before,' said Victoria.

'True. But I'm fine, and I don't like to borrow or be a burden to anyone, especially not to my favourite friend.'

'You're never a burden, babe.' Victoria patted Emma's hand and they both watched William.

Emma broke the silence first. 'Go on, say it.'

'Say what, babe?'

'What you're thinking?'

'Well you must be thinking the same thing then.'

'Probably. You go first.'

'Fine. Is he cheating on your sister?'

'Well, we are talking about Helen.'

'The uptight, anal, know-it-all snobbymaterialistic cow,' mumbled Victoria in one word.

Emma laughed. 'I was just going to say the word bitch. But I like your description better.'

'Think I nailed it, huh.' Victoria crinkled up her nose. 'Well if her husband is, I wouldn't blame him.'

'William's not like that.'

'He's male.'

'What about Paul? He's male too, isn't he?'

'Paul wouldn't dare. He's been warned I'd chop his nuts off and use it as fodder for the pigeons roosting on our apartment building's roof if he did.'

'Poor Paul,' Emma said seriously for a nano-second before she burst out laughing. 'Bet he laughed at you when you said that.'

'That's what makes Paul beautiful, babe, he's one of the few who isn't scared of me. But didn't William give Helen a new eternity ring yesterday? Sounds like a guilt gift to me.'

'It's their business how they live, not mine.'

'It doesn't remind you too much of your dad's deal?'

'Dad's Dad.' Emma frowned as she snatched up her drink and swallowed hard.

'Honey, not all men are like that.'

'And my track record's perfect when it comes to men,'

Emma said with bitterness in her voice.

'Frank was a sick-prick who didn't know how good he had it. You deserve so much better. Don't you think it's time to move on?'

It'd been three years since the whole Frank fiasco. Was she destined to be single for the rest of her birthdays?

But she wasn't desperate either. 'I'm happy swinging in my hammock at sunrise, alone.' It made life so much simpler and drama-free, which is how it used to be.

Until her van got stolen.

SIX

S tuck at a set of traffic lights, Ryan sat behind the wheel of his work sedan. The hunt for the missing *Parte'* van continued to elude the police, and the two carjackers charges of armed robbery had now been upgraded to include attempted murder.

Another commercial van drove past and his eyes scanned the white panels for any branding and the number plate.

They were everywhere. Everyday white work vans that blended into the background like busy bee-drones doing deliveries amid the city traffic. Before this case, he'd never given them a second glance. Now, he was finding them all over the place. Except for the one he was looking for.

Ryan picked up his mobile from the passenger seat beside a *Jack Reacher* novel and pressed a number, listening to the dial tone. He didn't mind the task of keeping in contact with this particular member of the public.

'Hello, Emma speaking.' Her bright and friendly voice over the phone made him smile.

'Hi, Emma, it's Ryan.' He cleared his throat, remembering himself. 'Detective Ryan Lewis.'

'Oh.' She cleared her throat too.

He frowned. 'Is this a bad time?'

'No, all good.' Her voice was higher than normal, and again she cleared her throat. 'Have you found my van yet?'

'No. Sorry.'

'Not your fault.'

He was relieved to hear her say that, when most people blamed the police for everything going wrong in their lives.

'I hope it hasn't been up to anymore mischief since last night.' Her voice light, sounding the same as when he'd first met her, staring up at him with her oversized slate-blue eyes and that plump bottom lip that was so pink and kissable, he licked his own.

But then he winced, and it was his turn to clear his throat, again. He couldn't divulge the ugly truth about the damage the two men were causing in her van. He wanted to shield her from the horrors out there. He also didn't want to be the bearer of bad news for her, but if she asked, he'd tell.

'How are you handling the media attention?' Who were sensationalising the story making it worse.

'My friend Victoria's saying it's good free advertising, just like you said. I've scored a few new bookings from all of this, so thanks for that.'

'Don't thank us, I'm glad something good has come out of this.' The lights turned green, and he drove through the intersection checking the traffic for one particular *Parte'* van.

'Why complain when you can turn a negative into a positive. And I'm flexible and adaptable to my surroundings or situation. Have to be in my game, with clients who change their minds regularly.' Her tinkling laughter warmed him over the phone, again getting that loosening sensation around his ribcage, making it easier to breathe. He'd almost forgotten this was a business call where she was meant to be unapproachable — yet, he found her fascinating.

'I was told, you'd had a few people ringing your office to report they'd spotted your van?' As another white van passed him, city bound, but not hers.

'I rang the details through to the pretty receptionist at your office.'

'Who?'

'The receptionist.'

'I think her name is Kelly?'

'That's her. She's got great shoes and thinks you're hot.'

Ryan blinked several times at his phone. 'Well, um...' Christ, how was he meant to react to that? He hadn't noticed Kelly or her shoes. 'Sorry, I'm not a shoe person,' he blurted out, and her laugh put him at ease. 'Emma, do you have an answering machine at work?'

'Sure, I screen my calls all the time. Not really, but it sounded good, huh?'

'What does? That you screen your calls or you have a machine?'

'Both or neither. Are you getting as confused as me in my ramble?' Her laugh echoed and he had to laugh with her.

'I'm talking about an answering machine.'

'Why?' Emma asked.

'To keep a record of the sightings.' A light van caught his peripheral view parked down a side street and he slowed down, until he spotted the red rear door and kept moving.

'The radio said those boys did another armed robbery,

this time at a mattress factory, before the van died. It sounds like they're settling into the *Parte'* van, huh?'

More like creating a killing machine. 'What do you mean the van died?'

'The van I'd borrowed decided to not work anymore, and it's now sitting on the side of the road.'

'You're not sitting in a gutter again, are you?'

'No.' Emma's laugh was as warm as sunshine dappling through a monsoon forest's canopy of choking shadows.

What the— He wiped a palm over his face to wake himself up. He'd never been like this. He shouldn't be like this. Not when he was meant to be doing his job.

Yet he couldn't help himself with this lady.

'Where are you, Emma? Do you need a hand?'

'Um, I'm on South Road and you won't believe this, but the neighbours van I borrowed stopped right in front of this car yard.'

'Which one?'

'It's called Fred's Car yard. It's a huge place. So, now I'm shopping.'

'Weren't you hiring one?' Eyeballing the rear-view mirror, he spotted another white van a few cars back. He slowed down, shifted into the left lane, and let it pass as he checked the number plate. Unfortunately, it wasn't the van he was searching for.

'I was going to. At lunch, Victoria and my brother-in-law William tried to convince me into getting another van. Then when this borrowed van died right here in front of this car yard, it's like someone is trying to tell me something.'

'Could be.' Not that Ryan was superstitious, but he'd observed enough tribesmen who lived with their cultural superstitions to never joke about it.

'But it's a car yard. They creep me out like some clown-phobia, which is silly because I have heaps of clown costumes in my shed, and I know a dozen cool clown performers I hire for kids' parties. So here I am, trying to prove to my friends, and me, that I'm not suffering some silly car-yard-phobia. Aaaaaand I'm so sorry I blurted all that out to you.' She shared a nervous giggle.

'Have you ever been car shopping before?' Ryan asked, as his mind tried to catch-up.

'Not really. This is my first time alone,' she replied quietly.

Did she wince? 'Are you okay?'

'Honestly?' A truck passed blocking her voice over the phone. 'I'm a little worried about the car salesmen. Talking to you has allowed me to avoid them, even though it took me twenty minutes just to step into the yard.'

'Why? It's just a car yard. Do you have problems walking through a crowded carpark in a shopping centre?'

'No.'

'Think of it like that.'

There was silence again, except for the passing outdoor traffic echoing through the phone.

'You're my hero.' She may have said it quietly, but her smile came through loud and clear.

His chest expanded and his smile grew as he sat taller behind the steering wheel. Why was he putting himself through this—yet, he couldn't stop. 'So, what's wrong with the other van you borrowed?'

'I don't know. It won't start, and the owners can't come and get it for a few hours. I got sick of waiting on hold for the cab company, so now I'm waiting for my mum. And okay, I'll admit I'm worried. I've heard scary stories where salesmen in these places are skilled at talking people into buying what they don't want.'

She sounded worried, which bothered him. 'You seem like a smart businesswoman who wouldn't get talked into anything you didn't want.'

'I like to think so.'

'Don't you have a husband or boyfriend to help you out?' He held his breath waiting for her reply as he steered through the traffic.

'No.'

He smiled at her answer, easing back into his seat.

'Do you know anything about cars?' Emma asked.

'Some. Not that I know everything. I spent enough time in the traffic division to know how to find a car's faults.'

'So what car do you drive?'

'A four-wheel-drive ute.'

'Huh? You've surprised me. I'd assumed you'd be cruising in a modern sedan?'

He grinned at the modern standard sedan he was driving, with a dashboard containing radios, lights, and all sort of gadgets. 'No, that's the work cars.'

'So is your ute all beefed-up with shiny hubby-cappy-things, thick tyres, a large polished bull bar with three different aerials hanging off it, with tinted windows, and large spotlights?'

'No, it's stock standard.'

'Well then, I'm not standing in front of your car, am I?'

He chuckled, relieved to hear that her laughter had replaced the worry in her voice. 'I went through that phase with my first car, spent a fortune on it. I own a Harley though.'

'As in a large, noisy motorcycle?'

'Yes. I have a traditional Harley Davidson low rider, with a soft tail frame, dual tank and classic chrome, with a sweet Milwaukee Eight, V twin engine.' He loved his bike.

'Wow, again you've surprised me, Detective. Do you dress up like a big tattooed biker in black leather and chains, with a patch on your back when you ride?'

He laughed. 'No. I don't play dress-ups. Do you?' And his brain tripped to the possibilities she'd look good in the bedroom with, he could almost drool.

'I happen to have a huge wardrobe for hire. Hey, how do your ears handle the loud noise those bikes make?'

'They're not that bad.' Although his mind was being bad. 'I take the bike out for a spin on my day off.'

'Where do you go?'

'In the hills for those sweeping country roads or I'll follow the coast on weekends. It's good to get away.'

'To clear the head, huh?'

'Yeah.' Ryan tried to remember the last time he'd taken it out. It'd been too long. 'Do you need a lift?'

'Thank you for the offer, but my mum finishes work soon. That's why I'm killing time by confronting my make-believe-phobia by window shopping.'

He spotted the bright red sign for *Fred's Car Yard* ahead. 'Do you want a hand car shopping?'

'Really?' She sounded hopeful.

'I'm just down the road.' He searched for a car park.

'I wouldn't want to bother you.'

'You're not. Besides, I'm a guy who doesn't mind looking at cars. What do you say? I'm entitled to a lunch break.' He parked behind a diesel-smoke-stained van.

'Honestly, Ryan, I'd appreciate the help.' When she whispered over the phone, 'The car salesman has spotted me. Oh no, he's smiling at me with his gold tooth. Do they still manufacture gold teeth?'

He laughed at her description. 'Does he look sleazy?'

'Kind of?' Her giggle muffled like she was covering her mouth. 'Oh no, he's getting closer.'

'I'm not far. I've just parked behind an old white van that someone's written the words *Clean me* on the back window, and I think it's got glitter on it?' The glitter sparkled as it caught the sunlight.

'That's mine. Benjamin did that this morning,' Emma said so brightly he could hear her smile.

'Would it fall apart if you cleaned it?'

'I'm only paying for driving privileges.'

Ryan shook his head as he walked past the decrepit van with its bald tyres and a cracked windscreen. It shouldn't even be on the road.

'No way, this guy has no dress sense for a car salesman, and I shouldn't complain when I'm no fashionista myself, but he's getting closer.' Her voice may have sounded humorous, but it had an urgent edge to it that made him walk faster.

'I'm coming to the rescue.' He chuckled, craning his neck to peer over the many car rooftops. The yard was huge.

'I've never been rescued from a car salesman before,' said Emma. 'I sound like a useless female, don't I?'

'Not at all.' Ryan spotted the four-wheeled drive she'd described. 'I see you.' She had her back to him with her hair in a ponytail that looked so soft it reminded him of powdered buttery shortbread. Her shoulders square, and the curves in her skirt were doing wonders for his heart rate. Until she turned around.

Boom! Like a cardiac arrest, his heart flat-lined at the sight of her smile. Her oversized slate-blue eyes sparkled like pools of pure enchanting magic, clearer than any tropical lagoon.

'Hey you.' She waved at him while holding her phone to her ear.

He smiled at her. Had to. She was an angel in a car yard and he could hear the panpipes of the Solomon Islands singing. Christ, he had to get his mind out of the jungle!

He hung up his phone, and the closer he got the deeper he inhaled her aroma of tropical tangerine mixed with frangipani. Or was that a summer rose? It reminded him of the seasonal change from spring to summer, which was his favourite time of year for riding his bike. 'Hi, Emma.'

'Hi, Ryan. Fancy meeting you here.' They burst out laughing at each other. 'Nice tie. It suits you.'

'Suit, huh? Nice pun.' Tugging at his suit coat he loosened his tie. Her smile got bigger and brighter, the way her plump lips curved, it was beautiful. 'Thanks, I'm still getting used to wearing a suit and tie to work. You look,' —*amazing*—'great.' He stopped and sighed at her blush. *Now that was cute.* So glad he'd made that call.

* * *

'Um, thanks.' Emma tried to exhale the heat from her flush creeping across her face. He said she looked great. How? When her faded denim button-thru skirt was missing half its buttons. Her clothes were hand-me-downs from Victoria's glamorous wardrobe, where some came with tags still attached as gifts from her clients.

Emma didn't dress for fashion but for practicality, wearing what Benjamin described as Shabby-Chic-Shed style. Which was whatever Emma found in her cupboard that fit and suited what she'd planned for the day. She dressed to blend into the background, not stand out in a crowd.

Yet the way Ryan focused on her it had her trapped under the sun's spotlight. What should she do now? *Friend, just a friend!*

'I'm Max, how may I help you?' said the gold-toothed, car salesman.

'G'day Max, I'm Ryan.' He shook the salesman's hand. 'The lady, Emma, is after a work vehicle as an upgrade from her utility van. We're just doing some window shopping to get a few ideas.'

Ryan called her a lady. Should she melt now? Suddenly her jacket was too hot.

'I'm sure we'll find something suitable, with lots of room?' Max asked.

'Yes please,' said Emma tearing her eyes off Ryan to the car salesman. That killed her buzz. Although, she was grateful Ryan was here. So out of her comfort zone in this place full of cars, she'd run if he wasn't here.

Did she really have a phobia of car yards? Or was it avoidance?

For years she'd refused to step inside such a place. Today, it'd taken twenty minutes before she'd crossed into this car yard's boundary. Why?

Her silly make-believe phobia had cost her heaps, having knocked back dozens of launch party requests from car yard businesses in the past. Why did she ever think she had one? When did it start?

'All our larger vehicles are at the back,' said Max, leading the way.

'You let me know what you like or don't like,' whispered Ryan, stepping in beside her.

She inhaled his sophisticated, yet surprising scent, so much stronger now up-close. It was of toasted cardamom and nutmeg, with a twist of mint, and lots of other complex mysterious aromas, turning it into something sensually amazing, just like the man. So glad he was here to play her hero.

They inspected large family wagons, utes, four-wheeled drives, and chunky vans. All with plenty of backspace to cart her gear for parties. Thankfully, Ryan asked the technical details which he was able to interpret for her.

'Made any decisions?' Ryan asked as they left the office, returning the keys to Max. Ryan had made her test drive a van, which was fun. Nothing like her experience with William helping her, where he'd kicked a tyre, shrugged, then sat on the bonnet to call his car-club.

'Not sure,' said Emma. 'Their stereo systems suck.'

Ryan chuckled. 'Cars are more than just a stereo, you know.'

'For you, maybe. For me, music is meant to move, and cars are just touring speakers of sound.'

'Like your music, do you?'

'You could say that.' Well, she was a long-time collector.

'Got any favourites?'

'All of them. Old, new.'

'For parties?'

'Music helps to create and compliment the overall atmosphere, no matter the party theme. But I'll do some more research on the car thing, using what you taught me, now I know how to ask the questions. Thank you.'

Ryan smiled wide and her tummy tumbled like a laundromat's spin-dryer full of ticklish glitter. He was still way too hot for a friend.

'Smart move, and I was glad to help.' Ryan's mobile phone rang. 'Excuse me.' He side-stepped away as his expression changed to the steely stare he wore so well. Even his speech pattern was short and sharp over the phone, it had to be work.

He pocketed his phone with a frown, took a deep breath, and as he approached her the frown disappeared. 'Sorry, Emma, I have to go.'

What a shame, when she'd had so much fun with the guy. 'It's okay, I'm meeting Mum in a minute. Thank you for your help in curing me of my car-yard-phobia.' She shrugged with hands waving to the rows of polished cars wearing coloured Sale signs. Whatever was she worried about?

'My pleasure, I had fun.'

'Me too.' She smiled so wide her cheeks ached.

'What are you going to drive until you get a car?'

The way he'd said that, it was obvious her van was on some extended vacation. *Oh no, how much was this going to cost the business now?* Not when she had parties booked this weekend.

She screwed her nose at the decrepit van she'd been forced to borrow. It wasn't the right look for impressing her clients, and it was making her sick from the fumes.

Ryan pointed to the curb where her borrowed van was parked. 'Don't say you're using that van, Emma. You're risking your life if you get behind that wheel again. Please don't make me put a yellow sticker on it for not being roadworthy.'

Was the delicious Detective going to book her? 'I won't. I'm hoping Mum will let me borrow her car, she's going to South America for four weeks.' She'd beg if she had to, because she'd be seriously stuffed if her mum said no.

'Good. I won't have to worry about you in that other van.'

Aww, he cared. Her stomach took flight in a rain of glitter that made her fluttery and female all at the same time. It was so foreign. Yet nice.

'Call me if you ever need a hand, and let me know what you end up getting.'

'Sure, and you'll call me about my van?'

Ryan's smile fell to a frown.

Did he have more bad news about her van?

'I will. Take care, Emma. Thanks for lunch.' He shared a slight smile.

She flinched as the siren screamed, as hidden red and blue lights flashed on Ryan's car that sped away.

Had her *Parte'* van been spotted? If so, what destructive trail had it left behind now?

SEVEN

Stu bolted across the carpark and jumped into the passenger seat of the waiting *Parte'* van.

The tyres screeched like a runover rat as Jae crunched through the gears, manoeuvring the long van past the smaller cars. Van-driving was an artform Jae had yet to perfect. 'Why do they make these carparks so small?'

'Dude, that was awesome.' Stu caught his breath, clutching assorted brown paper bags to his chest. The smell of cooked burgers and fries filled the interior, along with Stu's excited laughter, as he waved the handgun around. 'That's the best buzz.'

Jae ducked from the near pistol-whipping, while trying to steer, almost hitting a parked car. 'Hey, put that thing away before you shoot me, you little turd.'

'I'm not little, I'm taller than you.' Stu dumped the handgun into the glove box and booted it shut. 'You just killed my thrill, man. Not cool.'

'Sorry, Stu. I didn't mean that. But we should be aware of this thing called gun safety. It *is* a fully loaded weapon, you know.' Even though Jae still had no idea what type of handgun it was. 'Did you get enough for lunch?' Jae's stomach rolled with hunger spurred on by the aroma filling the cab.

Stu rummaged through the bags displaying the golden arches. 'This is yours, double the bacon with a jumbo frozen coke. I'll add the bourbon while you drive.'

'Thank you, kind sir.' Jae hunched over the steering wheel and unwrapped his burger. He took a bite of plastic cheese and salty bacon, moaning at the flavour. He didn't care it was forbidden. He loved pork and was in a non-halal-approved hog-haven with sweet music surrounding him.

'And this, my friend, is a stack of cash.' Stu held up a large bag full of loose bills in various denominations.

'Well done, young man,' Jae mumbled with a mouth full of bacon and sweet bread as mayo oozed on the side of his lips. He had manners, but he was making a pig of himself and didn't care.

'Check this out? Our *Parte'* van is famous.' Stu held up the second page of the newspaper displaying a photo of the van. 'We're famous. *Us.'*

'Always wanted to be a somebody.' Jae pushed his spectacles higher along his nose and focused on the paper. 'Are those sketches meant to be us?'

'Think so.' Stu shoved a few fries into his gob, folded back the pages, and read aloud. 'The witnesses state the van's driver is six foot two, with a well-defined muscular build, wearing round glasses, black hair, black eyes, and of Mediterranean appearance. He is considered armed and dangerous.'

Jae stared at his scrawny arms that didn't even bulge slightly as he raised his drink in a bicep curl. 'Mediterranean? Do they think I'm Greek or something?'

'Suddenly you're taller than me. And scary.' Stu chuckled

with his mouth full of fries.

'I know I'm as threatening as a unicorn-cupcake, but what does it say about you?' Jae turned down a side street and followed the road as he leaned in for another bite of his burger.

Stu frowned as he read, 'I'm an average sized, Caucasian male, wearing sunglasses and cap. Since when did I become white?'

Jae chuckled at his indigenous brother. 'Same time I became a tall buffed-up Greek God-of-War.'

'They've got a great photo of the van though, like it's more famous than us.' Stu held up the paper showing off the *Parte'* van.

'That's not right. An automated vehicle is just a piece of machinery that is a mere tool to be used by the driver.'

'With the sweetest surround sound system. The owner must've spent a fortune on the speakers on this thing, and all remote controlled. I like it how it echoed across the beach.'

'I'd never camped on a beach before.' Where he'd kicked back on the sand, listening to the music, drinking long after the sunset. It was a whole new way of life, free from all forms of parental restrictions. 'Hey, now you've found us more cash we should go score?'

'We should go visit those girls again, let you work on that hooker-lingo and give 'em mattresses in the back another whirl.' Stu play-punched Jae's skinny shoulder. 'Hey, you're no longer a virgin. I reckon you've ruined your new reputation as a good Greek boy.'

Jae used his napkin to dab at his mouth to hide his grin. 'Who knew being famous-dangerous, we'd get laid? Or is it this

Parte' van leading us astray?' They both chuckled between bites of their meal. With the music playing, the van took them deeper into suburbia.

The *Parte'* van stopped in front of a simple brick house. There was no car in the drive and no traffic on the street.

Jae screwed up his lunch-wrapper and tossed it into the back. The yellow paper ball bounced off the ceiling and rolled off a large blue esky, landing among the empty beer cans and bottles of spirits spread across the mattresses. Tiny sparkles flashed bright in the sunlight from glitter. He pushed up his glasses and wrinkled his nose at his reflection in the rear-view mirror. 'We should clean out the back, show the van a bit of respect.'

'Not here. The Munster wouldn't like it, and his folks would get cranky.' Stu slurped through his drink's straw as he scrolled through the playlist on the tablet. 'The music on this thing is endless.'

'Are you coming in?' Jae was still new to this, he'd hadn't gone inside alone before.

'Nah man, I'll stay and watch the van. We don't want anyone stealin' it, now it's famous. I reckon I'll make our own playlist from all these other playlists. I'll call it our *ruleless-road-tour tunes.'*

'Good idea, Mr DJ.' Jae grinned at Stu's wide white-toothed smile that contrasted against his dark skin. 'Back soon.' Jae slammed the driver's door, shoving money into his baggy jeans' pocket and pulled them up higher on his scrawny hips. The shoes always fit—but his pants never did. The sun caught a few tiny pieces of glitter on the denim hem and he wiped it away. 'More glitter.' It was showing up everywhere.

He strolled toward the back door of the house with its dead lawn. As long as he just acted cool, he could do this.

Ten minutes later a gunshot rang out, its echo ricocheted down the silent suburban street. Jae tore down the driveway as fast as he could with a backpack in one hand and a new handgun in the other.

Stu opened the driver's door and Jae jumped in, tossing the bag to the passenger floor.

Before the driver's door had shut, Jae pressed the accelerator pedal flat to the floor. The van's engine whined in low gear and kangaroo-hopped as the tyres screeched like fruit-bats.

'Toota. Toota. Clunka. Clunka. We're goin' cruising in our big blue car,' sang the overly-happy male voices that carried through the speakers.

Jae inhaled deep and let it all out in one breath. The hot barrel of the black pistol poked against his denim thigh on the driver's seat. His shaky hands gripped the steering wheel tight as he turned left down one street then right down the next.

'What did you do?' Stu asked.

'Toota. Toota. Clunka. Clunka. We're goin' travelling near and far…'

Jae frowned at the van's ceiling. 'What are you playing?'

'Toota. Toota. Clunka. Clunka. Check us out in our Big Blue Car.'

Stu turned down the stereo and scrolled for the next song.

'It's a kid's group, *The Giggles,* my little brothers love 'em. I'll admit I did as a kid too. Haven't you heard of 'em?'

'Nope.' His parents didn't like music.

Jae's adrenalin-fuelled fear was soon exchanged for a burning ache in his chest. He'd missed out on lots of things thanks to his parent's restrictive lifestyle. Now he was determined to enjoy life his way, with no rules or plans.

Jae changed down the gears and drove slowly, keeping to the school zone's speed limits, hiding the new handgun in the back of his jeans. Kids played on the bright playground equipment, their laughter and squeals of joy carried through his open window. He hated school and had feared it every day. But he wasn't scared any more.

'Check out what I scored.' Jae nosed towards the bag on the floor. He was doing so much more than he ever thought he could, every hour of the day, ever since he got into this van.

Stu scooped up the flimsy backpack and his eyes opened as wide as the pack's unzipped mouth. 'Oh maaaaan, we've got enough dope to last us for a year.' He pulled out bags of hooch, powder, and pills. 'You've got more cash here than what you took inside, Jae?' Stu held up thick wads of rubber-banded rolls of cash. 'You stole from the Munster?'

Passing the school zone, Jae slammed the van into a higher gear and sat taller behind the wheel. 'I did.'

'You are so *dead,*' Stu squeaked.

'No, I'm not. But our dealer might be?' Jae reached for a cigarette which he lit with trembling hands. 'Roll another joint, Stu.' He needed to dull the edge off his emotions. He needed to forget.

'You killed the Munster?'

'Had to.'

'Why? You had enough cash to buy plenty.'

'The Munster was lecturing me for pulling up out front with the *Parte'* van. He was elbowing today's newspaper showing the van that sat right next to his pistol,' explained Jae. 'He was calling me all these rude names, especially a Lebanese Muslim. I'm not Lebanese. Or Greek. Why can't people take me for who I am? Not what I look like. Or my family's restrictive religious beliefs. This is supposed to be a country that embraces multiculturalism.'

'You're preachin' to the wrong-colour-choir, man.' Stu sat up and used the tablet as his lap-table and began to construct another herbal rollie. He licked the paper's glue, lit the end, inhaled the weed deep, and handed it Jae. 'Did you really shoot the Munster?

'It wasn't planned, it just happened.' Jae inhaled the hot smoke, held his breath and let it roll around his lungs. Soon a slow sleepy wave rolled through his bloodstream and the world shone once more.

'So, he's dead?'

'I didn't mean to, I'd aimed for the kitchen cupboards behind him, I wasn't expecting it to be loaded. His pistol is bigger than the one we've got. Yet, I went inside unarmed, and he had it loaded, on the table, waiting for me. I didn't know he even owned a gun.'

'I did.'

'Could've warned me, because it was either me or him. So, yeah, he's either dead or a vegetable by now.' Jae's frown faltered against the drug fuelling the feel-good buzz in his brain. 'It was his own fault.' Munster was the type to set the rules and never use them. Sure, rules were created to stop chaos. But then there were rules that showed self-respect that Jae was learning for himself.

'What happened?'

'Munster sat at the kitchen table eating a bucket of fried chicken like Buddha's blobby big brother. It was disgusting. The grease was dripping off his triple chins, licking his fat fingers with that tongue like that alien war-lord slug, Yaba the hun.'

'Jabba the Hutt. Did you miss Star Wars too?'

'It's part of my own assimilation programming for university.' He still had a lot of catching-up to do. Taking another deep toke, Jae passed the spliff back to Stu.

'So, what happened to the Munster?'

'Well, that sitting-advertisement for all things obese, screamed at me for putting him at risk. Calling me names, sucking pure fat from this chewed on chicken bone — that he threw at me like I was some dog. It was disgusting.'

'That's gross.'

'That's when I snatched the pistol before he could, and pulled the trigger.' Why was he always bait for bullies to pick on daily? Jae screwed up his face, mirrored by Stu. 'I could do with a shower. I can smell his greasy crap all over my clothes.'

'Head for the gym.'

'I don't do gyms, and since when do you?'

'Mum was their cleaner for a while. I helped, and used to mess with their machines. Which might be why she got fired? I've still got a stack of passes.' Tucked behind his seat, Jae rummaged in his bag and soon held up a white plastic swipe-card. 'They've got these big fluffy towels in their flash showers. It'll be deserted this time of the day.'

'I'm in.' Jae flicked on the indicator, got into the right lane and waited for the traffic lights to turn green.

Stu took another hit from the hand-rolled. 'I didn't mind the Munster, even if he was an obese drug dealer.'

Jae frowned. 'He was a rude racist and a bully.' Another bully who wasn't going to hassle him anymore.

'He was rude to everyone, that's what the Munster is. Was. And he's got connections to the bikers.'

'Does not. The Munster only big-talked himself up to scare us. He was nothing but a small-time dealer, who, at thirty-six, still lived with his parents. I couldn't wait to attend Uni and experience the world.' Where his life experiences didn't truly start until this unplanned road-trip of self-discovery. Jae patted the van's dash as if it was his trusty steed.

'I like living on campus too. But I miss my mum's cooking.' Stu sighed, then slurped on the straw of his near-empty cup.

'You're always thinking of food,' Jae said. Stu might be skinny but he could eat more than ten men.

'My mum's a great cook. Isn't your mum a good cook?'

'Sure. But my mum spends all day in the kitchen preparing meals, then cleaning up after Dad, and never leaves the house.' With the heel of his palm, Jae rubbed over his aching heart. The last image of his mother wasn't anything like the farewell he'd gotten when he'd started university. Back then his parents gazed at him with pride, and Jae had given them everything for that look

Until he wanted to do something to make himself proud, and that was the day that look died. So too did the world he once knew.

'Go right here, down to the end, then left for the gym. You can park at the back in their basement.' Stu pointed out the directions while Jae drove. 'Don't you take your mother out?'

'I tried to. We lunched a few times. She hardly ate. Said she didn't trust the food and wanted to go home.'

'Is that because of your culture?'

'They've lived in this country long before I was born. They're missing out on so much by playing by their old-world rules.' A world he was only truly experiencing now. Jae sighed as he steered past a series of shops on the ground floor to a set of apartments. He turned down the rear laneway and stopped at a set of roller doors. 'No matter how much I tried to tell them they never listened.'

Stu reached over and swiped the gym's key-card at the carpark ticket machine. The front panel's light turned green and the roller door curled upwards. 'My mum's the same, giving up so much to look after us mob. She wouldn't let me help her when I told her I'd get a job. She wanted me out, said it was better this way, less mouths to feed. And I do eat a lot. She's got this new boyfriend now who says he helps her with the bills. But he hits her, man.'

Jae faced his mate while the large roller door rattled as it curled into the roof. 'How do you know that?'

'My littlest brother told me on the phone. He said Bob gave Mum a black eye for dinner bein' cold.'

'Which brother?' Jae asked, because Stu was one of six.

'Gavan.'

'Isn't he your cousin?'

'Yeah, but he's been with us since he was two so he's like my little brother. Gavan said he got so scared he hid in the cupboard where we keep the cereal.'

Jae scowled. 'No one should hit women and scare children like that.' The roller doors stopped and Jae drove through slowly while his eyes adjusted to the dim light. The place was deserted except for a few cars parked by the elevator doors.

'I so wanna get-up that arsehole, but Bob's this massive truck driver.'

The roller door closed behind them and Jae aimed for the back wall where the fluorescent lights weren't working. He reversed into the car park's shadows, turned off the engine, silencing the music. He cleaned his glasses, put them back on, and focused on the blinking broken light near the lifts. Lights on. Lights off. Darkness. 'We should go visit that guy after we're done here.'

From the passenger seat, Stu searched the vacant underground carpark. 'What guy?'

Jae scowled, his knuckles whitened as he tightened his grip on the steering wheel. 'No one has the right to hit anyone's mother.'

'You'd do that?'

'I would.' Jae needed to make up for what he couldn't do himself, so he'd do it to help others. 'We're friends. No, you're my family.' Stu was his only friend, loyal to each other since the day they'd met on campus, and that was all Jae needed for a new family.

'Are you ever gonna forgive your father for what he's done to you?' Stu whispered with empathy heard in each word.

Heat pricked at Jae's cheeks and neck while his stomach clenched tight. He knew his father would never forgive him and neither would his mother. They were already grieving for him. 'Why waste my time, when I'm only living for today.' He didn't want to know about yesterday, or any long-term-tomorrows, only today. Not when he was finally free from penitentiary.

EIGHT

Under a hooded awning, between large potted palm trees, Ryan walked along a red carpet. He turned the diamond handle and pushed open the glass door. Cool air with a hint of florals and vanilla washed over him as his eyes adjusted to a bright white showroom. Plush white couches rested in the centre, surrounding a coffee table holding hardcover portfolios of assorted themes. Still images of glamourous couples in ball gowns, of balloons, champagne, and fireworks, hung like art in a museum. It was classy and he peered back to the carpark.

This upmarket chic display room was not what he'd expected — from a shed.

'Hi, I'm Benjamin. How may I help you?' He gave a big white-toothed smile behind the large white desk. The teeth and desk matched.

'I'm looking for Emma?' Ryan approached a clean desk that only held a PC screen, a keyboard, and a mouse. It was nothing like his new work-desk covered in paperwork, courtesy of David. Ryan didn't say no, because he understood he had to prove himself. He wasn't going to screw up again and risk his job, so he'd obediently follow orders, because his life was all about the job.

On the side of the clear desk sat a photo frame of three people. Ryan recognised Emma and Benjamin with another woman, guessing it was Victoria, who Emma had mentioned a few times. The trio were hugging each other wearing towers of tacky coloured party hats. Glitter shone from their cheeks and hair, while they were wrapped in oodles of streamers as if wearing an entire supermarket shelf of party stock between them, and having a ball.

'And you are?'

'Detective Ryan Lewis.' His new title sounded foreign in this silent room. Should he flash his badge too?

'Oh, yooour Ryan. Why didn't you say so?' Benjamin bounced to his feet with a big grin and wide eyes. 'She's out the back, follow me.' Benjamin turned another diamond crystal shaped doorknob that was part of a cleverly hidden door within the wall. It opened into the shed as Pitbull's *Bad Man* made his heart bounce. Ryan had the song but he'd never played it this loud.

Through the magic door, Ryan did a full circle inside the expansive shed. Except for the surprising front showroom office, this was what he'd expected to find. A large shed, full of assorted equipment neatly stacked on large wide shelves.

It was divided into the thirds. The showroom office occupied the front area, with the roof space used for storage. At the back wall, a wrought iron staircase disappeared into a mezzanine floor with a small landing. *Was that another office?*

On the right, sliding doors opened up the entire wall to face a row of trees as part of the carpark. A red sports car was parked inside with heaps of space to spare. In the centre of the shed floor stood a large workbench surrounded by bar stools.

Music pumped from the speakers while Emma worked at the centre table. She swivelled on her paint-stained tennis shoes. Her eyes shone, painting while she sang, having her own party, oblivious they were there. He had to smile at her. Tilting his head, his hand in his pocket, it was the cutest—and the best thing he'd seen all day.

Benjamin bounced over to the table and grabbed the remote control. *'Emma,* Ryan's here.' He hollered over the lowering volume.

'Ryan… Oh crap.' Emma's big eyes widened, wiping glitter off her face, and trying to tidy her hair that hung in messy pigtails.

'That has got to be the longest string of pearls I've ever seen anyone wear.' Ryan admired her blush that was so bright against her powdered complexion. It'd be hotter than a campfire in the middle of the outback desert and something he could warm his hands against.

'It's what we put on the tables,' Emma mumbled as she began unravelling the long string of pearls around her neck. Round and round, it uncoiled like rope that was long enough to moor an oil-tanker to the wharf. 'I got attacked by Benjamin.'

'I was being creative, sweetie. Anyway, I'm going now.' Benjamin paused, grabbing the door jamb to the office, his head tilted and scanned Ryan from top to bottom. 'I'll lock up on my way out. Bye.' Benjamin gave Emma the thumbs up and the door closed.

'Did he just check me out?' Ryan had caught all of it in the reflection of the red sports car's shiny panel.

Emma's giggle made him smile a little. 'You should be honoured, Benjamin's very picky. I won't ask about my van.'

'Why not?' That's why he was here on his way back to the office to finish off his day.

'Rough day, huh?'

His shoulders sagged, sliding his hands into his pockets. 'Is it that obvious?'

'Yes. Bar's open.' She walked to the corner of the shed.

'No'—freaking—'way.' Ryan's jaw dropped as he wiped a palm over his face and eyeballed the area again. Rarely was he surprised by anything, but never twice in the same place.

Emma had a bar.

A proper, upmarket, wooden bar, with brass rails and leather barstools tucked into the corner of her shed. Mirrored walls displayed various neon signs with glass fridges full of assorted bottles and glasses. It even had a jukebox and a pinball machine.

It was not what he'd expected to find in the corner of a shed, with black-and-white tiles covering an area big enough for a dance floor. There was even a mirrored ball in the low ceiling, smoke machines, karaoke machines, costumes on a rack and so much more. 'So, it's a real Party Shed?'

'I have been known to indulge in after-hour creative staff meetings.' She gave a wry grin from behind the bar.

'Do you charge people for drinks?'

'No, otherwise I'd have to get a liquor licence. Name your beverage preference?'

Should he? He glanced at his watch. He had officially knocked off work. 'Beer?'

'From what country?' She waved her hand over an assortment of pale ales through to the stocky stouts.

'Er, lite beer, please.' He tugged at his shirt's collar, uncomfortable over the fanciness of the humble beer. 'Why do you have all of this alcohol?'

'I have tasting sessions for clients. When I have a party theme, I like to create cocktails to match, which makes it all part of the experience.' She grabbed two beers from the fridge, expertly popped the top and passed him a bottle.

His eyebrow arched and he nodded at her bar. 'How did you end up with so much?'

'Call it a hazard of the trade. They're either tips from satisfied clients, leftover party stock, or alcohol distributors trying to keep in my good graces. Take a seat.' She returned to the large work table in the centre of the shed.

Ryan took a seat and winced at the various dog paraphernalia on the table. But it was the way the glitter reflected on her face and in her hair that was dazzling him more.

'Um, how are you going with the prank phone calls?' Ryan sipped the ale to soothe his dry throat and tugged at his too-tight tie. No matter how pleasurable a distraction she was, he was meant to be here for work. Even if he was still amazed at what was inside this shed.

He then gazed at Emma. If this was what her workspace was like on the inside, what was Emma like beneath her shy shell?

* * *

How dare Benjamin let Ryan inside and then leave her alone with the guy! She swallowed hard on her beer while wiping glitter off her face. It was everywhere. She looked like crap and hadn't expected visitors.

But then, they were just friends, considering Ryan worked with Kelly who was gorgeous. 'Kelly would've told you, huh?'

'Kelly mentioned you've had a few pranks calls.'

'No doubt she did.' Probably pounced on the guy from her perch in reception as soon as he walked in the door.

'What sort of calls are you getting?'

So, this was a work visit. Why did she ever hope for more?

Emma had work of her own to do too, so she put down her beer, picked up her paintbrush and dabbed at the dog bowl. 'My van's famous now from the media attention, and there's these girls who sing and hang up all the time. Aren't prank calls meant to be when you call up a cute guy, but then when he answers you get all tongue-tied and can't speak so you hang up?'

'When did this happen?'

'What? Me pranking a cute guy?' The heat pulsed in her cheeks. She had to be glowing.

Ryan grinned at her. 'I meant your answering machine. When?'

'Late at night.'

'How many people know you live here, Emma? Where do you live?' His neck arched as he peered around with wary eyes.

'Up there is my apartment.' She pointed to the back staircase. 'I don't like to advertise.'

'Why?'

'I live in a shed. What do you live in?'

'At the Police barracks?'

'Why?'

'What do you mean why?'

'I'd assumed a house, garden, kids, glamorous wife.'

'I assumed this was just a shed.' He pointed to her bar and back at the showroom.

'I have to surprise my clients, it's how I get their business. People come to me when they're either too busy, too lazy, too unsure, or want to be surprised.'

'I get it. And you surprised me from your first magic trick of pulling a prawn head out from behind your ear.'

She laughed with him. His smile was enthralling dynamite.

Ryan shrugged, saying, 'I haven't been back long enough to bother finding other accommodations yet.'

'Where have you been?'

'I was with the AFP'

'What's AFP?' She'd heard that word twice now.

'Australian Federal Police.'

'What were you doing there? Here, make yourself useful.' She gave him a paint brush and a silver dog bowl, hoping to keep him occupied. She couldn't wait for his reaction.

'What do you want me to do?' Ryan frowned at the paintbrush and dog bowl covered with a sticker.

'Paint the name on it and then embellish it however you like.'

He raised his eyebrow at her. 'On a dog bowl?'

'Yes.' She laughed. Would he do it? 'I have a Pampered Pooch Palace party tomorrow night.'

'Say that three times real fast'

'No.' They laughed with that same comfortableness shared at the car yard the other day. *He was just a friend.*

'Any colour?'

'No, dogs can't read and I hear they're colour blind too.'

He took off his suit coat, loosened his tie, tucking the end into his shirt, and rolled up his sleeves. 'Better pay for my beer somehow. So, what do I do?'

She was impressed he was willing to give it a go. 'Pick a colour and paint.' She waved over the assorted coloured pots spread across the table amongst the glitter.

'I can't believe I'm sitting here painting a dog bowl with the name Cujo. Let me guess, like the book, Cujo is a big dog?' Ryan painted gold on the side of the silver dog bowl.

'Didn't know there was book? Cujo is a hairless Mexican Chihuahua with attitude. Want a dog biscuit?' She held up a plate of bone-shaped biscuits.

'No thanks, they're dog biscuits.'

'They're yummy.' She grinned coyly taking a bite.

'They're dog biscuits. Do you eat cat food too?' Ryan asked with an arched eyebrow.

'No. These are human biscuits made to look like dog biscuits that go into these doggie bags full of fabulous doggy delights.'

He chuckled, shaking his head. 'What's all this for?'

'A doggy day spa owner is launching her designer dog clothes with a fashion parade for the A-list's crowd of pampered pets.'

'Dog fashion parade?'

'Oh yeah, I can't wait. I've co-ordinated the music for the cat-walk for canines in these cute coats and jackets, they're very stylish. My friend Victoria has a bulldog called The Prime Minister, he'll be wearing a vintage styled, silk smoking jacket and cravat. My cat's running around in a bow tie somewhere.' She searched the shelves for the feline's favourite haunts. 'There he is, that's Mister.' The grey striped cat with yellow eyes stared down with his top hat and bow tie, unimpressed.

Ryan swore under his breath, then burst out laughing. 'How does the cat handle the music? Like from before?'

'Mister's deaf, living the good life now he's retired from the streets. He lives up there on the shelf. It's his gym.' With walkways of rope and long tree branches that intermingled with the shelving system.

'Is the cat completely deaf?' Ryan asked.

'The vet says he is. Mister's sensitive to vibrations. I tap the shelves if I want his attention, or to warn him I'm moving stuff. He'll sleep through the music, but he loves the mirror ball and will chase the lights across the floor for hours. Do you have any pets?'

'No. We moved around too much. Hey, how's this look?' He held up a crappy mass of gold paint.

'Good, now bling it up. Use whatever you like. Glitter goes with everything and it's considered a must-have party accessory.' Emma pointed to the open jars of coloured glitter.

'Like you're wearing?'

Again, she wiped what she could off her face. 'Another

hazard of this industry, it gets everywhere.'

'Can't believe I'm doing this,' Ryan muttered. 'Don't tell anyone, okay? It'll ruin my reputation.'

'Your secret's safe with me,' said Emma. 'What were you doing with the AFP?'

'I worked with the State Police prior, and the opportunity came up to be part of the AFP exchange programme, so I took it.'

'What did you do? Or is it all secret squirrel stuff?'

He chuckled, focusing on her with those chartreuse eyes of his that made her thirsty. She took a deep swig of her beer hoping to drown that glitter storm inside her tummy.

'No, I did relief work for AFP members while on call for certain parliamentarians daring to leave Canberra. I got posted to Fiji, and the jungles in New Guinea, the Solomon Islands, and a few remote outback Indigenous communities in the Northern Territory.'

'You really got around, huh?'

'Guess that's why I had trouble settling down when I first got back.'

'Are you settled now?' Emma asked, sprinkling glitter on her dog bowl. Was Ryan a loner? The type to never marry and leave a trail of broken hearts behind him like a sailor?

Who was she to judge, when she was at her most sociable home alone with a deaf cat.

'I'm happy with my new promotion. I'm looking forward to a routine,' said Ryan.

'Until the next adventure comes along?'

'I guess so.' Putting down his paintbrush, he winced at his

dog bowl. 'Is this any good? It looks like crap to me.'

She took the dog bowl from him and removed the sticker giving a perfect outline of the dog's name. 'I'm impressed, Detective. I think you've missed your calling in life. This is great.'

'You're just saying that.'

'I'd tell you if it was crap, because this is my reputation on the line.' She put it among the others and grabbed another bowl. 'Here, you can paint Tinkerbell's.' She bit on her bottom lip to stop the snort-laugh.

'Let me guess, a big dog?'

'A rottweiler. She'll be wearing a fairy costume with a purple tutu in the doggy parade. Glitter is a must on this one to represent fairy dust.'

He chuckled, taking the bowl in one hand and the paintbrush in the other. 'Well, if she's in a purple tutu, I'd better co-ordinate with the rest of her wardrobe.' He dabbed his paint brush into the purple paint and then onto the silver dog bowl. 'How many more do you have to do?'

'Just these two and I'm done until tomorrow.'

'Do you have a big weekend planned for parties?'

Emma examined the to-do list on her tablet where nearly all her items were checked off for today. 'Not too bad. Tomorrow there's a luncheon at the Council Chambers for the Mayor. There's the Pampered Pooch Party, and a cocktail soiree at a new hairdressing salon tomorrow night. Saturday there's an elite picnic on the river's Esplanade, and a swinging sixties hippy night.' But with no van for deliveries, all her profits were disappearing into transport fees. 'I might stick around for that one it starts at five.' It might cheer her up.

'Why so early for a party?'

'It's at the Southern Cross Aged Care lodge and they have dinner at five. They're fabulous people, great dancers, with this amazing zest for life.'

'Sounds like you visit often?'

'I offer weekly craft lessons there, which is my cheap way of keeping a highly experienced labour force. They've lived history, making them an excellent resource for details with theme-parties.' And they might be the perfect crowd to cure her post-birthday-aging blues.

'For free?'

'Bargain, huh?'

With purple paint on the tip of his brush he paused, with questioning eyes and a slight curl to his lips. 'Really?'

'They won't take any money from me. They don't drink, can't have certain foods for their health, and no matter what I've offered, they refuse payment. The least I can do is let them use my equipment for their monthly parties,' said Emma.

'How did you get into this?'

'By accident. I worked in a few office jobs and worked for a hire company. There I met a wedding planner who gave me a job after-hours.'

'I thought you hated weddings?'

'I don't hate weddings. I don't get involved with the planning, or deal with brides and their over-emotional parents.' *Never again.* 'I feel sorry for some of the grooms. They have no idea what they're marrying behind the white veil and shiny smile.'

'I can relate.'

'You're married?' Her heart froze solid and checked out his hands that were vacant of any rings.

'Divorced.'

'No way.' She gasped at her heart's reaction that had instantly started to thaw.

'My ex-wife demanded the whole white wedding,' said Ryan. 'It cost her dad a fortune. All that effort to marry a woman who acted so normal—at first. Have you been married?'

'No.' She didn't date longer than a week. 'How long were you married for?'

'Three years. Separated for two of them. And the divorce was finalised by the time I hopped onto the plane for my first posting with the AFP.' His head and shoulders dropped as he said, 'Thankfully, no kids.'

He seemed so sad about there being no children. 'Messy divorce?'

'Oh yeah. She wanted everything. In the end, I gave her the furniture and crap because I couldn't be bothered fighting anymore. When the house got sold, I got half, bought my Harley, and took off for a few years.' He sat there staring at his beer bottle while the music played in the background. 'Are you going to ask me?'

'Ask you what?' Not that anyone bothered asking Emma for her opinion before, she was used to staying quiet so others could speak.

'Why I got divorced?'

'None of my business.' Dabbing paint onto the bowl, she tried to appear nonchalant. But she was dying to know.

'You sure?' He lowered his head giving her that sexy steely stare, she had to reply to his police interrogation.

'Okay, I'm curious.' How could anyone dislike Ryan?

'My ex said it was my shift work that made her have an affair with the guy who'd been building my car shed.'

'That's rough. Car sheds have a lot to answer for, like my make-believe-car-yard-phobia crap.' While her own mode of transport was lost in the world somewhere without her.

'My fault.'

'How?' She paused painting to frown. Surprised she'd been so blunt to ask such a question, when it wasn't her business.

'I'd heard rumours in the beginning, she'd been screwing around on me. We'd only been casually dating for a few months when she told me she was pregnant. Sadly, she lost the baby not long after we'd married. Then, when we separated, she told me it wasn't even mine.'

'Bitch.' Emma slapped her palm over her mouth.

His lips tugged into a grin that soon disappeared. 'Tell me about it. I caught her in bed with this guy—in my bed, with my wife, in my house.'

'Did you shoot him?' She said through her fingers covering her mouth to stop the verbal spillage.

He chuckled. 'No. I punched him, put him in the hospital and almost lost my job over it.' He sat up straighter and frowned so hard she swore her table was going to crack under his stare.

'But you didn't lose your job, you said you got promoted?'

'I'd completed my degree in criminology a few months before I got married, and was offered a Detective's position. But then it all went wrong… I lost the promotion and almost lost my job, so I took an immediate transfer with the AFP. I finally got accepted back in as a Detective four years later.' He paused. 'Wow, four years.'

Was he still bitter towards his Ex-wife?

'I'm sorry.' He winced, dropping his brush and bowl onto the table to rub his palms over his face. 'I've never confessed so much about myself like that.'

If the guy had only just come back, did he have any friends in the force? 'Hey, what's said in this shed, stays in this shed. It's company policy.'

'I like that, thank you.' He nodded at her, picked up his brush and stabbed paint at the dog bowl. 'How come you never got married?'

She shrugged, taking a gulp of her beer hoping she appeared calm. 'Too busy and my work hours suck.'

'It'd be similar to my shift work?'

'Maybe. I spoke with your partner, David's wife earlier. They're using me for his parents' fiftieth wedding anniversary.'

'That's great. You'd see the good side of life with your job.'

'I assist in the celebrations of others.' From the sidelines where she would set it all up and leave before the guests arrived because she never stayed for the end.

'Except weddings.'

'Ah-huh. You'd notice the crappy side of people's life?' Kicking herself for saying that because it dimmed the shine in his eyes.

'I do.'

'Why did you become a Police Officer?'

'Dad was in the Army and wanted me to join. I liked the

Police more because you don't move around at the mercy of the Defence Force like Dad. I still get to shift in the Police, and there are different areas including the Taskies.'

'Is that some Eskimo code word for Canadian Mounty?'

'No, they have a Mounted Police division as part of the Riot Squad. The Taskies are the Tactical Squad.'

'The heavy-duty shoot-'em-up crew?'

'Yeah, I was a sniper. We worked as bodyguards for politicians and other visiting VIPs, I did the same for the AFP.'

'You're like a real live Superhero.'

'Don't think so. I'm just a bloke who wants to do his job.' Again, his frown flickered.

'Me too,' she said, putting down her completed dog bowl to dry. 'Except I'm not a guy.' Just a girl without her van.

'No, you're not.' His eyes walked over her, she felt naked while fully dressed in a sack with sleeves. 'Here. Is this any good?' He handed her his bowl.

She removed the sticker to reveal the perfect outline of the name painted in purple with glitter, and put it alongside the others. 'They look great, you should be proud.'

'I'm never looking at a dog bowl the same after this. I'd better leave you to it.'

'I'll let you out.' She led him through the open side door. 'Thanks for your help and the visit'

'Thanks for the beer. But tell no one I blinged up dog bowls.' Slipping on his jacket and adjusting his collar she saw his gun in its hip holster and badge and handcuffs on his belt.

'Your reputation's safe with me, Detective.' Emma opened the double gates that ran along her wide driveway.

Ryan stopped at the curb and scanned the quiet deserted area. Her shed stood at the end of a cul-de-sac among other dark industrial sheds, where his sedan was the only car parked on the street. 'You don't get scared being here on your own?'

'No, I like the privacy and there's no noise restrictions being industrial. And once I've closed those doors, you can't tell anyone's here.' Two large rottweilers ran along the neighbouring fence line.

'Are these the neighbour's guard dogs you mentioned?'

Wow, he remembers everything. 'That's Jack and Jill. They're harmless.'

'Are they going to get personalised dog bowls too?'

'No, but they were my test dummies for the dog biscuits we made.' She patted the two dogs vying for her attention through the fence.

Ryan cleared his throat, tugging at his tie he asked, 'Emma, would you want to go out to dinner sometime?'

'What, me?' She froze, blinking at him, then she peeked over her shoulder to see who else he was talking to.

'You're the only one standing there.'

Did she hear right?

'When was the last time you were asked out?'

'Um, years,' she squeaked with shoulders up to her ears. Why did she admit that? 'Sure, um, I mean, yeah, okay. But, only, if you want to?' *Eeek.*

'Great. I'll call you.' As he leaned over, his sophisticated exotic scent wound around her. He kissed her cheek and heat exploded beneath his lips like electricity, catapulting to all her nerve endings. She found it hard to breathe against her palpitating heart as floating glitter whirled like a cyclone in her stomach. *All that from one peck on the cheek!*

'Lock up and keep safe, Emma.'

'I will.' Her voice sounded as shaky as she was on the inside. She was grateful for the cool night air fighting against the heat in her cheeks. *I am so out of my league.*

She locked her gate in a daze.

No one ever asked Emma out, especially not handsome detectives. She'd assumed he'd felt sorry for her and was just doing his job and hadn't seen it coming—was he that desperate?

And not once did Ryan mention what her *Parte'* van had been up to. So how bad was it?

NINE

Victoria held her champagne in one hand and an unlit cigarette in the other. Her hips swayed in her black dress as her heels clicked on the polished marble. She swanned through the crowd leading her waddling bulldog, The Prime Minister, in his red vintage smoking jacket and cravat to stop in front of Emma sorting out party gifts for guests. 'Oi, I just heard Detective Adonis asked you out. When were you going to tell me?'

'I've been busy,' said Emma, putting the last of the delectable doggie bags out. 'I've scored another three puppy parties from today's event. There's this whole new untapped resource of clients using pet stores I could use for the future.'

'It's going viral on Instagram, link it to your website, babe, milk-it while it's hot.'

'Good idea, oh guru of advertising.' From her bag Emma grabbed her spare tablet, entering the details. She'd lost her other one in the van that the insurance company still had three weeks to cash in on.

Victoria lowered her sunglasses at Emma. 'By the way, babe, I like what you threw on today. I'm glad you're taking the anti-gravity challenge and wearing boots with heels.'

'Only way to go.' How long before she kissed concrete

though?

'Did Benjamin dress you today?'

'Not today.' Some days Benjamin refused to let Emma go out in public until she'd changed. He'd even had Victoria join him to do an intervention, attacking at her wardrobe with scissors, while giving her a lecture that clothes were not sacks with sleeves.

Emma dressed to blend.

'I'm learning,' Emma said, admiring her tailored houndstooth dress that hid the dog hair. With its oversized white cuffs and collar, it complimented her long black boots.

Heeled boots she could do. Normal heels were disastrous. Her feet just couldn't get co-ordinated and she'd fall over without fail. Like a good wine, she was improving with age.

'Hey, did Ryan ask you out or not?'

'Who told you? And you both look gorgeous.' Emma leaned over to pat The Prime Minister who wagged his whole body.

'The Prime Minister always looks gorgeous, he's with me, isn't he? And stop changing the subject. Benjamin told me.'

'Trust Benjamin to not keep a secret.' He'd walked into work this morning demanding details. After a few hours of his relentless badgering Emma confessed. It was a personal record to last that long.

'Benjamin was bursting with the news like he hadn't been able to pee all day.' Victoria stepped in closer. Lowered her sunglasses, narrowing her eyes, as the scent of Chanel No.5 wrapped around Emma. 'Again, you've changed the subject.'

Emma could skip bits of the story with Benjamin.

However, when it came to Victoria, it was an interrogation for details. She swiped Victoria's champagne glass and took a deep mouthful.

'Wow, that bad.' Victoria signalled to the drink's waiter with her empty glass and unlit cigarette. 'Come on, babe, grab a glass. I'll need to light the sucker up to hear this.' Victoria handed out fresh champagne. She then wrapped her arm around Emma's and guided them through the crowd of stylishly dressed pets and their owners, while The Prime Minister dutifully followed.

'I'm waiting.' Victoria demanded, exhaling a stream of cigarette smoke towards the dark sky in the open outdoor area that had fake grass and a lap pool.

Emma sipped her champagne and explained Ryan's surprise request for dinner.

'I hope you said yes? Benjamin said he's a stunner of a man in his suit, and we both know how picky Benjamin is.'

'That's the problem, this guy is so out of my league.'

'What makes you say that? Babe, the guy has witnessed you at your worst, wearing prawn shells for hair accessories, drinking from a wine bottle in the gutter. And he cured you of your car-yard-phobia. Oh, which reminds me, I've got a new car launch I'd love you to handle.'

'Sounds good. Hey, when did I start this make-believe-car-yard-phobia?'

'No idea, you just told me when I went for my first car you didn't do car yards, probably about the same time you refused to do weddings, except mine.'

Emma opened her mouth to speak. She knew when the

weddings stopped.

Victoria held up her hand with cigarette smouldering at her. 'Stop changing the subject. Are you going out with Detective Adonis or not?'

'I'd assumed Ryan was feeling sorry for me, and it was all work. I wasn't expecting it.' Emma leaned her back against the wall and sipped her champagne. The Prime Minister waddled over to the lap pool and teetered on the edge. 'Should the Prime Minister be drinking that water?'

The bulldog's bum was high in the air, leaning precariously over the pool's edge, with his tiny tail wagging at the sound of his name.

Victoria shrugged, blowing a steady stream of cigarette smoke a coal-run power station would be proud of. 'It's a doggy day spa, I'm sure it's tested for quality assurance. Has Ryan called yet for a time?'

'No. He knows I'm busy with work this weekend.'

'Are you excited?' Victoria asked.

'I'm terrified.'

'You got on well when you went car shopping, and he's been ringing you, right?'

'To keep me updated on my van, considering it's in the news all the time. Please, don't make a big issue out of this.'

Victoria smirked and pointed her long red manicured nail at Emma. 'No, you're out of practice. Detective Adonis is using the whole work thingy as an excuse to call you.'

'Is that how he normally scores?'

'Mixing business with pleasure isn't illegal, you know.'

'Ryan has this receptionist at his work, who's gorgeous,

young, and thin, drooling at him all day long.'

'You're gorgeous too.' With a hand on hip, Victoria took a sip of her champagne glancing sideways at Emma. 'You really like this guy, who isn't in *your league.*'

Emma rolled her eyes as she sipped on her glass of bubbly, her league was way below ten thousand oceanic bubbles in the deepest hole of the ocean.

'Have you used those vouchers we gave you?' Victoria grabbed her mobile from her handbag and scrolled through the numbers.

'No, but—'

'Shh, I'm speaking.' Victoria held up her palm to stop Emma, gave her a wink and smiled as she spoke over the phone. 'Stella, it's Victoria. Remember those vouchers for Emma the *Parte*' Babe's birthday bash… Ah-huh, that's right. So how busy are you?' Victoria puffed on her coffin-nail, then sipped her champagne, looking every part the glamorous rich socialite, while Emma slouched against the wall.

'I haven't got time. I should—' She went to move but Victoria held her back.

'Great we'll be there within the hour. Love your work.' Victoria disconnected the call and faced Emma. 'It's settled, you're coming with me.'

'I've got work to do.'

'Don't argue with me. We both know Benjamin's brilliant at finishing things for you because you never stay for any party, making you mine.'

Emma's shoulders slunk as she pouted with her fat bottom lip. 'I'd rather go home to bed.'

'Where has your spark gone?'

'I think they stole it with my van.' Along with her privacy from the prank calls and unwanted social media attention. Once, her bubble-of-bliss music machine had brought her so much joy travelling from one party to the next—now it was soul-crushing to see her business logo on the news linked to armed robbery, assault, and now murder.

'Considering all the crap over your *Parte'* van you *need* this. Let's give Benjamin the good news. He can show up for the unveiling. Consider this practice for when we're doing our hair for my wedding.' Victoria hooked her arm around Emma's and guided her out the room.

'I haven't said yes—' Not to the wedding or the hair appointment. Not like she had a choice.

'We'll need more champagne. Have you got your customary alcoholic tip yet?'

The door closed.

The Prime Minister waddled from the pool to sit and stare at the door.

It opened a few moments later. 'I'm sorry mummy forgot you, darling. Let me make it up to you, I'll take you out to dinner.' Victoria patted the bulldog who wagged his whole body. 'You look so handsome. Let's find your lead and more booze for mummy.' And the door shut behind them.

Celebrating the new-do, and a kilo in hair loss, Emma shared dinner with Victoria and Benjamin at a sidewalk restaurant. There they ate and watched the foot traffic and cars in the city while The Prime Minister slept under the table.

'I'm so full after that feed, I want to curl up and go to sleep like The Prime Minister.' Victoria patted her tummy and reached for an unlit cigarette.

Benjamin leaned back in his chair. 'Me too.'

'Ditto on sleep and slippers.' Emma was full. Her eyebrows tingled from the waxing, and her feet ached after running around in heels all day. *How did Victoria do it?* She wiped away dog hair off her dress, keen to go home and shower because she had another big day tomorrow.

Emma sat back, wary of the waitress clearing their table and glanced across the road. *'Are you kidding me.'* She sat up, wide eyed.

'What?' Asked both Benjamin and Victoria looking around.

'There's my van.' Emma pointed across the road, while she dug around in her handbag for her mobile.

'What do we do, sweetie?' Benjamin asked.

'Christ, I need a cigarette, this is all too exciting.' Victoria lit up and puffed like a vintage VW's exhaust coughing in winter.

'I'll call Ryan, I think he's working.' Emma dialled his number.

'Hi Emma, this is a nice surprise,' said Ryan.

'Are you working tonight?' Emma narrowed her eyes at her van. It was filthy, but dent free.

The thief in the driver's seat seemed so young and yet so normal. Pushing round spectacles higher along his nose, flicking through a book, casually waiting, while parked across the road. He matched the photo from the police station, but he did not match the way the media had described him.

'Yes, I am. Are you okay Emma, you sound upset?'

'I'm staring straight at my stolen van.' Her car keys suddenly felt heavy in her bag.

'Where are you?'

'I'm at the Italian cafe on Smith Street. My van is parked out front of Tortilla's Mexican place.'

'We're on our way. Don't move.'

She heard Ryan give instructions to someone and what sounded like he was in a car.

Across the road she watched her *Parte'* van as another guy climbed into the cab. Again, the passenger was nothing like the newspaper's description. 'They're leaving. HEY!'

'Emma, don't you dare,' cried out Ryan on the other end of the line.

She tossed her phone to Benjamin. Dashed to the sidewalk as fast as she could in heels, waving at the car thieves while trying not to trip over the gutter. She was clumsy enough in bare feet, without adding fuel. But with the traffic's noise they didn't notice her. 'Hey, that's *my van!*'

Now was *not* the time to blend.

She ducked between the traffic and stood on the centre line of the road waiting for a break. 'Excuse me, can I have my van back, please?'

'Oh, hello,' said the driver, pushing up his glasses.

'That's my van you're driving, may I have it back, pleeeease?'

'Aww, that's cute.' The driver grinned at her as he leaned his elbow out the open window. 'Sure, when we're done, Miss.

By the way, you have great manners. What's your name?'

'Emma. What's yours?' She swayed on the spot, only mere metres away from her mission in life—to get her van back, and not get skittled by the traffic whirling around her.

'I'm Jaed. I do prefer to be called Jae,' he said with a smile.

He looked harmless, and spoke so well.

'Hey there, Emma, I'm Stuart. Stu.' Stu waved with a wide friendly grin, leaning forward calling out from the passenger seat.

She had to stall them until the cops arrived. 'Are you best mates?'

'You bet. We met in Uni, sufferin' the same law classes,' called out Stu.

Did law school teach van theft as part of its curriculum? 'Excuse me, Jae, Stu, that's my van and I need it for work. I'd appreciate it if you could give it back. Please? It's been a real hassle without it.' She pleaded, hoping for a break in traffic to cross the road and hang off her van's door until the police arrived.

'Not today, Miss, we'll take good care of it, promise.' Jae waved, then steered into the traffic.

'We love your music mix,' shouted Stu and then they were gone.

'Hey, come back?' Emma cried out, as her van disappeared down the busy road. 'No, no, no.' She stamped her foot in the middle of the street. A car tooted beside her, she almost jumped into their path, and scooted back to the café's sidewalk.

'What did they say?' Victoria asked, lighting another fresh cigarette from the butt of the other.

Emma sat heavily in her chair. 'They said they'll bring it back when they've finished with it. And I asked them nicely too.'

'You've always had nice manners, better than me, babe.'

'You're always good with people, even the rude ones,' said Benjamin, holding out Emma's mobile. 'Although, Ryan sounded ticked when I told him what you were doing.'

'I forgot about him.' Emma rolled her eyes and shoved her phone back into her bag. 'Can I go home now?'

'Yes, babe, let's find you a cab.'

A police car whizzed past with flashing lights and sirens blaring. Pulling up in front of Emma, flashing its police lights in the grill and dashboard was a dark sedan. Ryan jumped from the passenger side, slamming the door behind him as he approached Emma. *What do you think you were doing?*

Emma clutched her bag, blinking at his anger, it was sexy and scary all at the same time. 'Pardon me?'

'*Are you crazy?* Those guys are killers with handguns.'

'I just told them I wanted my van back. I even said *please.*' Not liking Ryan shouting in her face. *What the hell?* Only her sister did that and Emma was used to that. But not from Ryan.

'You what?' Ryan's eyes narrowed at her as his lips tightened in a line.

'I asked them to give me my van back.'

'Are you stupid?'

Her face stung like she'd been slapped, and her eyes widened as she backed away from him.

'Aw crap, Emma, I'm sorry.'

With hands on her hips she glared at him.

She was not stupid. *Silent—yes. Never stupid.* No matter

how many times she'd been told, she never spoke up. But right now, she couldn't stop.

'It's my van. I've paid for it. I own it. And it was staring right at me, when it's been running around the city on a crime spree. A van no one's been able to catch, that they're not even hiding, while enjoying my playlist. Yet, I'm the one being bombarded by consistent prank calls, trolls spamming my website, and the media hassling me for dirt. The insurance company's stalling my claim until my van's been caught. But hey, they bumped up my premiums anyway. I've lost jobs, my profits have died, my professional reputation is trashed, and I may have to rebrand my entire business with a new logo so as to not be recognised as the van of terror. When all I want is my life, my music, and my bloody van back. Is it too much to ask for?'

Ryan replied calmly, 'They could've hurt you, Emma.'

'Well I'm sorry, but it's my personal property, and I saw no harm in asking them to give it back.' She turned away from Ryan and said to Benjamin and Victoria, 'Let's go.' Before she ranted on much more—which was more than she'd ever done in her lifetime. Emma never complained, until now.

What had she become?

* * *

Ryan reached out and grabbed her elbow gently. He couldn't let her walk away while she was still angry at him. 'Emma, I shouldn't have yelled at you like that. I'm sorry.'

She stared at him with those big beautiful eyes but with

her plump lips pursed. Still beautiful, but her angry look was not her best. He preferred those plump lips to be smiling, at him—which was frighteningly addictive. 'Did you do something to your hair, it looks nice?'

She pulled her arm away from him angrily, turning away. He'd never seen her with her glossy hair down, she was stunning.

But he'd stuffed up—this time it wasn't about his job, but the woman. 'Come on, Emma, I said I'm sorry.'

'Oh, by the way, the driver's name is Jaed. He calls himself Jae. His friend's name is Stuart who goes by the name of Stu. They're best friends who met at Uni studying law together—which is ironic. Good night, Detective,' Emma said coldly over her shoulder. She walked away with head held high, arm in arm with Benjamin and Victoria, followed by a waddling bulldog wearing some formal red silk jacket.

Ryan wiped his palm over his face. He was used to doors closing on him where he was left to find his own way in the dark, but he wasn't prepared for her. Most people came with warning signs and he wished he knew how to read hers.

But he had work to do, and thanks to the beautiful, yet angry woman, she'd given him some excellent intel he could use.

'That's pretty ballsy, what Emma did. She's a pretty girl, especially when she's peeved at you.' David chuckled as he leaned against their car, hands in the pockets of his wrinkled suit, looking around the scene. 'Van's long gone.'

'Yeah, I stuffed up.' He'd never lost his cool like that with any member of the public when on the job. He was trained to remain calm and in control in all instances while under pressure.

Yet, hearing Emma risking herself like that made his blood burn and tastebuds sour with fear, he wanted to wrap her up in his arms and shield her.

He shouldn't even be like this.

Ever since his divorce, he refused to get involved with anyone, considering he'd nearly lost his job over a woman.

Yet, he'd never met anyone like Emma. There was no mask hiding her open honesty and kind-heartedness. But most of all, it was her ability to laugh in any situation, it was infectious.

David pointed in Emma's direction. 'Was that bulldog wearing a smoking jacket and cravat?'

'Emma was doing a dog fashion party tonight, that would've been The Prime Minister.' He remembered all his conversations with Emma from the first time they'd met. But he wasn't going to share that he'd confessed secrets while painting dog bowls. He'd never done that before.

Neither had he ever chased a woman before, because they flirted with him first. Except for Emma. Her total surprise when he'd asked her to dinner had been priceless. At the time, he hadn't expected to ask her out either. But he wanted to continue the conversation with her, to hang out with someone who wasn't involved with the internal sides of his job. Would she go out with him now?

Did he bother risking his job and his emotions for more?

'My wife would love an outfit for her lap dog,' said David. 'I should get one to hide for a future suck-up pressie when I land in the dog house next. What kinds are there?'

'All sorts of costumes, ballerina's, fur coats. Emma had

her deaf cat wearing a tuxedo that looked cool.' Did she hear his apology and would she talk to him again? He wouldn't blame her if she didn't. He frowned over his shoulder searching the street where she'd disappeared.

'Cheer up, mate, you were doing your job. You're not involved with her, are you?' David patted Ryan's shoulder.

'No.' *Shit.* 'I'm just doing my job—yeah I know, I overreacted. Sorry.'

'Let's hope she doesn't put a complaint against you.'

That's just what he didn't need to hear. Emma had every right to do so, because he hadn't acted in a professional manner expected of his occupation.

'But you're right, what she did was a stupid thing to do. Be grateful she lived to tell the tale. I understand why she's aggravated though, she's getting over a dozen prank calls a night.'

'It'd be annoying staring at your own van parked right across the road.' Ryan hadn't realised her frustration until now. 'I'll hunt down those names Emma gave us. Jaed's an uncommon name. I bet they're from the University where they tore up the campus rugby oval on their first night in the van.' Ryan climbed into the passenger seat and tapped away on the tablet to start his searches while David drove them away.

Ryan wanted to make up to Emma for what he'd done, but how? Should he bother, when he had a job to do?

* * *

The next street over, the *Parte'* van was parked on the deserted roof of the multistorey carpark surrounded by city lights. Its speakers spilled music in the background, as Stu and Jae ate their meal on the van's roof, staring at the stars.

'Hey, what did ya think of that lady?' Stu asked, with his mouth full.

Jae dabbed at his mouth with the napkin. 'Which one?'

'This van's owner, Emma. She seemed nice, huh.'

'She was pretty, and polite.' Jae bit into his burrito and chewed thoughtfully, washing it down with a mouthful of bourbon. 'You know what?'

'What?' Stu lunged at his burrito, devouring it in seconds and balled-up the wrapping.

'Ever since we started this *Parte'* van's journey, Emma's the only one who's asked us nicely to return the van.' Jae took another bite, halfway through his first burrito.

Stu rummaged in the bag and pulled out another burrito and tore open the wrapping. 'She said please and didn't even swear at us.'

'Perhaps we should give it back?'

'Give what back?'

Jae chuckled at his mate, who was loyal, amusing, and his one true friend in life. Stu was a brother. 'The van.'

Stu screwed up his nose with his half-devoured burrito hovering nearby. 'Why? Have we finished with it?'

'No, not yet.' Jae shrugged, unsure if they ever would finish when they had only just begun. 'Emma seemed like a nice lady, that's all. She's the only one who hasn't sworn at us or called us names, compared to the other people who've come near us and this van.'

'But what's with all this glitter, man.' Stu wiped the few sparkly bits of glitter off his jeans and then on his shoulders. 'Do you want to give the van back?'

Jae checked over his own jeans and saw a few glittering remnants on his sneakers that caught the lights of the city. 'Not sure?' He wriggled his foot watching the glitter sparkle like mini stars in its own galaxy on the tip of his shoe. 'But Emma is the one who's lost out the most.'

'How?'

'It's Emma's van I stole, I bet it's set her back doing her job.' What sort of business was party planning? Jae had never been to any parties prior to getting into this van. Now it was a non-stop unplanned party.

'Hey, we should give that Emma a present.'

'Why?'

'Because she didn't abuse us and spoke to us as human beings.'

'And we have stolen her van, and Emma had every right to abuse us for it, yet didn't.'

'That's why I reckon she deserves a present. I also reckon we should give the van back to her when we're finished with it.' Stu then wolfed down the second burrito in a few bites.

'Let's think about it for a bit.' Jae finished his burrito, folded the wrapping and put it into the bag. He then rested his head on his arm, laying back on the van's roof and stared at the stars.

Jae couldn't stomach the second burrito; he'd lost his appetite over meeting Emma.

The *Parte'* van wasn't just a van. It had become a vehicle

that allowed him to become so much more from the second he'd broken the lock and sat in the driver's seat. He'd never stolen a car before. Never shot at anyone. Never sat on a beach listening to music, nor tasted the saltiness of bacon, or experienced the kiss of a woman, until this van. Tonight, he'd tried Mexican food and had a short, polite conversation with a lady on the street.

Was he ready to give up these changes and deny new experiences ahead, for what?

A life he couldn't live anymore—playing servant to others?

'Man, them stars are pretty tonight. I used to like stargazing when we were camping,' said Stu, patting his bulging belly that would be empty in a few hours.

'I've never been camping. I've always wanted to, to study the environment and its structures in a rural setting.'

'Well, then, while we've still got the van, we should go camping in the scrub somewhere and you can do your sketching.'

Jae sat up. 'With a campfire?'

Stu also sat up, nodding fast with shiny eyes reflecting the city lights. 'For sure. We should do it, it'll be brilliant.'

'That sounds like an excellent idea. What do we need to go camping with, Stu? You'll have to pick the place because I have no idea where to go.' Jae gazed at the stars as if they could grant his wishes for once. To visit the bush and perhaps achieve his true dream.

And for the first time since they got into the *Parte'* van they dared to make a plan.

TEN

I
t coughed, mewled, shook, trembled, choked, spluttered, and then finally steamed. And it was done.

'Thank heaven for small miracles.' Emma turned off the ancient kettle as it shuddered in relief. It used to be black and shiny. Now it was void of any paintwork leaving just scoured rustic metal. But it still worked—just.

Her whole morning routine revolved around waiting for the kettle. She'd showered and eaten breakfast. Responded to her emails. Uploaded the Pampered Pooch Party photos to her website, and fine-tuned her to-do list. All before her kettle boiled.

At least it still boiled.

And it was these small miracles in her day-to-day life Emma enjoyed.

With a large cup of coffee in hand, she walked downstairs to begin her day. She unlocked the massive side door, reversed her mother's sports car out, and parked it under her avenue of trees that ran along one side of her shed.

She then opened the front gates and found a bulging, brown paper bag, bearing the MacDonald's golden arches. It lay in the middle of the asphalt by the entrance to her showroom. She scooped up the litter and threw it into her empty wheelie bins and walked back inside the shed.

According to the big clock on the wall, she had ten minutes before Andy and his khaki van arrived.

On the side bench, was her old answering machine where the small white box flashed red numbers on the screen. *Fifteen messages.*

She scooped up her coffee, and with a sigh she hit the play button.

'*We wanna Parte'*,' screeched out the young female voices singing over the answering machine. '*We wanna Parte'! We wanna Parte'!'*

Emma slammed on the delete button. Prank call number one was recorded at ten o'clock last night. Message two, through to message ten, were all by the same singing female voices who'd serenaded the machine until two o'clock in the morning. As time passed, their singing ended in unknown gibberish and giggles.

Emma grinned at their voices that sounded like they were being carried through an ill-fitting pair of headphones where the chord was almost chewed through by the cat. And her deaf cat, Mister, did that all the time, as if tasting the music vibrations on his tongue.

At least they were having fun.

The answering machine played the next message, received at seven o'clock this morning:

'*Emma, its Helen, your older sister, because we both know you're the bigger sister. Wake up. I need you to babysit today.*' Helen's screech echoed around the shed and bounced into the corners while Emma winced, turning down the machine's volume.

'No. Way.' Emma enjoyed deleting that demanding bitch with the push of a button.

That left four more messages.

The next message had been recorded ten minutes later.

'Emma, it's Helen. Get up you lazy thing, I need you to look after my children.'

'Oh, shut up.' Emma jabbed at the delete button and the small machine bounced from the after-shock.

'Was that your bitchy sister screeching?' Benjamin asked, walking inside with heavy shoulders, in dark sunglasses, dragging a plastic shopping bag in hand.

'Yes. Morning?' Where was the bounce to his step?

'It's a Bloody Mary morning. I bought more tomato juice.' Benjamin grumbled as his shoes scuffed towards her bar. 'Want one? Or four?'

'No thanks,' replied Emma, grinning. Benjamin was always immaculately dressed, no matter what condition he was in. As the creative die-hard party boy, he lived for his job as much as Emma did and always showed up for work.

'Hope you don't need me to drive? I had to catch a cab, I'm not fit to be behind the wheel, and Simon's still in bed sick.'

'What happened after I left?'

'Victoria and I ended up at my old nightclub and checked out the new show, that's where Simon and Paul joined us. You should've seen The Prime Minister, lapping up the he-bitches attention in his costume.' Benjamin stirred his spiked tomato juice with a celery stick and sipped. 'These things are addictive; no wonder Victoria lives on them. I'll make a batch for the road trip.'

'Good idea.'

'Were there many prank callers last night?'

'The usual.' She grinned at how quickly her flexible and adaptable nature had kicked in. Sure, the prank calls had upset her the first few days, then they made her furious, but now she was getting used to the irritation.

Emma pressed play on her answering machine.

'Emma, its Helen, answer your bloody phone. Why don't you have a mobile like most people in this century? And you call yourself a business woman? My size six arse, you are—'

Emma stabbed at the delete button again. Hard.

Benjamin carried his cocktail to the main table and scrolled through the checklists on her tablet. 'I don't blame you for not sharing your number with your sister.'

'I've given Helen my number dozens of times because she'll only ring me when she wants something.' *Or to brag about her perfect life.*

'Emma, it's Helen. I know you're there and guess what? You're babysitting today. I forgot Mum's in South America and I have a luncheon on with my husband. Yes, that's right, unlike you, Butterball, I have marital commitments, and need to get my hair done. I'm on my way, and YOU'D BETTER BE THERE.'

Benjamin winced, with hands on his head as if nails were slamming into his skull. 'What a horrid cow.'

'Bitch.' Emma hit the delete button. How many more messages were left?

'Emma, it's Helen, we're at your front gate and it's freaking closed. I know you're in there, stupid.' The recording continued playing background noises of a car stereo. A girl's voice

squealed, *'mummy we're hungry.'* Helen mumbled, *'Okay I'll take you to MacDonald's for breakfast.'* There was a series of clunks as if the phone had been dropped into the bottom of a handbag and that's where the recording ended.

Did Emma's sister toss that MacDonald's bag into her yard this morning? Was Helen going to throw her children over the fence with their food too?

The last message played over the speaker, *'Emma, it's Helen. We're on our way back and you'd better be bloody open or else.'*

'She rang five minutes ago.' Emma raised her eyebrows at Benjamin.

'*Quick*, run and lock the gates.'

'I don't run, you know that.' She didn't want to tempt fate with gravity today.

'Walk fast, while I die.' He covered his head with his hands and lay it on the table assuming a flight attendant's crash position.

Too late.

A bright red BMW drove into the shed where Emma had just removed her mother's sports car.

'Damn,' Emma said, while Benjamin groaned hiding his head under his arms.

'About time you woke up,' hollered Helen from the driver's side window. 'Get out, kids.' They scampered from the back seat, slamming the door behind them.

Emma approached her sister's car with caution. 'Sorry, Helen, I can't look after them today.'

'Too bad, you already are. We both know you have no life.'

'I have work to do.' Emma didn't have a husband to buy her the fancy car, house, clothes and jewellery. Emma worked. Unlike her sister, sitting in her fancy red BMW.

'You don't work. I have to go, I'm late for my hair appointment because of you.' Helen reversed out of the shed. 'Bye kids, your aunty can drop you home tonight.' She waved as she drove off, leaving the two children with Emma.

'Hi.' Emma shrugged at the short duo. 'You've both grown.' Her niece, Jamie, was the seven-year-old know-it-all who resembled her mother.

Beside her was her little brother Toby. 'Still sucking the thumb, huh?'

Toby's thumb-sucking habit was to annoy his parents, having outgrown it well before he'd turned five. And they both knew it. Toby, who took after his father, pulled his thumb out and poked out his tongue.

'Quick, put the thumb back in your mouth, I think your tongue's trying to make a break for it.' Emma grinned at the kids who grinned back, then they bolted forward to hug Emma, who adored them just as much. 'So, your mother dumped you again, huh?'

'She had a hair appointment for some fancy lunch. But this time she gave us breakfast.' Jamie held up the large brown paper bag displaying the golden arches.

'Mum never lets us eat junk food,' said Toby with eyes as big as Wonder Woman's shield.

'Excellent. Go eat your breakfast and stay on the stools, there's a van coming in to load-up in a minute. So please remain seated until I give you the all clear to exit your seats.' Did she sound like an air-hostess?

With a rustle of their brown bags, they moved towards the large work table. Toby climbed up onto the stool beside his sister. 'Hey there, Benjamin.'

Benjamin gave a limp wristed wave without lifting his head from the table.

'What are we doing today, Aunty Emma?' Jamie asked.

'There's an elite luncheon by the river and a dance at the Lodge.'

'Is it a children's party or grownups' party at this lodge?' Jamie unpacked her breakfast with a straight back and pinkies raised, unfolding the wrapper. Unlike Toby, who'd ripped the package open and stuffed his face.

'Older than me,' replied Emma, still a little delicate on the age issue after her birthday last weekend, that felt like aeons ago. 'Older than your Nana.'

'Can we go with you?' Toby asked with his mouth full.

'We'll see,' replied Emma.

'Saw your van on the news,' Jamie said.

Crap. Why did they bring that up? Emma was still annoyed over her van being parked right in front of her last night. But what hurt more and made her punch her pillow and toss and turn last night, was that Ryan had yelled at her.

He did say he was sorry.

But it wasn't just that—she'd yelled at him too. She'd never done that.

And she'd never tried to get armed killers' attention before, when she was all about blending.

'I like your hair, Aunty Emma,' said Jamie, Toby nodded

beside her with bulging cheeks.

'Thanks.' Emma touched her hair. She'd forgotten the new haircut, that had shocked her this morning in the shower, to wake and wash less.

Andy's khaki van drove into her yard and she waved it into her shed. 'Look alive, Benjamin, it's party time.'

The cool breeze flowed with the slow-moving river. It caressed the grassy edges that led toward the white marquee where a long table was set for sixteen people. Alternate blue and white crockery rested before each white chair wrapped in blue bows. Blue scented candles in glass domes sat amongst mini lifebuoys of blue and white flowers. A buffet table and bar waited within a scene carefully curated for that Olde English high-class nautical experience.

Mary Poppins had been Emma's inspiration, all that was missing was a couple of penguins and a merry-go-round.

'Okay troops, is everyone done?' Emma asked her team made up of Benjamin, Jamie, Toby, and her hero of the day, Andy with his khaki van. They all nodded at her, holding their boxes of ribbons and other garnishes needed for setting up.

She got the nod from Betty, the gourmet caterer with her own wait-staff, who were so skilled they'd never spill food on guests. Because five-star service was required for today's elite packaged party.

Emma spotted the first of the guests arriving. 'Okay, back to Andy's van everyone.'

Her team carted empty boxes and rubbish to Andy's khaki van parked beside the red sports car. Emma only set up parties and rarely stayed because her motto was to *blend and never attend and never stay for the end.*

'Emma, is it?' called out a male voice behind her.

'Yes?' Emma turned to face a robust man in a long-sleeved white shirt, long navy slacks and boat shoes, he belonged in the yacht club, not here.

'I'm Graham Tottsner.' He held out his hand to shake hers. 'I'm the director of Tottsner Constructions.'

Tottsner's were paying for this luxurious luncheon. Emma had no idea for who, and frankly, she didn't care why. She'd dealt with politicians, billionaires, prominent Doctors, lawyers, and magistrates. Then all of their wives. She knew she was the humble staff. Yet she treated all her clients the same, right down to the little old ladies throwing a surprise party for their bridge partner, it was those parties she put the extra oomph into.

'Pleased to meet you, Graham.' His hand was huge shaking hers.

'I see you had no problem in getting the Council approval for having lunch at this site in particular.' Graham adjusted his trousers as he inspected the table.

This side of the river was part of a large wide grassy parkland with sweeping paths, made for bike riding or Sunday strolls. On the other side of the river, it was a rundown dump full of disused warehouses.

'No, not at all.' She catered for the Council office, their public shows, and monumental private occasions for staff, who'd mentioned this was a first for this area. There were better places to have such a fine-dining experience than here.

'I'm developing that land across the river, so I'm glad you could access this area.' With his hand shading his eyes like a sea captain surveying unchartered waters, Graham frowned. 'I see you have the rowboats ready.'

How could he not like the rowboats, they were cute? 'Each boat has a basket of snacks and wine cooler for your guests to enjoy their trip across the water. There are towels, padded cushions, sunscreen, with a large umbrella on board. Life jackets are under the seats.' She was all about the details.

'I see… You came highly recommended by a colleague, William Martin. He owns Martin Finance Investments. Have you heard of him?'

'Yes, I've done a few functions for Mr Martin's firm over the years.' After all, Mr Martin was her brother-in-law. She side-glanced to William's off-spring running amok, screaming in the car park, swinging off light poles.

Emma called out to the waitress. 'Crystal, would you care to offer Mr Tottsner a drink, please? He's today's host.'

'I'll get it. Would you join me, Emma?' Behind the bar, Graham poked around the assorted beverages, like all hosts did before every party.

'Thank you for the offer, but I'm on babysitting duty, and have another party to set up. The wine and beer menu are as per your assistant's specifications, I hope it's up to your expectations?'

Graham rummaged around in the ice. 'Are you a champagne girl, Emma?'

'Yes.' Was this her alcoholic tip if she'd done her job well enough, or would she be sent away by row boat?

'Well, if you can't have a drink with me now, have one for me later.' He pulled out an icy bottle of Dom Perignon Vintage champagne. At two hundred dollars per bubble bursting pop, this guy had money to burn.

'I couldn't accept that, Graham.'

He laughed at Emma's reaction. 'My compliments on a job well done. I saw how you orchestrated your team here this morning, like a well-oiled machine. Now, take it, it's yours.'

Was the guy perving on her? *Nah, he was just a man watching where his money was being spent.* 'Thank you, Graham. I hope you enjoy your lunch. Your guests are arriving.' She started her exit stage right on her flat shoes, navigating the terrain to not trip and dance with gravity, carrying yet another bottle of booze for her simple bar.

'Right on time. By the way, Emma, do you do weddings?' Graham called out.

'No, everything but weddings.' Why did everyone keep asking her that?

'Could you recommend anyone? My daughter's getting married and if I'm footing the bill, I'd want someone that's reputable.'

Woah! She was reputable? Obviously, he didn't know of her true-reputation as a wedding planner. 'I can email a few wedding planners I've dealt with to your assistant, if you like?' Along with her bill.

'Good. One last thing, I wanted one big boat, why the little rowboats?' Graham frowned at the eight rowboats waiting in a row.

'Water level, Graham,' replied Emma.

He raised his eyebrow at her as if she was stupid.

She wasn't stupid, no matter how many times she got told. 'On this side of the river and due to the curve of the embankment, the water level is lower, and I didn't want your guests to wade in the mud. The rowboats float in shallower water and it offers a unique extra to the scene.' It made it romantic. 'Don't you think so?' He'd already given the approval for it through his assistant.

'It should make for a memorable occasion.'

Which was another one of her mottos. Always offer a surprise and leave an everlasting memory. It's how she operated, where her work was carried via word-of-mouth advertising—but not like the soul-crushing saga of her van on the news. 'Enjoy your lunch Graham, and thank you for the champagne.'

Emma returned to Andy's van. Her niece and nephew were still swinging off light-poles nearby, while Benjamin lay on the van's floor with his legs hanging out the door. 'Okay boys, the next lot of boxes are to go to the Aged Care Lodge. Please drop them off at the front reception area, they'll take care of the rest.'

'No worries, Miss-Em.' Andy was the driver and lifter of heavy things. As a retired furniture removalist, he was the best man to unpack and put away a job faster than anyone Emma had ever met—who worked for beer money. 'What time are this mob finishing up then?'

'Four o'clock. Are you still okay to be here at four thirty to collect the gear?'

'No worries, luv. Out, you drunk,' Andy said to the

partied-out bounce-less Princess Benjamin.

Like a vampire rising from the dead, moaning into an upright position, his complexion was pale and his eyes bloodshot. Benjamin mumbled, 'I won't be. I can't. I'm done.'

Emma grinned at her assistant. 'I'm surprised you'd lasted this long. Andy, could you please deliver Benjamin home, just add it to my bill?'

Andy chuckled, shaking his head at the pale-faced-passenger. 'He can pay me himself.'

'Gladly, in gold.' Benjamin rolled back into the van.

'See ya Monday, luv.' Andy closed the van's side door and headed for the driver's side. 'By the way, Miss-Em, I like what you've done to your hair, makes ya even prettier.'

Her jaw dropped and she nearly smacked herself in the head going to pat her hair with the champagne bottle. She wasn't used to getting compliments because no one really saw her. Although, Ryan complimented her last night too—and yelled at her.

At her mother's small red sports car, the caterer had supplied lunch that was resting on the front passenger seat, and it was always brilliant food. Tucking the champagne bottle into the boot, she spotted her mother's blanket.

'What are we doing now, Aunty Emma?' Jamie asked, with her brother rushing over, both breathless from their pole-dancing tour of the parklands.

'We should have our own picnic.' Why not take advantage of the Saturday sunshine by the river?

'What's a picnic?' Toby asked.

'It's where we sit on a blanket under the shade of a tree.

Eat amazing food, with fabulous company, and count the clouds in the sky.' There was only few in the rich Indian blue skyline, it was glorious weather. Emma grabbed the blanket, closed the car boot then spotted the bumper sticker. 'Bloody hell, mum.'

Toby pointed to the bumper sticker. 'What does *Cougars Rock* mean, Aunty Emma?'

'Well, um…' How do you describe what their sweet little old grandmother did in her recreation time? 'Maybe it's a sports club Nana is into?' Irene's sport was sex and she was a club member of her local sex shop. Emma wanted to block her ears to not think about her mother like that. *Bloody hell, Mum.* Quite the change from the woman who'd stayed home and baked butter biscuits.

Emma missed those butter biscuits—but her hips didn't.

'Let's find a spot for lunch, shall we? This way.' Emma carried the food and blanket to the grass beside the river and had an impromptu picnic.

A little while later, a small rowboat glided toward then with its single passenger. *'Ahoy there.'*

'It's Daddy,' Jamie said, pointing at the lone boat.

'Daddy!' Toby cried out, chasing the boat. Emma was impressed at the little guy's ability to run and wave his arms around without falling.

William rowed up to the bank. 'What are you lot up to?'

'We had a picnic lunch with Aunty Emma,' replied Jamie.

'Can we go for a ride, Daddy?' Toby asked.

'Sure, hop on.' Togther William and Emma, still on dry land, helped the children climb on board. 'I didn't know you were looking after the kids today, Em?'

William may be the best big-brother-in-law she had and she wasn't going to burden him with what a bitch his wife was. Her sister had always been like that. 'It was a last-minute thing.'

'Well, come on then.' William held his hand out to Emma.

'You know gravity and I don't agree. I'd fall in.'

'Come on, Aunty Emma,' said Jamie, 'it'll be fun.'

'I won't let you fall or let the boat tip with my children on board,' said William. 'Hey, I like your haircut. Looks nice on you.'

'Thanks.' It's not like she'd never had a haircut before, but she wasn't used to being complimented—especially from men—when she was all about blending.

'Just get in, Em?' William's question was more of a demand.

'Okay, okay.' Even if her feet lacked coordination, she grabbed William's hand and stepped gingerly onto the boat.

It was a personal milestone. She'd won another challenge with gravity and didn't kiss concrete, or get her face wet falling into the water. *Whoohoo*—next it was astronaut training for the moonwalk.

'Did you enjoy catering Tottsner's lunch today?' William asked, seated beside Emma at the back of the boat. They watched the children in front, rowing furiously with their backs to them. He poured a glass of white wine for Emma then one for himself.

'I did. Thank you for your recommendation.' Elite parties were rare, but brilliant.

Emma leaned back against the cushions. A glass of crisp white wine in hand, and an umbrella resting over her shoulder, she floated like queen of her own river. *Ah, this is the life. I wonder what were the rich people doing? Oh, they were looking at derelict sheds on the other side of the river.*

'How come you're not over there?' Emma pointed to the group of rowboats on the opposite riverbank.

'I've been there before. Graham's offering large river view properties.'

'And you're the man to find the buyers and investors, huh?'

'With the commission to go with it.' William smiled at the derelict site as if it was diamonds. 'I've purchased a property for our new family home.'

'Where is Helen?' Shouldn't her sister be with her family enjoying this moment? It's something Emma would love, a life partner, not a husband, but someone to share a family with, and to be a decent father toward their children—which she knew would never happen. Ever.

'Helen didn't want to come, she's back in the marquee,' said William. 'The rowboats were a great idea, yours I'm assuming?'

'Yes. It's fun.'

'I agree. Hey you two kids, you have to row together or we'll be going in circles forever,' called out William. 'So how are you coping with your stolen van on the news every day?'

'Day by day.' Emma didn't watch the news anymore, preferring to avoid it all.

'No luck in catching them?'

'No. But you'll never guess what happened to me last night?' She relayed last night's van spotting saga to him.

'You bloody idiot!' William shook his head at her. 'I don't

blame the guy for yelling at you, I would've done the same. On the radio this morning it said they'd held up a camping store at gunpoint. They've shot at two men and their ute. Wounded one guy for delivering bread, killed a drug dealer, with a total of seven armed robberies. You were lucky they didn't have a go at you too. I'm glad this Ryan yelled at you, you could've been hurt—*or killed.*'

'I know, I didn't think.' Emma winced from William's lecture and at her own stupidity, staring at her fingers wiping the condensation on her wine glass.

William took a deep breath and took a mouthful of his wine. In a calmer tone he asked, 'How long has the van been missing now?'

'It'll be a week tomorrow.'

'Are you getting a new one?'

'I'm looking. Hey, I went to a car yard the other day.' She sat up with chin high. 'I'm cured of my make-believe-car-yard phobia.'

'You, in a car yard?' William grinned, cocking an eyebrow at her.

'Okay, so it took me twenty minutes to get in there, but I did it, with a little help from a friend.' William had helped her buy all her cars in the past; she'd known him longer than her father had stayed at home.

'Who did you go with?' William asked.

'Ryan met me there. He was driving past on his lunch break.' But he never ate.

'Ryan, the Detective? Sounds like the guy's sweet on you, Em.' William playfully nudged her, as the heat rose from her neck. 'Aw honey, you're blushing'

'Stop it.'

'Might explain why this Ryan yelled at you last night. I would've done the same thing, or worse.'

'Are you siding with Ryan? It was quite unprofessional for a detective to yell at me like that.' She'd never yell at a client. Nor had she ever blurted out her problems while angry like she'd done to Ryan.

'I'm not sticking up for him, I don't know the guy. But if he likes you, he'll call.'

'For work. Ryan is assigned to the case for my stolen van.' Otherwise, why would a guy like Ryan bother with her?

'Are you still having trouble with the insurance company? I bet they've bumped up your premiums by now.'

'The bastards,' she muttered.

'Now, as my little sister, I'm giving your number to the insurance guy who works for me. I'll have him go right through your business insurance, including the new car, to find you the best possible deal, at no charge to you. I know you've never accepted before, but this time. I'm not taking a no for an answer. He'll call you on Monday.'

'Um, thank you.' At the moment she hated insurance companies.

He put his arm around her shoulders and gave her a tender brotherly squeeze. 'Cheer up Em, it'll all work out.'

'Hope so.'

'What have you got planned for the afternoon?' William asked his children as they rowed in a zigzagged pattern.

'We're going to a hippy sixties dance party at the old

people's home,' said Jamie.

'They're older than you and Mum, even Nana,' called out Toby. His tongue hung out of his mouth as his little muscles strained on the oar, rowing with all his might.

'You guys have more of a social life than me.' William then asked Emma, 'Are you still volunteering weekly craft lessons?'

'They're actually my secret design specialists,' she replied with a grin.

'They still giving you dancing lessons for their parties?' William asked.

'Yep. They had me doing the foxtrot. You know how uncoordinated I am, so my dance card's vacant for their own safety.'

'I'd love to learn ballroom dancing.'

'Really?' Emma smirked at William in surprise.

'It looks like it'd be fun?'

'It's fabulous fun and they're great teachers.'

'I like the fact you find your fun anywhere. I haven't had much time for fun these days.'

'Don't you have the glamorous rich and fabulous lifestyle of lunches and parties that Helen tells me about?'

'I don't think so. I'm expanding my business where I'll have an accountancy firm with a few bankers on board, instead of out-sourcing that part to my clients. I've put in long hours for this to work. Remember that group you saw me in the restaurant with?'

'With the blonde?' Emma remembered the clingy leggy blonde from her lunch with Victoria.

William nodded. 'She's keen to sell her father's business in accordance with his Will. That business lunch was with the board of directors of that firm and we'd completed negotiations that day.'

'Congratulations.' She clinked her glass against his in a toast.

William smiled wide with pride. 'Thank you. It's been a lot of work, and I swear all these luncheons and dinners are making me put on so much weight, I'm over it. It'll settle down soon and I'll be able to start enjoying myself and spend more time with the family. Hey, I'll get you to cater for the grand opening.'

'That'd be good. Will the touchy-feely blonde be there too?'

'Hope not.' He frowned over his glass as he sipped his wine. 'You thought I was having an affair?'

They both looked at the children in the front of the boat too busy rowing to hear them.

She gave a slow shrug. Did she dare voice it?

William laughed. 'I was wondering what Victoria was prattling on about.'

'Have you ever cheated on Helen?' She slapped her hand over mouth for daring to speak.

'Don't get me wrong, I love my wife. Always have, and I always will, but—' William shuffled in his seat and stared at his glass in hand. 'I did lapse, still feel stupid for it.' His shoulders drooped and his head lowered as if sinking into his seat as he spoke. 'It wasn't an affair, it was a stupid one-night stand, too drunk to know what I was doing. Helen knows all about it. I've never lied to her, and I couldn't keep that from her.'

Emma sat there with wide eyes, stunned. William looked so sad too as she patted his arm. 'We're all human.' Even if her sister was Satan in designer gym-wear where many wishful exorcisms had failed.

The children were busy counting aloud, trying to coordinate their strokes, the boat didn't know which way to float.

'Thanks, Em.' He patted her hand giving her a slight smile. He then leaned over and whispered, 'But, lately, I've been wondering if Helen isn't cheating on me.'

'Why do you say that?' Helen may have trillions of faults, but to cheat on her husband?

'The kids are in school now, and I haven't been around home much, not until this deal is completed. But when I ask Helen what she's been up to she says shopping, or gym, or lunch, and kid's stuff. Lately, we have nothing in common. She's always mad at me. Never interested in what I have to talk about anymore and doesn't listen. You should've heard her this morning, going off about today's lunch.' He waved his glass at the marquee behind them. 'Helen was telling me off for not giving her time to prepare. But I know I told her a month ago, and I reminded her plenty of times these past two weeks. This is a good deal for me. If those people buy into Tottsner's proposal, it'll practically pay for our new home. But there she is yelling at me, at the kids, at the hairdresser, and someone else copped an earful about the kids on their message bank.'

'That was my answering machine.' Emma put her hand in the air. They both chuckled, sipped their wine, and gazed over the water that barely rippled. While the kids counted, the oars splashed, and the boat floated nowhere.

William said under his breath while watching his children play, 'I've given her everything. Anything Helen asks for, I get it for her. I truly adore the woman. But no matter how much I try, or the kids try, there's no pleasing her.'

'Is it that bad?' Emma was surprised at William's candidness.

He nodded as his shoulders sunk, cradling his hands in his lap, openly displaying his sorrow.

'Hold on, Helen's always telling me that it's perfect. Last weekend she was showing off a new eternity ring you'd bought her.'

'I didn't give her a ring. I don't buy Helen anything because the last couple of times I gave her anything it wasn't good enough for her. I just pay off the credit card. Life's far from perfect for us, Em. In my eyes, it's your life that's perfect, as the one without the stress and the fun-loving lifestyle.'

'Mine? No way. I'm waiting to see how long before my kettle dies. My van has been stolen and making headlines for all the wrong reasons. I got yelled at by a Detective, who'd met me while I was sitting in a gutter, drinking straight out of a wine bottle, covered in prawn muck. And that was just last week.'

'Yes, you do, Emma. You love what you do, you can see it. You don't care who or what the client is, you love the job itself, right down the intricate attention to details. Graham Tottner was impressed with your work.'

'You didn't tell him we were related, did you?'

'Of course, I did.' William laughed at her expression.

'Helen would have been mortified.'

'It's wrong the way Helen treats you like staff. You're a successful businesswoman with a great professional reputation. I admire you for it because you've created something out of nothing. Even though my father owned the firm, I'm getting it to a stage to be like yours.'

'I don't make money like you do, William.' Nowhere near the amount.

'But you seem comfortable where you are in your life. Your business is growing every month. You've planned ahead with your vision when you bought your shed. You've come a long way from that kid messing up Irene's kitchen with your latest craft project where glitter floated in the air.'

'Mum got sick of me doing that, glitter gets into everything.' It got so bad her mother moved Emma into the car shed—her first shed.

Without a social life, Emma sat listening to the music on the radio while she created decorations all weekend, and loved it. She adored it when all the individual pieces she'd created came together for one big moment. It was the only thing she enjoyed at school, volunteering for the school's annual play, making sets. She didn't deal with actors—where most were lousy. But Emma was in charge of the sets, creating the scenes that made it a magical experience.

It was that same small magical moment that still meant more to her than the surprised expressions on arriving guests and the client's pride in receiving them, where she happily walked away to plan her next party.

William continued, 'I'm jealous of the way you laugh at

the worst and smile at the smallest things in life. You're one of the rare who've found their happiness in life.'

'Have I?' Emma sat back. Was she happy? 'Of course, I want to be happy, doesn't everyone?'

'You know, happiness is a choice, not a destination and that is something you've worked out,'

Emma shook her head unconvinced.

'Okay, what made you smile first thing this morning?'

'My kettle worked.' She snickered at his fluctuating frown.

'Your kettle?'

'It's ancient and takes forever to boil, but it worked.' Her whole morning routine revolved around that decrepit kettle.

'And the next time you smiled?'

'Um, Benjamin's hungover condition, while he was making himself Bloody Mary's for breakfast.' When he was whining about Helen, but she couldn't share that with the husband.

'I like your bar. You know, I think your sister is jealous of what you have.'

'No way?'

'It's why Helen is always putting you down, so you wouldn't discover she's nothing more than a miserable rotten cow—but god I love that woman,' he said, chuckling. 'We need to find someone for you. Hey, there's a guy from —'

'Oh no you don't.'

'Aunty Emma, your phone's ringing in your bag,' called out Jamie from the front of their row boat. 'Can I get it for you?'

'Sure.'

'Aunty Emma's phone, Jamie speaking. How may I help you? … Whom may I ask is calling, please?'

'Does Jamie work at your office on weekends?' Emma laughed with William.

'Who are you? … I'm her niece, Jamie.' She paused to listen over the phone. 'Aunty Emma's here, we're spending the day with her. We set up this party. Then we had a picnic lunch. Then we fed the ducks. And now we're rowing a boat with my daddy… Yeah, it's a real rowboat. I'm rowing on one side. My brother Toby's rowing on the other. And we're going in circles!'

The adults laughed, looking at the slow whirlpool they were creating with little Toby trying to row with the heavy oar.

'Sure, I'll get her for you… Nice talking to you too, Ryan.' Jamie held out the mobile.

'Oh no.' Emma didn't want to talk to Ryan in case he yelled at her again, or he had some really bad news about her van.

William nudged Emma with his elbow. 'Told you he'd call.'

'Aunty Emma.' Jamie stood up and the boat tipped to one side.

'Honey, careful,' said William, 'don't rock the boat.'

'Aw, Dad, Jamie's rocking it.' Toby held his tongue to the side, and with as much determined force his little body could muster, he pushed the side, rocking it.

'Jamie, sit down, please.' William leaned forward, and the boat tilted sharply.

'Please be nice, gravity. Please be nice.' Emma's wine tipped overside. She bonked her head with the umbrella and it landed in the water. Unlike Mary Poppins where her umbrella flew, Emma had to grip the handle tight to stop it sinking, almost getting dragged overboard.

On the other side of the boat, Jamie lost her balance and fell hard onto her seat. Her hand let go of the mobile and it flew like a released pigeon off on a mission to deliver a message, only to sink fast like the flightless brick it was.

Plop. Emma's mobile phone splashed into the brink. Sunk. Gone. Now a new home for whatever lurked beneath the silvery surface.

'Everyone, sit still.' William pointed at Toby.

With shiny eyes and flushed cheeks, the boy smiled wide showing off his missing tooth, and the boat soon stabilised.

'I'm so sorry about your phone, Aunty Emma,' whimpered Jamie, peering over the side.

Emma rescued the umbrella that rained all over her as she shut it down and put it out of harm's way. At least she didn't fall into the water—but was just as saturated, and burst out laughing. There'd be no more calls today. *Sorry, Ryan.* For Emma, no news was good news. She didn't want to hear it, not today.

ELEVEN

'H'ey, d'ya reckon that lady will find her present?' Stu asked, passing a smouldering hand-rolled to Jae in the *Parte'* van.

'I do.' Jae, while steering the van with his elbow, inhaled deeply, then passed it back to Stu. He pushed up his glasses and peered through squinty eyes as he drove along a wide street.

'Reckon she'll know it's from us when she gets to work on Monday? Left, man.' Stu pointed, and checked the map. The tablet was resting on the dash, charging, as it continued its playlist of never-ending music.

Jae steered the van left, noting there were only a few cars around this late Saturday afternoon. 'That's a good question.'

'We should call and tell her. Bein' a small business she'd have an answering machine. Reckon we should find a pay phone before we hit the campsite coz we'll be outta range from everything out there. I wonder what Emma's number is?'

Jae laughed so loud it filled the van, now crammed with camping gear and food. He wiped at the happy tears steaming up his glasses.

'What's with you, man?'

Jae wheezed for air between belly laughs that made his body shake. 'Emma's number is on the side of the van, dickhead.'

'I forgot.' They both laughed as white smoke filled the cab.

Jae wiped at the happy tears, slowing down as he approached the intersection. 'Which way, navigator?'

'Huh?' Stu sat up, waving at the smoky air, he cracked open the window to let it escape and peered through the windscreen. His eyes widened and he leaned closer. *'No bloody way?'*

'What's wrong?'

'It's that wanker, Bob, driving that truck.' Stu pointed to a small box-truck waiting at the stop lights. Its massive driver was covered in angry tattoos. His belly pressed against the steering wheel and his massive chest rolled upwards to tuck under his chins. His oily black hair was pulled tight into a man-bun wearing the look of a sumo wrestler with clothes on.

'Remind me, what is Bob to us?'

Stu scowled, his voice deepened as he said, 'He's my mother's boyfriend. Another one of her boyfriends. But this arsehole hits her.' Stu craned around in his seat never taking his eyes off the meat-sack.

'Oh, that butt-less-blunder.' Jae crunched the gears and did a U-turn. The van leaned dangerously to its side as it turned, wobbled, and with a few tyre squeaks like a mouse's screech, it stopped in front of the truck. He could never get those dramatic exits right in this van with pink bubbles on the side.

'Oi, what are ya doin', ya bloody moron,' yelled Bob, sticking his head out of the driver's window. 'Stu is that you?'

'You've gotta stop beating up on my mother,' yelled out Stu.

Bob waved a beefy arm at them. 'Nick-off back to your fancy college and get outta the way. I've got work to do. Real work, book-boy.'

'Book-boy?' Jae frowned and saw red. '*Excuuuse me. Don't you dare speak to my friend like that. No one talks to us like that anymore.*' Jae pushed Stu back against the seat, and pointed the handgun out the passenger window.

Bob's eyes widened and his jaw dropped.

'And don't you dare hit his mother again.' Jae squeezed the trigger. The bullet hit the truck's windscreen which shattered like an ice pick slamming against a frozen lake. But it didn't break. It just held together like a dew-covered spider web in the wind.

Jae dropped the gun in the console and put the van into gear and the van shunted off.

'Man, you shot at his truck. Good job.' Stu sat tall, wearing a lazy side grin, nodding to himself.

'It should scare him for abusing us. We won't be bullied anymore, and no one should hit anyone's mother.' Would his own mother be proud of this moment? 'Woops, wrong way.' The tyres squealed and the van leaned over as Jae did another U-turn and drove past the intersection where the truck still sat there. They couldn't see beyond the cracked windscreen as they drove by.

'Dude, there's glitter on the gun. Where is it coming from?' Stu reached for the gun as the tiny sparkles caught the light of the late afternoon sunshine. 'Hey, what were you aiming for?'

'The passenger side-mirror.'

'Huh. The glitter must've got in your eye, mate, coz, you missed.' Stu snort-laughed swapping the pistol for the cigarette packet on the dashboard. 'All I saw was the spidery crack covering the front window.'

'I've never had lessons. And just because my parents come from a country with neighbouring terrorists, doesn't automatically grant me prior knowledge of firearms.' Why was he continuing to speak so posh when his parents weren't around to check on him?

'We'll do target practice at our campsite. Can't wait to test out all that camping gear.' Stu rummaged in the back and pulled out two cans of cold beer.

'So, Mr Navigator, which way is it to our campsite?' Jae waved at the empty road before them, excited. He'd never been camping, and it was another new world he was about to experience. Except this one he'd dreamed about.

Stu cracked open a beer can and put it in the cup holder for Jae, and the other for himself. He grabbed the map and traced the road along with his finger, peering at the sign as they approached the next intersection. 'Go left. Left here.' Stu pointed and Jae slowed down to make the turn.

Behind them, the truck's shattered windscreen crackled. A piece of broken glass dropped like melting ice. Then another. Then another. And then the entire windscreen fell away at once to reveal the driver stuck behind the wheel.

Mouth open, drool spilled from the corner of his lips, while glazed eyes stared at nothing. As Bob's lungs expressed his last breath, he slumped over the steering wheel. The seatbelt snapped and his chins hit the truck's horn. Blood flowed from the bullet wound and trickled down his neck.

BEEEEEEEEPP. It whined, droning on and on and on.

Curtains shifted, doors opened, and people peeked through windows. A car pulled up at the intersection with a young couple sipping their takeaway lattes. Open-mouthed they stared at the truck with a broken window, horn screaming, and a dead man behind the steering wheel. And just ahead of them, the *Parte'* van's tyres screeched like a pre-schooler's choir where it disappeared around the corner.

TWELVE

At her kitchen bench in her upstairs apartment, waiting for her decrepit kettle to boil, Emma rested her head in two hands and stared at the instructions for her new hi-tech mobile phone. *How do you turn the freaking thing on?*

The kettle choked out its steam-train scream that filled the room as she smiled—it lived.

She made herself a coffee using the French Press, with freshly grounded beans, savouring the aroma and remembered William's words from yesterday. Was she happy?

Most people would've been annoyed about a decrepit kettle that was taking twenty minutes to boil. But it was a game to her.

Most people would've been annoyed that their lifeline-link to the world was at the bottom of a river. Yet it kept bad news away.

Did that make her happy?

She smiled slyly to herself—so her sister wasn't so perfect after all and lied about the new ring too.

Tink... Tink... Tink...

Emma stared at her ceiling.

Something dropped onto her roof, rolled down the slope, and tumbled off. Through the large wall of windows that was framed by her lush canopy of trees, the morning displayed clear Indian blue skies.

Tink... Tink... Tink... Followed by a rumbling noise that ran across her roof.

Was her tree or a bird dropping seeds?

Curious, Emma went downstairs in her socks. She unlocked the side door of her shed and pushed it open. Shoving the keys into her pocket, her palms shaded her eyes from the sunlight and she stepped outside scrutinising the sky. She walked out further toward her trees to gawk at the tall expansive roof but saw nothing. Not that she could see the top either.

'*Hey*, why don't you answer your phone,' called out Ryan, standing at her padlocked gates.

'What are you doing here?' Emma wasn't dressed for visitors, wearing socks and a baggy house dress that kept slipping off her shoulder. But it was the last of her old wardrobe she'd snuck past Benjamin and his scissor-intervention. Maybe she should've surrendered it and not get caught like this. *Meh, we're just friends.*

Or were they?

She approached the cop cautiously.

Ryan dropped a hand full of rocks and dusted the dirt from his palms.

'Were you throwing rocks on my roof?'

'Yeah.' He nodded with a boyish grin that stirred up her tummy of floating glitter—or she was hungry?

'Why?'

'I had to get your attention somehow. I'm assuming from my conversation with your niece, yesterday, your phone went swimming?' He slid his hands into his jeans' pockets that were deliciously moulded for his build.

Should she close the gap or leave a nice, safe, padlocked gate between them? 'Yes, my phone is on a new adventure to be unearthed as a relic of the distant future.'

'Did you get any of my messages on your answering machine?'

'No.' It was her day off and it was early-ish for a Sunday morning. 'I only came downstairs to search for that noise.' She glanced back at the sturdy metallic structure.

'I want to apologise for yelling at you like I did. I was way out of line.' He shrugged in his tight grey t-shirt that showed off his amazing torso.

She'd never realised how muscular and fit he was, and tried not to notice.

'I was worried you might have gotten hurt, and I'm sorry, okay?'

Aww, he cared. 'No, you were right. It was a stupid thing to do.' It was Emma's turn to shrug, shoving her hands in the pockets of her sack-with-sleeves. 'When I told my brother-in-law what I'd done, he agreed with you and gave me a lecture for being an idiot. I just saw my van and didn't think because I wanted my property back.'

'I get that. So, please, don't do it again?' His lips curled into a slight smile as he lowered his head giving her that stare where his dynamic chartreuse eyes made her thirsty.

But did she want the hangover that might follow that drink?

'I won't do it again.' She licked her lips and stared at her roof so as to not focus on the Adonis standing at her gate. 'Did you really throw rocks on my roof?' She scrutinised the sheer height, trying to calculate the distance from where Ryan stood on the other side of an eight-foot mesh fence that had three strands of barbed wire running across the top.

'Yeah.' His grin grew to that dynamite smile.

'That's got to be at least fifty metres or more, what did you use?'

'Those.' He toed the gravel mix of stone and dirt with his biker boots. In his denim jeans and t-shirt, the man was too hot to be standing at her gate on a Sunday morning.

'Here give me one.' She held her hand out, and he picked up a stone.

'Are you going to let me in?

'I'll swap you.' She pulled the key out of her pocket and swapped them for a gritty cold stone. While Ryan unlocked the gate and let himself in, Emma tossed the rock as hard and high as she could. It hit the upper panel of her shed. A mere ten metres away.

'That was a pretty poor effort.' Ryan chuckled, passing her keys back.

'I'm not known for my athletic abilities. Gravity is not my friend, so for me, that was a pretty good throw. Hey, *you threw rocks at my roof.* Did you do that to get your girlfriends' attention in high school to sneak them out of the house?'

Ryan's dynamic smile was accompanied by his laugh that made her smile with him. How could she stay mad at that?

'No. But it got your attention.'

He had that just by breathing. 'What were you ringing me

for? Please don't say bad news about my van.'

He shook his head with a palm raised in half surrender. 'I wasn't, and I won't, not today. It's my day off and I don't want to talk shop, I swear it.'

No news is good news was her new motto in life. 'I like that.'

'And, I was hoping you might want to join me for a ride?'

Yesterday she rowed in a boat. She also drove her mother's sports car with the top down, with her niece and nephew in the back seat, screaming as if on a roller coaster driving up and down steep hills. There's no way she'd get on another living animal like a horse. And she'd never viewed bicycle seats the same since falling off one in her last attempt at going to the gym. 'A ride on what?'

'My bike.' Ryan pointed to the edge of her driveway where a large Harley Davidson motorcycle was parked.

'On that?' It was huge. How come she didn't hear it pull up?

'Have you ever been on one?'

'No. It's very shiny.' All the steel and chrome sparkled in the sun. 'Will I be tone deaf for the rest of my life if I do?'

He chuckled. 'No. I brought you a helmet and wanted to take you out for lunch, unless you've got something else on?'

'I was just putting numbers back into my new mobile phone as my challenge of the day.'

'Well then, go get ready. You'll need jeans, a jacket. Boots would be good.' He grinned at her socks where she wiggled her toes. 'Hey, how did you get a new phone on a Sunday morning?'

'Well now, if I told you that I'd have to shoot you,

Detective. Although, I only have water pistols in my shed. Do you want a coffee or something?' She led them inside. 'It's a good time for a coffee. I'd just boiled the kettle so it's still hot, that should shorten the re-boiling time.'

'Why? How long does it normally take for your kettle to boil?'

'It took twenty-five minutes this morning.' She climbed her wrought iron stairs trying to think what she had to wear. She couldn't sit in her skinny jeans, she'd faint from lack of air. 'Hey, does this make me a bikie-witch if I'm on the back?'

'Don't think so.' His laughter echoed in the silent shed as he followed up the internal staircase to the landing where she opened the door to her apartment. 'I'll give the coffee a miss if it takes that long to boil the kettle.'

'Okay then, your loss.' Or was it hers?

* * *

Ryan walked into Emma's apartment and froze.

'I won't take long. Do what you do.' She slid across the floorboards on her socks as if skating on ice, and through another doorway to the right.

THUMP!

'Are you okay, Emma?' He peeked around the doorframe to find her getting up off the floor.

'I'm okay. Just gravity doing its thing. Excuse me.' Bright red in the face, on her hands and knees she slammed the door shut.

He chuckled, then examined her apartment. 'Damn.'

She'd surprised him, *again.*

Ryan glanced back to the landing that gave a bird's-eye view of the shed with the red sports car parked below. The exterior to the apartment was a simple set of wrought iron stairs that led to a landing facing a simple weatherboard wall. It seemed like an office for a shed on the outside. But the inside…

He closed the door and surveyed the large open space that had nothing white compared to her pristine showroom downstairs.

Here, it was warm, earthy colours, with wooden floors, and where corrugated and brick walls blended with exposed steel girders. Its large wooden pieces of furniture with couches in the centre of the room were made to lie on. Near a wall of windows, a wooden dining table stretched below a bank of black hooded industrial lights, with room for over a dozen people, made for intimate dining leisure.

Directly above was an internal balcony in the apex of the roof that ran across the wall of windows. The side walls were bricked and lined with empty shelves from floor to ceiling. And in the centre was another comfy couch, bathed in natural light, perfect for reading. It was a great spot for a library, but she had no books.

Yet, she had music records. A bookcase that stretched across the wall, full of vinyls and a record player. Emma did say she liked her music. His eyes widened as he inspected her impressive collection from jazz, blues, classical symphonies, show tunes, right through to today's current covers. She had music for every mood.

Ryan did a full turn, taking in the details. It was big,

classy, with an industrial rustic appeal to it. And he liked it.

This wasn't a shed, it was like a spacious New York City loft that was a well-concealed piece of paradise she'd turned into a home with a view. Ryan stepped closer to the wall of windows framed by the treetops giving an uninterrupted view of the skyline. No sheds. No rooftops. Nothing but open sky.

No wonder Emma lived here. So why did she talk it down for?

Emma rushed out with her boots clopping across the floorboards, as she slipped on a duffel coat. 'Is this okay, I don't own a biker's jacket? I've never ridden on a bike before.'

His eyes scanned over her figure, the legs long, curvy hips and man, those jeans fit good. He saw what he liked and wanted to hold onto her. Was she the words he'd been missing in his book of life?

'Ryan?'

'Huh?' He shook his head to wake up. 'Sorry, um, yeah. That's fine. I should've put in a spare jacket but most of my stuff is still in storage.' Boxes and boxes of books he'd collected over the years that were as homeless as he was. Now they were tossed around his storage unit as a result of his last-minute decision to invite Emma, that had sent him on a mission. She needed a helmet, so he needed to find his spare.

Last night, after leaving another *Parte'* van murder scene, he'd knocked off work to face his tiny room. Unable to sleep. Unable to read. He sat on his tiny back veranda beside his bike that was hidden under a tarp.

Eating cold pizza leftovers found in his tiny fridge, with music low to not disturb his neighbours, he drank beer and polished his bike. He hadn't stopped thinking about Emma, where guilt had strapped itself across his shoulders for how he'd shouted at her and needed to make amends for his actions.

He was determined to spend his day-off away from the cube he lived in, because he always felt better after a ride. He hoped she'd come along, because if he felt crappy over Emma's *Parte'* van, then Emma with her sensitive nature and frustrations would too.

He didn't care if it might be considered against the rules of his job—because today he wasn't working. 'Come on, let's beat the traffic.'

'Where are we going?'

'I have to drop off my library books first, or they'll never let me borrow again. Then we'll hit the hills.'

'You read?'

He cocked his head at her surprised expression. 'Why, is that weird for you? Do you read?'

'I try to. Sometimes.' She stared up at her empty shelves. 'I end up getting crafty and want to make something. My mother suffered years of glitter and glue smothering her house, so I swore to myself I wouldn't do it in here in hope of making more time to read.'

Shaking his head, he again regarded the room. 'You've surprised me again, Emma. It's really comfortable up here.'

'You surprised me too, starting with the impromptu stone-chucking call out.'

He grinned at her. He'd never done that before. 'Good thing I wasn't aiming for your windows.' He pointed to the wall of windows with a great open view.

'Those windows are bi-fold doors, I have to put in a fire exit, so I'm putting a deck out there. I've got a barbecue and a hot tub I'm retiring from party hire that'd fit perfectly there.'

His jaw dropped just imagining it.

'What do you read, detective books for research?'

'Anything but romance.'

'You don't like romance?'

'Not my genre. I'm a guy, okay.' He shrugged. He wasn't a non-romantic. Or was he? 'I just like stories.'

'Why?'

'Because in my line of work I witness all the crap, it's nice to slip away somewhere else for a change. I'm always carrying a book because of my work. If I'm doing a stakeout my partner watches, I'll read. I work odd hours and miss all the prime-time TV to not get hooked on them, so I read. I've worked in places that don't have internet or mobile reception, so I'd read.' He'd spent countless hours sitting on roofs, in airports, cars, office waiting rooms, and in the hallways of many embassies, reading. With his sniper's rifle secure in its case beside his backpack at his feet, he'd wait for his superiors to tell him where to go and what to do, so he'd read.

For years that's all he had, carry-on luggage and books he'd send back to his mother like postcards of places he'd been. Now packed away in his storage unit until he found a place to call home.

'Do you have any favourite books?' Emma asked.

'Ah, yeah.' He shrugged, toeing the rich wooden floor panelling with the tip of his boots. 'I've got my keepers.' Boxes of them. 'With Dad in the army, shifting around as a kid, friends came and went. But my books, they're old friends I revisit. I've told no one that.' Why did she do that, make him confess things he'd never meant to say?

Was she the friend he'd been missing?

She smiled so brightly, her large eyes reflected the windows and softened the skies as if bringing sunshine to rain. It was the strongest love potion on the planet.

'So, shall we?' Before he spilled all his secrets, he held out his hand with hope. 'I don't want you to trip and fall again.' Not while he was around.

Like a timid bird, she lifted her hand. Hesitated, and then put it in his. All while chewing on that plump bottom lip he wanted to taste like summer cherries plucked straight from the tree.

But why rush what may grow and sweeten more with time.

'Let's go have some fun, Emma.' He gave her hand a squeeze and her smile reached her large eyes, shedding light on his rigid world of darkness. It was a smile that said more than words ever would and he proudly escorted her out the door.

* * *

A few hours later, Ryan pulled his Harley Davidson into a car park area that stood on top of a hill and turned off the engine.

Emma sat behind him, holding his shoulders, she tried to get off the bike modestly without kissing concrete.

'You okay?' He asked, wrapping his arm around her hips to steady her while her body still vibrated from the ride.

Emma wore a smile so big her jaw ached and her cheeks tingled, and surprisingly, gravity was kind. 'That was awesome.' She wanted to jump high in the air while performing an air guitar solo, it was that good.

Ryan chuckled, casually getting off the bike. He removed his helmet and hung it off the handlebars.

'Oops, am I supposed to act all cool or something?' Because Ryan was so cool while looking so hot.

She tried to undo her own helmet, but the adrenaline made her fingers clumsy.

'No.' Ryan helped remove her helmet. 'Did you enjoy that?'

She patted down her hair and pointed at her smile. 'See this smile, what does that say?'

'I like that smile.'

She was too happy to blush or shy away, and only smiled wider. How did he do that? 'I understand why you do this, now.'

She then spotted the view and her eyes widened. 'Wow. Where are we?'

It was a scene that stretched over a sea of green tree tops and sloping hills, where a river wound lazily in the far distance. Her eyes strained to peek past the horizon where clouds hovered above the ocean giving it that silvery lining.

'Mecket's Point. I haven't been here for ages. They used to make the best hamburgers.' He pointed to the small kiosk behind them. 'Do you want one?' Then he stopped and crinkled up his nose, sliding his hand into his denim pocket. 'Sorry, forgot my manners. Do you eat meat?'

Aww, he cared about her meal choices. 'I do. I'm not fussy.'

Let's hope she didn't spill her food over her shirt like a pig either. 'This is a great view.'

'Come on, this way.' Again, he held her hand and the tingles scurried up her arm. She just about floated as she followed.

They shared lunch sitting on a picnic table, facing the amazing view and chatting with the ease of long-time friends.

'We should head back,' said Ryan, noting the time on his phone.

'Sure.' Emma followed his delicious derriere. She didn't want to get caught perving so she faced the magnificent scenery.

'Don't you want to leave?' Ryan asked, holding out her helmet.

'It's a spectacular view. I wonder if they'd allow parties up here?'

'Are you thinking of work?'

'No, yes—it's a really great location.' They'd agreed to not talk shop today and she liked that, especially with Ryan's work she understood why. 'Cool, more helmet hair.' And plonked the helmet onto her head.

'Here let me help you.' He adjusted the straps, wiping stray strands free from her face. He was so gentle.

She sighed, breathing in his aroma that married perfectly with the clear air.

'Open your mouth,' said Ryan.

'Why?'

'I want to make sure your helmet straps aren't too tight across your jaw. Now open wide?'

She prayed there was no food stuck in her teeth and held

her breath to not breathe on the guy.

'No bugs.'

'Huh?'

He held the side of her helmet, leaned closer and brushed his lips against hers.

Emma didn't have time to panic. With a rush her thoughts were silenced, but for one…

Of Ryan.

And his kiss.

Which was the lip dance of the divine that she could slow dance to and never forget. It was the taste of a nourishing nectar, silencing all her doubts.

His lips pressed against hers and it swept over the songs in her soul that didn't sound so sad anymore. Coaxed by the rhythm of his stroking tongue, it was slow and gentle. There were no flashing lights behind her eyelids, no exploding fireworks, but a warm glow that made her weave and soar effortlessly.

He sucked on her bottom lip, giving it a slight nibble and pulled back.

She sighed, opening her eyes, brushing her teeth over her bottom lip that tingled from his touch. All she saw was his whiskey moonbeam eyes and she was drunk, listening to his music still humming her favourite tune.

'You okay?' He whispered.

'Wow.' Leaning into his chest, she stared at the awakening of a thousand daydreams she could linger over long after today.

A car horn tooted and a bird squawked overhead, as a bus's diesel engine roared up the hill and into the car park.

'Um…' She swallowed hard, trying to engage her brain into gear from the land of cotton-candy-fields filled with melodic heart songs and floating glitter. 'You surprised me.'

She'd surprised herself the way her brain and heart were reacting to his kiss.

'I didn't want you to panic. Come on, time to head back down the mountain.' He kissed the tip of her nose. Taking her by the hand, he guided her to the bike and started their journey.

Emma was flying as if made of weightless silk. She loved it on the bike. The view whirled past her from thick tree-filled forests, down winding roads that opened to wide windows of countryside spread below. All this while holding onto Ryan, as he skilfully guided the bike through the light traffic.

He'd kissed her in a way that made the ordinary around her extraordinary. His intelligence and logic mixed with adventure and spontaneity was a sexy combination she could get addicted to, she didn't want this day to end.

But soon enough they turned down her street. She waved at her neighbour, Mr Brunswick who lived on the corner in his caravan. Seated in his customary deckchair, with a beer in hand and blue cattle dog at his feet, he waved back.

'Oh no. Not today. Why today?' She whined at the red BMW parked in her driveway.

'Who's that?' Ryan asked over his shoulder as he steered the bike around the cul-de-sac. The throaty rumble of the Harley's engine bounced off the sheds.

'My sister.' Why did Helen have to ruin her day? Who knows what would have happened later? Perhaps another one of those kisses where she wanted this bike ride to last forever.

Oh no, was she picturing fairy tale endings of a happily ever after? All from one kiss!

'Younger or older sister?' Ryan asked as he pulled up at the front of her double drive. The BMW driver's door flew open and there stood Helen with hands on her hips, frowning.

With Ryan's help, Emma got off the bike semi-gracefully. Her body was still vibrating from the ride—or was that from what she was feeling for Ryan? 'She's my older sister.' *But not necessarily wiser.* 'You'd better go, it looks like she's having another diabolical follicle emergency.'

'Sure.' Ryan helped undo Emma's helmet. 'She looks like your mother, so I'm guessing you take after your father's side?'

Let's not talk fathers. 'Thanks for the best day, it was great. It put me in the best mood. Thank you.' She hoped it didn't sound overeager or desperate, but it'd been fun. Just like he'd promised.

'My pleasure.' He stepped in closer and brushed his lips against Emma's. Only this time she was prepared to dance on cloud nine's sunshine beam and meander along the moon's edge. She didn't care if it was glitter and rainbows that clouded her mind, she liked glitter. But it was his arms that held her, it was his kiss that deepened, and it was his flavour that had her flying.

'Ahem.' Helen coughed behind them, toe-tapping her stiletto on the concrete driveway.

Emma sighed as they broke apart from a kiss that spoke her heart's language in songless words. It didn't shout of goodbyes but whispered of a glorious goodnight.

'*Ahem.*' Again, Helen coughed.

'Bloody family,' muttered Emma, and Ryan smiled. Giddy from the adrenalin rush of the bike ride, and fabulously punch-drunk from his kiss, she didn't want it to end.

But it did.

His eyes on her, his thumb stroked her bottom lip sending tingles of pleasure to filter through her system. It was such an intimate gesture she'd never experienced before, she could swoon.

'I'll call you later,' Ryan said.

'Sure. Ah-huh. Yeah, that'd be nice,' she said, still trapped by his eyes.

He winked at her, returned to his bike that started with a roar. Giving a nod and a grin, her hero cruised down the street. The engine's throaty rumble echoed long after he'd disappeared around the corner while she stood at the end of her driveway daydreaming.

'*Are you sleeping with a biker?*' Helen bellowed out behind Emma.

'Ugh, I forgot about you.' Emma frowned at Helen for interrupting her fantasies, and for standing there like a glossy princess of perfection.

'What do you want?' It was like she'd crash landed on Mars with a hangover, Emma didn't care if she sounded bitter. 'By the way, whatever happened to the simple common courtesy of saying *hello*. Or, *thanks for looking after my kids yesterday*. Or, how are you sis, who's the dude?'

Emma had never spoken like this to anyone, and never to Helen. But she wasn't in the mood for a lecture, or to be treated like a second-rate, stupid staff member. Emma was a sibling, not an errand boy.

'I don't say *dude*,' squawked Helen with her nose screwed up.

'You just did.' Emma unlocked her gate and stepped inside, prepared to leave her sister on the street. She couldn't slam the gate in her face when it was made of mesh, but the idea was still tempting. 'What do you want Helen? If you're here to abuse me and treat me like crap, you can leave right now.'

'What did I do to you?' barked back Helen, pushing her way inside the yard.

'You showed up and ruined my entire afternoon by being here.' Emma didn't bother looking back as she headed to her side door.

Helen's heels echoed down the concrete drive following. 'You should be grateful I just saved you from that biker. They deal in drugs, carry knives, and are dangerous people, you know. You shouldn't be hanging around with them.'

Emma spun around and faced Helen. 'You are so wrong.'

'I'm never wrong.'

'Bull!'

'Don't tell me he's your latest desperate fling? Because we both know you don't do boyfriends, and marriage scares you. You should thank me for being here to save you. They're dangerous people, god knows what he might have done to you.'

Emma pointed her keys toward the empty road. 'That guy who rode off on that large beast of a motorbike, his name is Ryan and guess what? He might be dangerous because he carries a gun too. And do you know why?'

'Because that's what drug dealers do?'

'No, he's a detective. One of the good guys who happens to own a Harley that he likes to ride on his day off. And you know what? It was fun riding on the back of his bike and I was having such a brilliant day—*until you showed up.*' She turned her back on her sister and unlocked the shed door.

'Is he really a detective?'

Emma flicked on her lights and headed for her bar. 'Yes. Ryan's been working on the case of my stolen van.' She didn't want to think about her van on its misguided adventure, even if she missed it. But again, she was proving to be adaptable and flexible in any situation.

But did she need to be like that with Helen?

Emma faced her sister from the other side of her bar. 'What are you doing here, and where are my niece and nephew?' Was she expected to babysit again?

'They're at the movies with William.' Helen put her bag on the bar and climbed onto a stool. 'Why do you have so much alcohol? You should sell it and live somewhere nicer.'

Emma liked where she lived. Few people understood why and today she didn't care. Ryan liked it. Victoria and Benjamin liked it. Emma didn't just *like* it, it was her home, her life, and she *loved* it. And she certainly didn't have to explain herself to her bliss-bubble-bursting sister.

'Got any flavoured vodka?'

Emma put a bottle on the bar, a brand no one drank. Grabbed a glass of ice and put it on the counter in front of Helen. 'Your drink, you pour; and it's my bar—my rules.' She wasn't going to serve her sister; she'd been doing that for too long. 'Why are you even here? You never come here.'

'My children told me I'm no fun to be with, and…and…' Helen's lower lip trembled as she poured a big shot of peach flavoured vodka and took a huge mouthful. 'William told me I wasn't fun either and they were happy to go without me. My family left me behind.' She whimpered into her glass, this time taking a sip.

With a glass of ice in hand, Emma examined her top shelf of spirits. 'Fair enough.' She wasn't going to offer any sympathy, not today.

'Are they right? Am I no fun?'

'Helen, I can't remember the last time I did anything fun with you, and I've known you my whole life. If you weren't my sister, I would've told you to get out of my life decades ago.'

Holy crap—was she a biker's bitch who'd found her backbone after one bike ride?

Had Ryan's kiss cracked the concrete that held her civil tongue in place for so long?

Yet, inside her chest it was like a belt had loosened around her rib cage, and an invisible weight lifted off her shoulders. Emma stood taller, and her soles connected firmly to the floor — where gravity was now an ally and not the enemy.

Helen's face dropped, then in the blink of an eye she pulled herself together. 'I'm not that bad?'

'Unless you want me to give it to you straight about what a heartless materialistic bitch you are, by all means, stay. But if you're looking for sympathy, go elsewhere. I have enough of my own problems to deal with than to listen to you rant.' Emma faced her wall of exotic spirits, refusing to think about her problems. Did she dare concoct a new cocktail to match her new mood?

'But, I'm here to talk to you about my problems, not yours. My family doesn't like me.' Helen drained her glass and slammed it on the counter. She then clutched the bottle like a gold-rush miner coming in from the western desert, sloshing more spirits into her glass.

'That is so typical of you, Helen. Guess what? Your problems are yours, and it's your responsibility to deal with them, not me.' Emma crossed her arms over her chest and glared at Helen. 'Please do me a favour—go phone a friend or something and be fake-nice with them, not here.'

'But, I have no friends to go to.' Helen whimpered, cradling her glass with two hands.

'Oh, come on, you're always bragging about the ones you have lunch with. The ones you go shopping with, the ones you go to the gym with. Surely, one of them will pat you on the shoulder and feed you all the niceties you want to hear?'

'It's not my fault.'

'*Yes, it is,*' said Emma. 'It is your fault your family doesn't like you. I don't like you. But we're blood, and that's the only reason we bother with each other. Or you use me for babysitting duties.'

Helen sniffed as tears started to trickle down her face.

'Not falling for that!' Emma had been caught too many times in the past by Helen sucking her in for the sympathy only to then use and abuse her. There was no way Emma was going to let that happen again, not now she'd drawn her line in the glitter of this sibling stoush. Emma wasn't going to take any more crap from her older sister, not today. And never again.

Woohoo—she deserved a twenty-one exploding cannon extravaganza of glitter for this epiphany!

'I could never discuss this with them,' said Helen. 'They have their own families to tend to, while you—'

'Oh, so you'd assumed I had no life, no family, and would be sitting here with nothing to do. You were wrong. *Again.*' Emma smiled as she faced her spirits shelf. Although she had planned to stay home, the day had panned out better than ever and she'd been kissed. Again, she gave a slight sigh at the marvellous memory.

Until Helen crashed her party.

'*I could've got laid*, but noooo you had to show up and ruin it for me. I need a decent drink.' Emma snatched up her bottle of Grey Goose and splashed a decent nip over crushed ice, then she added a dash of Galliano, stirred and sipped. 'Argh, now that's a nice start to a session.' Did she dare dance with the Chartreuse?

'You have all these best friends,' muttered Helen. Her hair stuck to her face while her tears created tracks through the makeup smearing down her cheeks.

'No, I don't, I only have two best friends, Victoria and Benjamin. If I had too many best friends, I'd be too busy spreading myself around. In school I had no one, and you had everyone.' Emma had her crafts with the radio to keep her company in her mother's shed, occupying the space that once used to belong to her father's car.

She still hung-out in a shed, but now she had an exceptional music collection with surround sound on remote. Emma picked up the remote control and selected a random playlist to surprise her. This is why she lived in an industrial area, because she had no neighbours to complain about the music.

'I'M SORRY,' shouted Helen over Macklemore's, *Good Old Days*.

'What?' Emma aimed the remote and turned down the stereo. 'Did I hear right?' Helen never said *sorry*. Helen was never at fault with anything and the word *sorry* was not part of her sister's vocabulary.

'I said *I'm sorry*.' Helen burst into a loud howl as real tears streamed down her face. It was like her mask melted in a mash of makeup and hot streaky tears.

It was pitiful.

Yet, it tugged at Emma's heart as she passed the tissue box to her sister.

Helen wiped her eyes in vicious swipes removing layers of mascara and false eyelashes. 'I miss Mum.'

'Me too, but her sports car has been fun.'

'My children were telling me what you did with them yesterday.'

'We had a great time together.'

'Am I no fun?' Helen asked, staring up at her with big black panda eyes.

For the first time Emma saw the cracks in her sister's perfect façade at how truly miserable Helen was.

Emma couldn't help herself and walked around the bar and hugged her sister. Helen sobbed out her whole sad and lonely life story while Emma listened, like always, until Helen spilled all.

A few hours later, Helen had her hair in a simple ponytail, no makeup on, dancing to the music in bare feet behind the bar. She added assorted liqueurs and crushed ice into the blender's open-mouthed jar, put on the lid and then hit the button. She twirled like a ballerina on a bad day and reached for clean cocktail glasses. Then spun back like an 80's Flashdancer, turned off the blender, popped the lid and tasted it with the tip of her manicured nail.

Satisfied, Helen poured the thick creamy concoction into the glasses. Sprinkled grated chocolate on top and added a glass straw. 'It needs something shiny on top. Can we eat glitter?'

'No, I mean yes you can get edible glitter, but I only stock craft glitter,' Emma said, returning to her seat. 'But it is the environmentally safe kind of glitter, that I'm sure over the years, I've inhaled kilos of the stuff. If you want shiny for drinks, in the wine fridge there's some crushed rock candy we use for that, it'll give an added texture.'

Helen spun around and found the container and sprinkled the candy over the cocktail. 'There, it looks like a creamy sundae made from snow on a Sunday.'

'It does.' *But how would it taste?* Emma exchanged her cordless phone for a cocktail.

'Who were you talking to on the phone?'

'William. I rang to tell him that you and your car were staying the night.' Emma sipped her drink and her eyes opened at the fluffy cocktail. It was a heavenly, creamy white chocolate blend with a hint of aromatic spice and nutty essence that had her tastebuds buzzing. 'I think you've missed your career path in life, Helen, because this is divine.' And she took another taste. 'Yum, what did you put in this?'

'No idea.' Helen cackled like a teenager, sipping from her cocktail glass.

'There are pens and notepads behind the bar, write down your ingredients. We're always searching for new ones for parties.'

Helen retrieved the notebook ready for the next recipe. 'So what problem are we talking about?'

'William told me you've been a horrible misery-guts complaining about your day.'

'I am not.'

Emma didn't justify that response with an answer but stared at her sister while sipping her cocktail.

'Okay, so maybe I have been.'

'Like every day of my life,' mumbled Emma. 'This is so good. I could eat this. We should freeze a batch and test it for adult ice creams to use for a future pool party in summer?'

'But I'm busy all day.'

'What do you do all day, Helen?' *It must be sooo exhausting doing the bare minimum in life.*

'I get up in the morning, get breakfast and lunches ready for my family. I take the kids to school. I go to the gym and go home and clean my house.'

'You have a housekeeper who cleans and shops for you, a gardener, and a pool guy. Hey, I've heard about pool guys and rich stay-home-wives. Is he cute?'

Helen screwed her nose up. 'The pool guy used to date Mum.'

'Ew.' So there went that theory.

'Then, I go wait until it's time for the school pickups,' said Helen, returning the lidless spirit bottles onto the wrong shelves. 'From there they have soccer training, ballet lessons, piano lessons, violin lessons. Then home for dinner, where I get the children to bed and do it all over again the next day.'

'What do you do while the kids are at school?'

Helen shrugged, putting dirty glasses into the small glass dishwasher and turned it on. 'I do stuff. I go to the gym daily where I may stay for a few hours.'

'You have a gym at home.' Anything athletic was dangerous in Emma's world where her form of cardio was all about perfecting the eye-roll.

'For this figure, I have to work for it,' announced Helen posing with her perfect fat-free figure.

'By feeding the parasites,' Emma mumbled and shrugged at Helen's frown. 'Come on, we both know you could always eat what you wanted and never put on any weight.' Which sucked for Emma who'd missed out on that hereditary trait. 'You're bored is what you are. Your kids aren't as dependent on you except as their glorified taxi driver.' Amazing herself at how philosophical she could get drinking cocktails. But was she making sense?

'Do you think so?'

'Have you ever considered finding your own interests?'

'Like what?'

Emma reached across for a spoon and scooped into her cocktail. She could eat it until sunrise. 'I dunno, what fun interests do you and William share?'

'Um…' Helen's mouth squelched to the side. 'The kids. But William's working all the time.'

'Oh, puh-leese! You're a stay at home mother driving a BMW with a wardrobe the size of my front office, don't complain how hard your husband works. Especially when he's almost completed the deal for a major expansion of his business to set you and your family up for the rest of your lives. William is working hard on this now, so he can cut back on his hours to spend more time with you and your children in the near future.'

'Did William really say that?' Helen asked.

Emma nodded with her spoon hanging out of her mouth.

'But what do we do?'

'I don't know, I'm not a marriage counsellor,' Emma said, savouring another spoonful of magic medicine.

'There must be something you can suggest?'

Emma swivelled on her stool in time with the music, scooping at her cocktail as if in a 1950's ice cream parlour with her own jukebox resting silently in the corner of her black and white tiled dance-floor. 'Dancing.'

'What?'

'Your kids had a ball dancing at the Aged Care Lodge last night, and William mentioned he wouldn't mind learning ballroom dancing. Didn't you do ballet or some other form of dancing at school?'

'I did tap, until Mum lost my shoes.'

'Mum didn't, I hid them in the roof. I wonder if they're still there?' Along with lots of Helen's belongings that used to annoy Emma as a kid.

'You did what to my tap-dancing shoes?'

Let's not rip that band-aid off today. 'Why not try dancing lessons with William? Make it a date night.'

Helen's eyes glazed over dreamily. 'That's not a bad idea, and the outfits I could buy—'

'I didn't mean buy a new wardrobe,' Emma said to the shopaholic with a platinum credit card. 'What I'm trying to say is you need to find your own happiness. Get a job during school hours or do a course. Get that brain of yours working, and Helen, you do have a brain.' She hadn't seen it in a while, but Emma did do her best to avoid Helen at all times. 'There's an entire world of fun out there and it's only you who can find it.'

'I will,' Helen said determinedly, as if making a solemn vow to herself.

'Good, now you can make me another cocktail.' Emma held out her empty glass to Helen. She sucked on the end of her spoon, swinging her legs under her stool like a child.

'I can't remember what I put in it?'

Would Helen remember this epiphany in the morning? 'Make up another one then. You're good at this. Remember, write down what you use.'

'Would you give me a job?'

'No.' Emma coughed, tapping her chest for air, and then remembered to be nice. 'But you can create cocktails after-hours as part of our creative staff meetings. I'll have to confer with the creative committee for their vote of approval first.' She grinned, picturing Victoria's and Benjamin's faces for daring to even consider such a proposal.

'I'm sorry I was such a bitch to you.' Helen then stood square in front of Emma on the other side of the bar and said, 'it was because I was jealous of you.'

'Huh?' Emma's eyes widened, pressing the spoon against the bottom lip of her open mouth.

'You're so irritatingly happy all the time.'

'Irritating?' Emma stared at the woman who'd turned *irritating* into a fine art.

'I got jealous because you'd created your own successful business without any support. You weren't known as someone's wife or someone's mother but just you, for who you are. I got jealous whenever I heard my husband recommend you for parties because you do a fantastic job. You surprise me every year with William's office Christmas party. It's the talk of the finance sector, you know.'

Emma stayed silent. As always, Helen did the babbling while Emma was trained to listen, and never complained because Helen never listened before.

Was it because of the ear bashing she copped as a child from Helen, Emma now had the patience for her clients? The patience to listen to people's nuisances? The patience to put up with so much bullshit!

But this was one confession worth listening to and she watched Helen's bitchy barriers crumble.

'Helen, you already have your own brand of happiness.'

Helen tossed chopped fruit into the blender. 'Do I?'

'You have a husband and a family who love you very much. They'd have to, considering they've put up with you as a crabby bitch for this long. They'll love you more when you find your extra layer of happiness. You're lucky to have such a wonderful family.'

Helen poured a dash of banana liqueur, white rum, and then a pinch of cinnamon spice into the blender's bowl. 'You think so?'

'I know so.' It's what Emma wanted, a family of her own. But she gave up on that dream the day she swore to never do weddings again. Both created too much drama, leaving an emotional hangover that still lingered in her life.

'By the way, I like your haircut. It brings out your eyes more.' Helen pushed on the lid and pressed the button blitzing the blender into life.

Emma had never received compliments from her sister before. Would Helen be like this tomorrow?

THIRTEEN

Emma heard the shed's roller door open below her, and she rolled over to wince at her bedside clock. 'Oh god.' She lay her head back on the pillow. How, in the blink of an eye, did it mysteriously turn into morning?

Dare she open her bedroom door to face the sunlight? At least she remembered to shut her curtains before dancing with her pillow.

There was a knock on her apartment's door. 'Yoo-Hoo,' called out Benjamin. 'Sweetie, you home?'

'I'm coming.' Emma groaned, sitting upright like Frankenstein's bride.

A tap turned on and then she heard the familiar clunking sound of her kettle. That meant at least twenty minutes before she could drink a coffee. *Damn.* Today she hated that kettle and hid her head back under the pillow.

'Knock, knock,' called out Benjamin on the other side of her bedroom door.

'I'm alive.' *I think?*

She threw back the covers and opened her door. It was like she'd died and gone to sunshine heaven when she preferred the darkness of hell.

'For you.' Benjamin held out a tall glass of a Bloody Mary

and painkillers.

'Is this where I tell you I love you forever and ever and ever…' She popped the pills and washed it down with iced-tomato juice, vodka, with a dash of Worcestershire sauce. '…and ever and ever.'

Benjamin cast a disapproving eye over her attire as she staggered toward her kitchen.

'Don't judge me, I'm not awake yet.'

'The cat does.'

'He's a cat! They're judgy creatures.'

'Mister ignores me too.'

She arched her eyebrow at him. 'Mister's a deaf cat who ignores everyone.' Except Emma who fed her favourite after-hours companion.

'So, I'm to assume you had a major indulgence with the bar downstairs? Or did Mister have a cat party with the rest of the stray alley cats?'

'Must be a mess for you to hand-deliver me a cocktail for breakfast.' Emma stumbled to her kitchen bench as the kettle clonked, whirred, whined, and churned to boil water. She frowned at the contraption. Was today the day she'd buy a new one?

'What was the occasion?' Benjamin asked as he bounced onto his seat beside Emma at the breakfast counter.

'Guess who I drank with last night?' Emma slurped on her straw, while Benjamin shrugged. 'My sister.'

'Noooo! Not the bitchy perfect princess. Not Helen.'

'Shh, she'll hear you.' Emma peered over to her couches where Helen lay asleep.

'Why is that bitchy cow still here? And you let her sleep in here and park her car downstairs. Helen's never been in here.'

Emma grinned and sipped her spiked juice, which was getting better with every mouthful. No wonder Victoria lived on these. 'Helen also told me she was sorry. And she told me she was miserable with her life and was jealous of ME.' She stabbed her thumb at her chest. 'Ow.' It was too early to be so hard on herself, and rubbed her chest.

Benjamin's brown eyes stared at Emma then flicked over to Helen, then back to Emma. 'How is that possible? Helen doesn't know the word *sorry*.'

'Helen's family told her she was no fun to hang out with.'

'So, then she came over here demanding your sympathy while putting you down at the same time, which you put up with, as per usual.'

Emma sat taller with chin up and shoulders back. 'No, I didn't. I'd been having the best day until Helen ruined it by showing up, and so I told her too.'

'You did? I don't believe it.'

'It's true. I don't know what happened. It's like I found my spine or something but I lost it. No, I found it. And, I told Helen exactly what I thought of her.'

'Well, it's about time.' Benjamin patted her shoulder. 'Shame I missed it. I've wanted to tell Helen to piss-off for years.'

'You already do, what's the difference?' They snickered at each other over the breakfast counter while the kettle clonked, whirred, churned, and groaned in the background.

'Morning,' mumbled Helen. Her hair was a bird's nest after a cyclone and she wobbled to her feet from the couch.

'Where's the bathroom?'

'That way.' Emma pointed to the small hallway. Was her bathroom presentable enough for the perfect princess, who didn't look perfect, stumbling across the room and closing the bathroom door behind her.

Benjamin sat up, slapping a palm over his heart. 'Helen said morning? Unless she's talking to the voices in her head, she never acknowledges our presence. What happened last night?'

'We made cocktails. Helen made some amazing concoctions. I hope I can read her writing for the recipes.'

'Why?'

'They were good,' said Emma, 'and we sorted out a lot of crap between us.'

'Does this mean Helen's on your Christmas card list?'

'Let's not be too hasty.' Emma patted Benjamin's hand. 'It's early days yet. For all we know, Helen could slip straight back into the bitchy princess persona as soon as she puts her makeup back on.' Emma sipped the last of her cocktail. 'Thank you for the Bloody Mary delivered with a smile.' And in only another ten minutes—if she was lucky—her kettle would boil.

Benjamin plucked the empty glass off the counter. 'Want me to get breakfast? Tina's smoko-van should be here soon.'

'Yes, please. Tell Tina I'd love one of her blue-collared bacon deluxe toasties. Get one for Helen and you too. My shout. I don't remember eating dinner last night.'

'Isn't Helen always on some strict diet?'

'Helen will get what she's given. But thank you for the wake up with the delicious delivery, Benjamin.'

'I was the mess the other day. Besides, it won't take you

long and you'll be bouncing down the stairs.' This from the man who bounced to the door with her empty glass in hand.

'Could you ask Tina for two of her coffees, please? The largest she's got.'

Benjamin caught the door jamb while halfway out the door. He stared back at Emma and flicked his eyes over to the decrepit kettle whining and coughing on the bench. 'Does this mean we can finally get a coffee machine downstairs?'

Emma face-palmed herself. She was such a traitor to her kettle. 'I have a guest? And, I have the perfect coffee maker.'

'Where are the keys for the cars? I'll move them so Andy can unload his van for our half-day Monday.'

'Um, inside the cars,' Emma muttered, laying her head back down on the cool steel counter. Her head thumped and her tongue was covered in fur. Her tummy rumbled from tomato juice and hunger while the kettle carried on in her ear. But she had work to do.

Oh great, it's bloody Monday again.

Would it get better… Or worse?

On the shed floor by the large industrial shelves, Emma packed away her equipment from the weekend's functions with the help of Benjamin.

Nearby, Helen sat at the central workbench sipping her coffee while talking to her husband on the phone. 'Darling, I think I might do a course or something.'

Benjamin stopped and stared, holding a box to Emma reaching down from her step ladder. 'Did I hear right?' he whispered to Emma.

Emma shrugged, putting the box on the higher shelf. Her short-haired grey and white ex-alley cat, yawned at her from his neighbouring shelf. It was a cubbyhole fit for a prince that oversaw all. 'Morning, Mister. Didn't keep you up all night, did we?' She gave the cat a slight scratch on his soft grey ears as he purred.

Helen continued her phone conversation. 'Yes… No, I'm okay. Spending time with my little sister has been good for me. Also, I want to say I'm sorry for being such a bitch, William.'

'She said what?' Benjamin froze with box in hand while gawking back at Helen.

'Yes, I said *sorry*… Don't laugh, William, I am sorry. Emma told me off for being rude to her and guess what? … I made cocktails last night, and I slept on her couch in her loft. I didn't know it was like that. It's nice…'

'Has Helen sobered up yet?' Benjamin passed the last box to Emma.

'It's still early.' Emma shrugged, then slid the box away and carefully stepped down the ladder. Gravity—and her sister—had been kind to her today.

'I'm sorry, baby, I've got a lot to make up for,' Helen gushed over the phone.

Emma rolled her eyes at Benjamin, who with hands on hips, stage-whispered, 'This isn't right. The material perfect princess is being nice. It's sickening.'

'Maybe I'm not just hung-over from the cocktails.' Emma put the ladder away. Her physical chores were done on her half-day Monday.

'Oh, honey what do you think about doing dancing lessons? …Yes, Emma suggested it… You would, that's wonderful. I'll tell her… Sure, I'll leave that to you then. I love you, honey, bye.' Helen hung up the phone smiling to herself and polished her wedding ring on the napkin from breakfast. She then held her palm up to catch the light streaming through the open side of the shed now vacant of all cars.

Emma didn't know whether to smile or gag with Benjamin. Instead, she took a sip of her takeaway coffee. *Sorry kettle, there's always tomorrow.*

'How's William?' Emma asked, while scrolling through her tablet's to-do list. Thankfully, Mondays were normally slow. That allowed her to follow-up on last weekend's events and to strategize for the oncoming week. Monday was also more of a long lunch as part of her creative meeting sessions with Victoria and Benjamin.

'My wonderful William is sending you some flowers,' Helen said to Emma. 'We both agree you deserve them.'

'Okay, *enough.*' Benjamin forfeited the bounce to storm over to stand in front of Helen. 'What the hell happened to you? You're being nice.'

'It's the new me.' Helen raised her arms like a model in an infomercial showing off a new brand of toothpaste. 'I'm sorry for being a bitch to you too, Benjamin, and thank you for fetching me breakfast.'

Benjamin narrowed his eyes at Helen. 'Are you still drunk from last night, or do you need drugs?'

'No. William asked the same thing. I'm fine.'

'What did you put into those cocktails? I want the recipes,

they're life-changing.'

'I wrote it down in the bar, I think?' Helen then patted her sister's hand. 'Emma?'

'Yes.' Emma sat back warily because Helen only spoke nicely when she wanted something, and leopards weren't known to change their designer labels overnight.

'I want to say thank you, because I think you've saved my marriage.'

'I hate to interrupt this love-fest,' said Benjamin, pointing to the side bench, 'but, you've got a few messages on your answering machine. Want me to delete them?'

'Thanks, but no.' Emma got up with as much enthusiasm as a harassed mother waiting at a supermarket checkout line guarding a trolley-full of groceries. It was time wasting, but necessary for operations. 'I'll deal with them. Hopefully there aren't too many prank calls today.'

Emma frowned at her machine blinking the number nine on its small screen. Compared to Saturday's messages, this was good.

She hesitated before she hit play. Had she deleted Helen's screeching messages from Saturday?

Too late now.

Emma pressed play for message number one that had been recorded on Saturday afternoon:

'Hi, Emma, it's Ryan, I'm assuming your phone has gone for a swim in the river. Can you call me, please, if you can?'

Emma smiled at the sound of his voice and hit the delete button.

'What happened to your phone?' Benjamin asked, while

seated beside Helen at the large worktable.

'Since when did you get a mobile phone?' Called out Helen.

'I've always had one. Well, I did until Jamie dropped my old phone over the side of the rowboat while talking to Ryan.'

Benjamin picked up the sleek silver smartphone from the table. 'So where did you get this new phone from?'

'Victoria, she's doing their campaign,' replied Emma. 'Although I'm having issues with that model, I can't turn it on.'

'Like this.' Benjamin pressed the side panel and the screen lit up.

Damn. Now she had to answer her calls.

'I wished I'd gone on the boat ride with William and my children. They said it was great fun.' Helen sulked behind her takeaway cup watching Benjamin work the new phone.

'You can do it as a future family outing when you move into your new riverside mansion.' Emma pressed the answering machine's play button.

'Biatch, how come Victoria didn't give me a new phone?' Benjamin asked, scrolling through the new smartphone.

'Why don't you call her and ask, while loading yours and Victoria's number into the new phone, please, Benjamin?' Emma gave him a hopeful smile; after all, she was his boss.

Message number two played over the machine's speakers:

'Hi Emma, it's Katrina the assistant to Graham Tottsner. I'm calling to send Graham's compliments for a job well done. I'm definitely using you for future functions. Christmas is a must; I'm locking it in now. It's such a pity you don't do weddings, but I look forward to that wedding planner's list you mentioned to Graham and your invoice.

*Also, Graham would like you to include a fifteen percent bonus on top
for your work too, bye.'*

'No way?' Emma slapped her heart as her jaw dropped.
Fifteen percent bonus, on a five-star elite package was HUGE!

'Congratulations, Emma.' Benjamin sat up and golf-
clapped. 'I'm so proud. Your attention to detail for that English
nautical theme was superb.'

'I owe it all to Mary Poppins.' With her hand still covering
her heart, Emma bowed.

'It was a great luncheon by the riverside, Emma, you did
such a good job, everyone said so. You too, Benjamin,' said
Helen, patting Benjamin's shoulder.

'Wow, when you drop the Princess-bitch-routine, you're
nice,' said Benjamin.

Message number three came on:

'We wanna Parte',' sang the girls' voices over the speakers.
'We wanna Parte'! We wanna Parte'!' Emma hit delete.

Helen's face screwed up as if she'd sucked an unripe
lemon straight from the tree. 'What was that?'

'Prank calls. Although, they're starting to sound a little
better.' Or Emma was getting used to them. She still gladly
deleted their singing messages four and five from late Saturday
night.

Then the recorded message number six played from
Sunday morning:

*'Hi Emma, it's Ryan. I'm standing outside your front gate
wondering if you wanted to go for a ride today. Are you there? I'll
throw rocks on your roof. Hope you don't charge me with property
damage. Just saying.'* His laugh carried over the phone.

Again, the sound of his voice made Emma smile.

'Was that Detective Adonis?' Benjamin asked. 'A ride on what?'

Helen sat up and explained. 'On this big noisy Harley Davidson motorcycle. It was so shiny.'

Benjamin tilted his head at Emma. 'You were on a motorbike?'

'I saw it. Emma rode up on the back with this guy, and then they kissed goodbye and Emma got all gooey.'

'I did not.' Did she? It had been a memorable kiss.

'Did Ryan really throw rocks on your roof?' Helen asked.

'Yes.' Emma glanced at her wide carpark area that now had three red cars parked under the trees. None hers.

'That's got to be over a gazillion metres, I'm impressed,' said Benjamin. 'But I want details on that kiss.'

Emma waved her hand at her eager assistant in his quest for gossip when message number seven played:

'Emma, it's Mum here. I just had the strangest phone message from your sister. She sounds so upset. Please check on her. No matter how she treats you, Helen is your sister. I'll owe you one when I get back. Gotta go, I'm having the best time.' Irene then crooned, *'Oh Mitchell, stop it, you dirty bugger, lower, oh, yes that's the —'*

Emma cringed, slamming the delete button on her mother.

'I'm sorry for being a bitch to you, Emma.'

'You should be, Helen. You've been such a bitch to everyone,' blurted out Benjamin.

'That cocktail history boat was floated last night. Today is a new day,' said Emma, waiting for message number eight to share the news. So far so good.

'*Emma, it's your father,*' came the male gravelly voice over the speakers.

'*Nooo,*' said all three of them, staring at the machine.

'*I saw this morning's news, I swear I spotted your business logo on some van, where the driver is shooting people. Call me and tell me you're not involved with this?*' The message ended.

There was no goodbye.

No hi, how are you?

'Dad never calls,' said Helen.

'When was the last time you spoke to your father?' Benjamin asked.

'Christmas time with the kids,' replied Helen. 'Emma, are you still trying to ring Dad once a month?'

'Nope.' She'd stopped doing that a long, long time ago.

'Emma, it's not your fault,' said Helen.

'What isn't my fault?' Emma stared at the perfect princess seated at her bench. 'You're the daddy's girl, did it sound like he was blaming me for those murders? You know what—I'll find out.' She snatched-up the cordless phone and searched for his number.

'Emma took it hard when Dad left,' Helen said to Benjamin. 'I think that's why Emma hasn't been in a relationship since Frank.'

'Is that why Emma won't work weddings? Is it because of your parents' marriage break up? We get people asking all the time.'

'Er…' Helen flinched, and so did Emma, turning her back on their conversation. 'Ask Emma.'

'I have,' said Benjamin. 'Is it because of Frank, her ex? He used to treat her so badly and talk to her so poorly, and Emma put up with it too. It was horrible. That's when Emma started to sleep in this shed, long before she'd built her apartment.'

'Why did Emma put up with Frank being so rude to her?' Helen asked Benjamin.

'Probably the same reasons why she put up with you.'

Helen gasped. 'Me?'

'Oh, spare me with the falsities, princess. Don't tell me you weren't relishing the public belittling of Emma where you treated her like the staff. You should be ashamed of yourself.' Benjamin wagged his finger at Helen. 'If you were my sister, I would've put a restraining order against you so you'd never come near me again. Then I'd sue you to pay for all the years of therapy I'd need—wow, Emma, sweetie, I'd never realised how strong you are for putting up with your sister all these years.'

Emma screwed her nose up at Benjamin. *Strong? Yeah, right—not!*

'All right, I know I was a bitch.' Helen's shoulders slumped as she fiddled with her fingers in her lap.

'Well, now you've admitted it, I won't give you such a hard time.' Benjamin pointed at Helen. 'I will warn you, if you dare go back to the way you were, I'll let Victoria loose with one of her legendary tongue lashings, your ears will be ringing for a fortnight.'

Helen winced. 'Victoria scares me, but I deserve it for what I've done, to you, Victoria, and Emma.'

'Fear is stupid. So are regrets, Marilyn Monroe said that.' Emma wished she could live by that motto, and walked away

from their conversation, trying to listen to the dial tone.

'Hello,' answered Emma's father on the other end of the phone.

'It's Emma.'

'You got my message then?'

'Yes. Nice surprise, Dad.' It wasn't nice. It was a surprise because he never rang—ever. All those years sitting by the phone as a child, when he promised he'd call, he never did. It was a harsh lesson learned.

'Was that your van on the news? You're not shoot—'

'My van got stolen on my birthday.' Which he always forgot. But never Helen's.

'Oh, err, happy birthday. Sorry, I've been swamped, can't remember what day it is.'

'It's Monday.'

'Yeah,' He gave a nervous laugh, but Emma wasn't smiling. 'So, how are you?'

'Perfect.' No way was she going to ask about the other woman he was playing happy families with, not when he'd forgotten about his first family.

'How's your sister?'

'Helen's here. Do you want to talk to her?' Because Emma couldn't understand why she'd bothered calling her father, when he really didn't know her and she didn't know him either.

'I'll talk to her later. I've got to head off. Maybe, next time I'm in town I'll call you and we can go out to dinner or something?'

'Sure, Dad.' It'd never happen. Like a spineless coward, he'd come and go from town and never call. She was surprised he'd had the nerve to show up to Helen's wedding; which was last time she saw him, and it was the last wedding Emma ever attended. Eight years ago.

'No worries, um, take care, okay?'

'Sure, you too.' Emma stared at the phone. Did he care?

She returned the phone to its cradle beside the answering machine where the final message blinked at her.

'Did you get through to Dad?' Helen asked.

'Dad says he'll call you later. Wished me a happy birthday.' Which he always forgot. But Emma never forgot his birthday, Father's Day, Easter or Christmas, where she'd send him special personalised gifts. She used to wait for a reply, a response, something more than a backhanded compliment as passing conversation.

But she got nothing.

And she'd learned to expect nothing.

From anyone.

'Want another Bloody Mary?' Benjamin asked.

'Yes please.' Emma pressed play for the last message.

'Hi, this message is for Emma, its Jae. I'm here with Stu. We're the guys who stole—Sorry, I should rephrase that...' He cleared his throat and said, *'We're the ones who inadvertently borrowed your van without your permission.'*

'Are you kidding me!' Emma stared in horror at her answering machine.

Jae's voice continued, *'After speaking with you the other night, we'd never realised how much we were putting you out and left you a present. We threw a large paper bag over your fence into your yard late Friday night. Because you'd spoken to us so nicely, we thought you deserved something nice, and, what with being a small business owner, we left you some money for hire fees. Please consider this a form of compensation for what we've done. Anyway, we hope you'll enjoy your present and we'll be returning the van to you, once we're done with it. Stu's decked it out and we're going camping. Can't wait. We hope you have a lovely week, bye for now, Jae and Stu.'*

A large truck engine roared over the phone message.

Jae said, *'Do you want to say anything, Stu?'*

'Should we send Emma a postcard from the van?'

Jae's laughter carried over the speaker. *'I don't think so.'*

'We'll take photos, the Parte' van's famous, you know.'

'Finish the call so we can go, please, Stu.'

Stu cleared his throat and said, *'Hey, Emma, we'll take good care of your van, and I love your playlist, reckon it's endless. We hope you like our pressie. See-ya.'*

The message ended.

'They know YOUR NAME!' Helen hollered in horror from her seat at the worktable.

Emma ignored Helen, it was a specialised skill she'd practised all her life, and replayed the message again. *What brown paper bag of money?*

'They were here! At your shed!' cried Benjamin in a panic beside Helen. 'We should call the police?'

Helen said, 'the fire brigade.'

'Alert everyone.'

'Calm down, you two.' Emma frowned at the pair over her shoulder. 'I'm trying to think.' She paced back and forth near the answering machine. 'He said brown paper bag. What bag? I can't remember—oh, wait a minute. Helen?' She faced her sister seated beside Benjamin, both with smartphones in hand ready to speed dial a national crisis. 'On Saturday morning you took Jamie and Toby to the drive-thru for breakfast and the gate was locked. Did you throw their rubbish from Macca's over my front fence?'

'No.'

'Are you sure? You were preoccupied at the time.' Having a personal meltdown classed as a curlers-crisis.

'No. We went to the drive-thru for breakfast because the gate was locked, and when we returned your gate was open. I don't litter, and I don't do it with my children. I'm always telling them to put their rubbish in the bin.'

'*The bin.*' Emma spun around, did a slight two-step to stay upright. She bounced off the bench, then headed back on course, upright and outside, with Benjamin and Helen in hot pursuit.

On the side of the shed stood a row of wheelie bins. At the nearest one, Emma lifted the lid and dug around inside.

'What are you doing?' Benjamin asked.

'That is so disgusting.' Helen gagged with her hand over her mouth.

With her head in a rubbish bin, Emma prayed the wind didn't blow up her skirt and bare all for the neighbours. 'Believe it or not, these are the cleanest rubbish bins in the city. Gotcha.' She pulled out the heavy brown paper bag with golden arches on the side.

Helen held her hand over her mouth and nose. 'It's a rubbish bin, how can they be so clean?'

'Mr Brunswick, who lives on the corner, owns a bin cleaning service,' said Emma. 'He visits weekly to clean these bins and has a beer with me.'

Benjamin nodded. 'He does a thorough job too. I'd recommend him to anyone. But I'd be careful with that bag, you don't know where it's been.'

'It just came out of the garbage,' said Emma, grinning with excitement, keen to peek inside.

'Benjamin's right,' said Helen. 'They might have put a bomb, or needles, or set a booby trap inside.'

'Or it could be a bag of dog poop,' said Benjamin with nose screwed up.

'Yuck.' Emma dropped the bag.

Benjamin and Helen squealed, clutching onto each other.

Emma quickly scurried to stand beside them where they stared at the brown bag sitting on the asphalt.

A large aeroplane flew in the distant. Traffic hummed in the background from the main road. A grinder from her neighbour's workshop whirled. Metal tools clanged as if dropped by the mechanics across the road and the sound of an engine turned over.

Still, the three of them stood and stared at the brown bag sitting on the concrete.

Benjamin said quietly, 'If it was full of dog poo wouldn't it have oozed out everywhere by now?'

Still, they waited.

And waited.

'Would they really leave you money inside that bag?' Helen asked.

'They have done a lot of robberies,' said Benjamin.

'Let's find out.' Emma took a deep breath and cautiously

approached the paper bag. She unrolled the top and peered inside.

Helen and Benjamin clung to each and took teeny-tiny steps away from the scene while craning their necks to watch.

'No way,' exclaimed Emma.

'*What?*' Both Helen and Benjamin asked, stopping their backward tiptoe of escape.

'It's full of money.' Emma smiled, reaching inside.

'STOP.' Helen's screech echoed down the drive. The grinder stopped and the revving car engine was silenced next door. 'Don't put your hand inside, it could have needles or razor blades.'

'Helen's right, it might be booby-trapped,' said Benjamin, nodding. 'Wait, did I just agree with Helen—in public?'

'You did. I'm being nice, remember?'

Emma wiped itchy palms down her skirt. 'You're both right, and can we please remain calm?'

'And do what? Call the bomb squad?' Benjamin asked.

'No. Not when their message sounded like a couple of guys excited about their camping trip and were sharing the joy of gift giving.' She knew that sound from her many satisfied clients.

Did the media fabricate those robberies and murders, considering how wrong they'd described Jae and Stu? Ryan hadn't given her the details on her van's escapades because she never asked. Did she need to know all now?

'I want to see. I have to.' Emma held her breath and picked up the bag's paper edge with her fingertips and carried it inside as if it was a ticking bomb.

Helen and Benjamin, still holding onto each other, followed at a distance.

'What are you going to do?' Helen hollered, still holding onto Benjamin, both hovering way outside the shed.

Emma cleared her work table and poured the entire contents of the bag.

It was cash. Lots of loose cash in all forms of denominations in a large jumbled pile. She grabbed a pen and poked around the money spreading it around. There were no hidden surprises except cash.

'All clear,' called Emma over her shoulder.

'I've never seen so much cash before,' said Benjamin, coming to stand beside Emma.

'Me neither.'

'I have,' said Helen, approaching with caution.

'You would,' said Emma and Benjamin.

'Hellllooooo,' called out Victoria, strolling in through the open shed door.

'AAUUGGHH.' The trio screamed in fright and grasped onto each other.

'I know Monday's are frightful, but there's no need to make it a horror movie drama.' With an unlit cigarette in hand, Victoria peeked over the rim of her dark sunglasses.

'What are you doing, Victoria?' Benjamin patted his chest as if to slow down his heart rate. 'I swear I've aged a decade from your grand entrance.'

'I needed a Bloody Mary and thought I'd come say hello on your half-day Monday.' Victoria put her shopping bag down, raised her dark sunglasses, and pointed her unlit cigarette at the table. 'What is that?'

'Money,' replied Emma.

'I see that. But what's it doing on the table like that, and why do you look so scared?'

'Those guys who stole Emma's van left all this money as a present,' explained Benjamin.

'When?'

'On Friday night. They left a message on Emma's answering machine on Sunday and…' He shrugged.

'You've just found it now?' Victoria flicked her lighter and lit her cigarette.

'Welcome to the drama party,' Emma said, reaching for an ashtray.

'Sounds like it, babe. That's a lot of cash.' Victoria placed the ashtray on the table. 'I need a drink for this. Who's up for a Bloody-Mary-special made by Queen Victoria herself?' With cigarette smoke trailing behind her, Victoria went behind the bar. The other three raised their hands while staring at the money. 'What are you going to do with the money?'

'We should count it to find out how much is there,' suggested Benjamin.

'I'm not touching it,' said Helen. 'You never know who's touched it or where it's been. I rarely carry cash anymore.'

'Suit yourself, I want to count it,' said Emma.

'Goodie, I'll get the gloves.' Benjamin bounced off to the shelves.

With plastic gloves passed out, a jug of Bloody Mary shared, and while the music played, the quartet sat at the work table and counted the cash as the grey cat, Mister, oversaw all from his shelf.

Victoria stripped off her plastic gloves like a mortician after an autopsy and sat back and lit another cigarette. 'Babe, they gave you $24,325 in cash. Why?'

'They said it was for hire fees for stealing my van.'

'You have enough here to buy yourself another van,' said Helen. 'Although I have no idea how much a van would cost. I've never been in one.'

'Why is Helen even in the Helen-free-zone? Who let her inside?' Victoria asked Benjamin.

Benjamin, with shiny eyes and wide smile, leaned forward and explained. 'Last night Emma yelled at Helen for being nothing but a heartless, materialistic, yoga-lite-latte-loving-queen-bitch—'

Victoria raised her chin at him. 'Who did you call queen?'

'Oh sorry, did I say queen? I meant bitchy princess. Then they had these magical epiphany inspiring cocktails that created Helen's rebirth into becoming nice.'

'What did you say about lattes, Benjamin?' Helen asked.

Victoria arched her eyebrow at Helen. 'You don't do nice. It's like me telling you it's nice to see you again, when we both know I'm lying.'

'Do I need to say sorry to you too?' Helen asked Victoria.

'Probably. I can't believe you said the word *sorry*.'

'It's a whole new me.' Helen raised her arms in the air like she'd won bingo at the Aged Care Lodge.

'What was in those cocktails?' Victoria looked to Benjamin who shrugged his reply.

Emma threw her balled up plastic gloves into the bin, then

pointed at the neat piles of money spread across her table. 'Hello, am I on the right planet, people? Can we focus back here?'

'You should keep the money,' said Benjamin.

Victoria raised her smouldering cigarette in the air. 'I second that motion.'

'Emma should give it back,' said Helen.

'Why?' Asked Benjamin and Victoria.

'Helen's right,' Emma said, and her friends stared at her with wide eyes and open mouths, horrified. 'I know, I agreed with Helen too—in public.'

'What is wrong with you?' Victoria leaned over and touched Emma's forehead. 'Did you drink those life-changing magical cocktails too?'

'We should give the money back,' said Emma. 'These guys have done armed robberies from all those small businesses. It belongs to them. Not me.'

'But those boys gave it to you as a gift,' said Benjamin. 'I never return gifts, it's poor taste if you do.'

Victoria exhaled a stream of smoke and said, 'I'm sure those businesses have insurance cover for robbery and have already been reimbursed.'

'Or they're having as much trouble as I am with my own insurance company.' Decision made. Emma reached for her cordless phone.

'Who are you ringing, babe?' Victoria asked.

'The Police.' Emma dialled the police station's number from memory. It had become part of her daily tasks to pass on the messages left for van sightings—*amazing what you get used to.*

'Are you calling Ryan? Hey, you forgot to fill me in on the

details of his kiss,' called out Benjamin.

'Who, Detective Adonis? How, when Emma was furious at Ryan for shouting at her?' Asked Victoria as Emma walked away and made her call.

Emma soon returned and took her seat back at the table covered in money. 'Well, that was Kelly who's contacting David.'

'Why didn't you call Detective Adonis direct?' Victoria asked with a sly grin.

'I still haven't worked out how to use this new phone you gave me.' Emma pushed the sleek silver gadget across to Victoria.

'Hey, where's my new phone? Don't you love me anymore?' Benjamin gave a childish pout at Victoria.

'Behave, yours is at home. Babe, what do you mean you haven't worked out how to use it? You're part of the test group.' Victoria snatched the phone from the table, when it rang in her hand. 'Hello Emma's phone…Oh, hold on, I'll get her for you, Ryan. Detective Adonis wants you, babe.'

Emma's cheeks burned as she snatched the handpiece from Victoria. 'Hello?'

'Hey, Kelly rang and said the van thieves left you a message?' At the sound of Ryan's deep silky voice, her toes curled.

'Yes, we found a bag of cash, and before you ask, I still don't have your number to call you direct.' Emma turned her back on the trio making faces at her while she tried to talk and keep a straight face on a serious matter. Instead she giggled.

'Well, you have my number now,' said Ryan. 'We're on

our way, should be half an hour.'

'Okay, I'll put the kettle on, shall I?'

'Considering it takes that long to boil why not give it a head start. Hey, are you okay though?'

Aw, he cared. 'Yes, I'm fine, thank you. Bar's open and Queen Victoria's making Bloody Marys for our half-day-Monday so be warned.'

'Ah-huh? Please, do me a favour, don't go anywhere or delete that message until I arrive. Talk soon.'

Did Ryan think she'd do something stupid, *again*?

'Victoria, how do I save Ryan's number into contacts?' Emma passed the phone to Victoria.

'Only if you tell me all about riding Ryan.' Victoria grinned behind her glass, with Benjamin sniggering beside her.

'You mean, Ryan's ride.' Emma had managed to avoid it most of the day—a personal record. 'It's a deal.' She got a lesson on using her new phone, while dissecting her date, drinking Bloody Marys, before a table of stolen cash.

It seemed so normal for a Monday at the *Parte'* shed, waiting for the police to arrive.

It's funny what you get used to.

FOURTEEN

Half an hour later Ryan and David drove up to the *Parte'* shed where music filtered from inside. Ryan grinned at the music, relieved Emma wasn't scared and hiding, locked up in her shed. He was looking forward to seeing her again.

'Sounds like a party's happening,' said David as they approached the side of the shed.

'Emma warned me it was a half-day Monday session — which I have no idea what that means.'

'Maybe they're like hospitality workers who have Mondays off. Nice cars. Must be money in party planning?' David pointed to the four red cars parked under the row of trees.

'The sports car belongs to Emma's mother. The Beamer is her sister's, and I'm assuming the Alfa and Merc belong to Benjamin and Victoria.'

'Getting to know the girl, are we?' David asked with a raised eyebrow and a cheeky smirk on his face.

'Told you I took Emma out yesterday.'

'As your senior, I'm gonna be straight with you.' David came to a standstill and slid his hands into the pockets of his crinkled suit. 'I know I've warned you a few times about getting involved with Emma while we're working on this case. Can you separate your emotions for this girl or do I need to pull you off the case?'

'No.' He didn't want this. 'I can do my job.' It's all he had. Ryan followed orders and let his superiors make the plans and the decisions, because whenever he did, it was disastrous.

'Do you reckon Emma's the type to keep any of this cash they found?'

Ryan frowned while David watched. David may appear casual, even dopey, but he was a brilliant detective and someone Ryan could learn from.

And it was his job that mattered. But did it?

Ryan studied the simple shed that blended with the industrial sheds in the district. He thought about all he'd learned about Emma. She was a surprise you wanted to explore, once you got through the front door, just like her shed.

But would she keep the money?

'No, Emma isn't that type. She's one of the few people who can find fun in her day, no matter how terrifying it can be. Last week was the first time she'd stepped inside a Police interview room. She's never had a speeding ticket, nothing.'

'Do you have any doubts?' David asked, narrowing his eyes at Ryan. 'I've seen women con cops before.'

Ryan had seen plenty of pretty eyes that told the sweetest lies. 'I divorced a con, and Emma's not like that.' Her facts were a story he wouldn't mind re-reading.

'True.' David's eyebrows rose. He tugged at his loose tie and swivelled on his heel for the door. 'Sorry, mate, I had to ask.'

Ryan grabbed David by the arm. 'Look, I told you I took Emma out yesterday to keep this transparent. I don't want this to interfere with my job in any way, and if you think it is, tell me.'

'Would you stop seeing Emma?'

Ryan frowned. 'We just took the bike for a spin. That's it.' But it'd been more than that. It'd been the luxury of holding her hand, sharing a meal and a conversation away from the job. It was like finding a home in her smile and the way she wore her heart, wide open for the world to see. She was brave and beautiful all in one breath.

Ryan was also aware of the need for patience, like waiting for that right song to play before he dared ask her to dance.

But how could he lose what he never had?

And he slid his hands into his pockets and said, 'If you want me to stop, I will.'

David squinted at the yard, brushing his nails on his three-day stubbly chin. 'Did Emma tell you she's doing my parents' fiftieth wedding anniversary?'

'She mentioned it, yes.'

'Made my life a helluva lot easier. My wife adores Emma, so do my parents.'

'They do?'

'Yeah, Emma's booked the original hall where my parents got married. Got my parents going through their wedding album to make posters as decorations. All their family photos they're collating with the grandkids to make a slideshow. Emma's even put on the invitations, no gifts, and created this go-fund-me link to accept donations towards a holiday for my folks. They've never been so excited about a party before.'

'That's good, right?'

'Did you know Emma volunteers her gear at the children's hospital at Christmas time?'

'No, I didn't. How come you do?'

'My wife is on the fundraising committee, she said they'd never be able to throw it without Emma's generosity.' David patted Ryan's shoulder. 'My old man told me what his father told him… When you fish in a murky river full of flashy bony carp, once in a while a shy little brim tries to sneak by. That's the one you want to keep. This is a big shed.' David strolled towards the shed with tie loose and hands in pockets of his crinkled suit, as if it was a Sunday stroll. 'Do you fish?'

'Used to go with my dad a lot, up north.'

'We should go sometime.'

'Sure.' But was Ryan ready to do some serious fishing of the female kind when he'd almost lost his job over a woman? He couldn't risk it again.

Ryan caught up with his senior partner and they entered the shed. The first thing he saw was a table of neat piles of cash, where Helen, Victoria, and Benjamin sat.

Emma worked behind her bar and smiled at him. Even if it wasn't physical, he'd felt her touch. It was like he'd been running an obstacle course, blindfolded, where even in the darkness she still sparkled.

Yet, he'd read plenty of stories where it was only pages between a cover, they were never real, but only a momentary escape.

Should he dare, when he'd never believed in the dream itself?

'Wow. Nice bar.' David's eyes lit up as the music was

turned down.

'I told you about the bar.' Ryan spotted another unmarked police car pull into the carpark. It was Detectives Mannis and Bercher, the men he shared desk space with, that made up David's team. 'Rest of the crew are here.'

'Good, we'll need photos and statements. You take a copy of the voice recording and cash. Leave Emma and her friends to me to interview.'

'Agreed.' Ryan didn't want to jeopardise his job and the investigation in all of this. No matter how much he daydreamed about nibbling on her bottom lip. She was a plot twist best left for later. Much later.

If only he could keep his eyes off her.

Ryan, with Detective Mannis, counted the cash and bagged it on the bench beside the answering machine. He may have had his back to the room but he saw all through the reflection of the white board. At the centre table, Emma and her friends were interviewed by David and Mannis's partner Bercher.

Every chance he got, Ryan kept his eye on Emma. Again, she was a distraction. He wanted her attention on him. But he couldn't go near her. Wanted to—but couldn't.

'Let's take it to the station or we'll never see sunset,' said Mannis.

'Sure, I'll jump in with you.' Ryan scooped up the bags of money with Mannis. He wanted to say something to Emma but didn't. Surely, she'd understand he was working and following orders.

'Oi, David, Bercher, we're going to lock this up back at camp,' cried out Mannis and waved as they headed out the door.

'We're ten minutes behind you,' said David.

With bags in hand Ryan nodded to Emma and gave her a sly wink. It was all he could do, especially with David watching. But the smile she gave him in return, he felt like some superhero coming home from a battle. It was like he saw home in her smile.

How is that possible?

'They'll be busy typing statements while we add this to the evidence vault,' said Mannis.

Ryan just nodded and followed, trying to get his head back on the job. He could use this time to get to know the rest of the team and not play puppy to David, which was expected. He was new and had a lot to learn. Thankfully none of his past had come into question, yet.

Two hours later, they were still counting cash at the counter by the evidence room at the Police station.

'There, $24,325. Just like Emma said.' Ryan put the last sealed bag on the counter and passed it to David to sign off as the senior.

'She never kept any of the cash.' David pointed to the clear plastic bags of bundled money. 'Is that glitter?'

Ryan grinned, couldn't help it as he wiped the few tiny dots of gold off the notes and handed the bag to David. The glitter on his fingertip sparkled under the bank of fluorescent lights like tiny stars.

Emma. His ribs expanded as he breathed in deep.

She did warn him glitter was a hazard of the job. Compared to the hazards of his job, glitter was so small, sparkly yet fragile, like the lady herself.

'Rare, for a member of the public to not keep any cash as finder's fees,' mumbled Mannis, ticking through the sheet and handed it to David for his signature.

'Not really.' David scratched his pen over the board and passed it to the officer behind the cage to lock it all away in evidence. 'We're just used to dealing with thieves.'

Ryan frowned at his senior. 'But you said—'

David held up his hand. 'I know what I said.'

'Do you know about my ex?' It wasn't a secret, he worked with cops who were nosy by nature. So why not clear the air now in the corridor where there were no cameras or others around, except Mannis? So why not hit that rumour mill now?

'I know you took a long time to get to this job when you aced your scores years ago. Why?' David asked.

'I almost got charged for assault after punching out the guy I caught my ex-wife in bed with,' Ryan replied coldly. He felt nothing for the ex or that incident, when it used to flare a deep-seated hatred in his chest, mixed with shame. Now nothing. *When did that change?*

'Woah.' Mannis froze alongside them mid-step. He rubbed the back of his head as he leaned against the wall in the corridor. 'I did that too. Kind of—I got lumped with a trumped-up restraining order and ended up in Comms for months until the lawyers cleared me. Where did you go?'

Ryan was relieved he wasn't alone. 'Out bush, as far away

from here as I could.'

'You were wasted out there with your skills and intellect, doing your tour,' said David. 'I get why you did it, I do. But if you'd hassled the Super more, he would've let you come back because you weren't charged, you were cautioned. Up until then your record of service was exemplary, still is.'

Ryan frowned at the shorter Detective. 'Is it? I stuffed up, I know it.' He'd reacted emotionally instead of rationally. It's why he just followed orders now and did as he was told. Simple.

'There's nothing on your record of service stating why you didn't take that detective job. Except that you turned it down.'

Ryan couldn't face it, not when he'd put a guy in hospital, and the place he thought was home, wasn't. All those dreams once of having a home, a family, and not rotating stations with the job were gone. 'How come you know about this, David?'

'I had to ask when your name came up in the list of applicants for this job. With your test scores, your degree, your service and skills, it was a straight career path to this job. Then bang, you're out island hopping with the AFP.'

'I'd love to do that, but my missus wouldn't let me,' said Mannis.

'I'd do it for the fishing,' said David. 'But I'm too unfit for that kind of work now.'

'It wasn't hard work.' Ryan shrugged. It was just constantly moving with hand luggage, at the beck and call of the department, never staying anywhere longer than six weeks. Until he got this job. The AFP wanted him permanent, but he was over it. He'd come back, hoping for a fresh start.

So why the hell was he risking it by going near Emma?

'What was it like? Not the postcard version, mate, the real deal?' Mannis asked. 'You were over there in that coup in Fiji? Didn't you get a medal for it?'

Ryan shrugged, slipping his hands into his pockets. He got a medal for doing his job and moved on to the next posting and never thought about it again. 'Let's not make this weird, hey fellas?'

'Lad's humble, I like that,' said Mannis to David. 'So, what was it like?'

'Um, it was danger money. Some places were hostile, some beautiful. The tropical islands were great, there was no one in sight, with plenty of good fishing. I really learned how to handle a basic four-wheeled drive in all sorts of terrain.' It was an adventure almost every day on that job, it didn't leave him time to think about anything *but* the job. Not like this. But it's what he wanted, the mental stimulation of this game.

'Now you're making me jealous on the fishing.' David said, then patted Ryan's shoulder. 'Listen, Ryan, we're cops, not robots. We're also human beings and not superheroes.'

'Am I missing something here?' Mannis asked.

'This guy's got more medals than our entire team, and we've only got 'em for years of service,' said David.

Ryan cringed, he wasn't a superhero. He was paid to shoot. And he did. He also wasn't paid to think and was glad to leave it all behind.

'Young Ryan's also dating Emma Toplin,' said David, waving his thumb back at Ryan.

Ryan dropped his head, so close to face palming himself.

Was this some sort of initiation where the new guy had to air-out his issues in a corridor. 'Shouldn't we do this with a beer in hand?'

'That Emma's bar is the best. Can we go visit?' Mannis asked.

'Not my place.' Ryan did not want to jeopardise his job again. Or was this another one of David's tests? 'Don't know if I'll go back.'

'Why?' Mannis asked. 'Because you're doing this case? Shoot, if we're not sleeping with other officers, it's how half of us find our partners in this job. Emma was cute and she was watching you.'

Like Ryan watched her.

'*Knock, knock,*' said Kelly at the end of the corridor and they all turned to face the receptionist. 'Ryan, this urgent parcel came through from the University's registrar.'

'Thanks, Kelly.' Ryan took the package and ripped open the envelope. 'I'm hoping we'll find out who the driver is of Emma's stolen van, the one with the name Jaed.'

'You can go, Kelly,' said David.

'She's sweet on you, you know that?' Mannis tilted his head, watching Kelly with her heels echoing down the hall. 'Great legs on her.'

'Didn't notice,' mumbled Ryan as he scanned over the pages.

David put his hand on the stack of papers Ryan was trying to read. 'How about you share that file and we all go through it together? We'll knock it over quicker so we can all go home, on time, and you can go visit that girl.'

'But we're working.' If Ryan couldn't see Emma, he'd do his best to make sure he got these guys who'd stolen her van. It was a priority now they'd been to Emma's shed.

'I know what I said. I'm also worried Emma isn't taking the threat seriously enough about those boys coming back with her van. Do you?'

'I didn't talk to her.' Ryan knew he was being watched like the new kid under supervision.

'I did, and she's a sweet kid,' said David. 'I suggest once we're done here, you go and talk to her too. She needs to realise the danger she's in.'

'I'll call her later.' Ryan handed out the paperwork as they made their way to their desks where sunlight streamed in from the outside windows. He had time; it was still daylight. But it played on his mind. Emma was at risk, out there alone in that shed at the end of the cul-de-sac. Especially now that those thieves, the murderers, had been there and said they'd return with her van. They were doing everything that went against statistics, making them the unpredictable kind of killer—and that's what made them terrifying.

FIFTEEN

Emma was headed for her front fence when a large white four-wheeled drive ute drove into her yard with Ryan behind the wheel.

'Is that your vehicle?' She grabbed the right gate and walked it to the centre while Ryan did the other side.

'Yes. How come you're only locking up now? It's dark and you're alone.'

Emma clicked the sturdy padlock in place. 'I've been busy. There were lots of distractions today, I needed to do some work after my guests left. Don't you work late too?' She turned her back on him and headed inside.

'I was hoping to finish earlier. We were putting the money in the evidence locker and kept losing count all the time.'

'Took us a few times too.' She giggled and started to pull the corrugated side door.

'Here, let me.' He pulled it shut with ease. But the way his biceps moved, she had to chew her bottom lip to stop herself from drooling. 'You're turning this place into a car yard. Or is this to make sure you've cured yourself of your car yard phobia?'

'I hadn't thought of that.' She eyed off the four red luxury cars parked in a row inside her shed. 'Bar's still open. Thirsty?'

'Sure, beer's good. So, the convertible is your mother's, the BMW is your sister's, the other two cars belong to?' Ryan leaned down to check out the cars like he'd done in the car yard.

'The Alfa Romeo is Benjamin's and the Mercedes belongs to Victoria.'

'I would've pictured Victoria driving a Rolls Royce,' he said, approaching the bar.

'She's working on it.' Emma cracked the top of the beer and put it on the counter.

'They're all red.'

'And they're all luxury models, parked in my shed, and none of them are mine.' She sighed at the four cars reflecting the neon signs from her bar.

The grey cat jumped down from its perch and slinked around her ankles. 'Hi, Mister, nice of you to show up.' She stoked her cat's soft fur feeling the loud vibration of his purring.

'No monkey suit for the cat?'

'Not today. Mister didn't come near me for a few days after that. He's not keen on crowds.' She opened a tin of tuna for her favourite after-hours companion. 'Have you had any dinner?'

'No. You?'

'I've got a great lasagne if you want some?'

'Did you make it?'

'No, one of the caterers made it for me.'

'Another perk of the job, like your tips that fill your bar?'

'Guess so.' Emma set the dish in the microwave in the far corner of her bar. Did she dare invite him to dine upstairs?

'David and the other detectives are in love with your bar,

they're trying to find some excuse to come back.'

What was Ryan's excuse for coming back, when he'd practically ignored her this afternoon? 'My bar's been getting a workout these past few weeks.' Ever since her birthday.

'Is that normal?' Ryan asked, taking a seat on the other side of the bar.

'No. I'm not an alcoholic or I wouldn't have this much stock. This is tips from clients.'

'You have a lot of satisfied customers.'

Was Ryan like the other men in her past who liked her bar more than her? 'Do you think those boys who stole my van will come back?' Was that why he was here?

'Not sure.'

'They won't, because you guys will catch them before they do.'

'Thanks for the vote of confidence. Aren't you worried at all?'

'I was in the beginning, but they gave me that money and said sorry for stealing my van.'

Ryan frowned, but by the time he'd walked around the bar and gently held her upper arms, it was gone. 'Emma, please listen to me. They're armed robbers who have killed people, and if you're not worried, I am. That's why I'm here.'

'I thought it was because you liked my bar?'

'I'm being serious, Emma. The other reason we finished so late is we've got a positive ID on those two men. It's being released to the media tonight.'

'Who are they?'

'Their names are Jaed Zaraf and Stuart Beckett.'

'Jae and Stu? What else did you learn?'

'Jaed's family are from Al Bukamel in Syria, right next to the Iraqi border. His father manages a small medical practice with his eldest son, who are well respected within their Muslim community. When we informed his mother, I couldn't understand a word she said, but she was inconsolable. It was like she'd gone into mourning.'

Her hand to her heart. 'Oh, the poor woman.'

'The mother may have been visibly upset, the father not so much. He's a proud man. The department's trying to work out how much to release to the public so they don't turn this into a racial-hate-crime-by-media.'

'I kept thinking the media descriptions were wrong.'

'They are. But who knows what the witnesses are telling the journos?'

'What did you learn about Stu?'

'Stuart Beckett is from the poorer side of town. He lives with his mother who has six kids, looking after another two kids that they're related to.'

'How did she take it when you spoke to her?'

'Stuart's mother is in shock, already grieving.'

'Why?'

'Those two boys shot and killed Ms Beckett's boyfriend on Saturday afternoon.'

'Why are they both doing this?'

Ryan shrugged. 'All we've learned so far, is that Jaed and Stuart met at University. Stuart is on an indigenous scholarship programme. Jaed was being paid to be his tutor and they shared the same dormitory.'

'They sounded so normal and excited to go camping. What made them go on this...' Her van had many headlines where some called it a *criminal carnival on wheels* through to *the portable party of pain.*

'We're still trying to work that out. A few weeks ago, they both stopped showing up for class. Their parents weren't aware.'

'So, they're smart guys, doing dumb things. But why?'

'Drugs and alcohol, we're guessing. We've found evidence of both in their dorm rooms. Jaed's family are Muslims, they don't drink.'

'Is Jae rebelling against them?'

'Not sure. Jaed's family aren't talking and we're hoping that their community's cultural liaison officers can find out more. The van was spotted leaving the murder scene of a known drug dealer, yet, when we searched the place, we found minimal contraband. So, we're assuming they stole from their dealer, which may be some of that cash you've received.'

'They paid me in drug money?' She slapped a palm over her mouth. 'How is that possible?'

Ryan led her by the hand around the bar to sit beside him. 'I'm aware this is a lot for you.'

'It's so foreign. Surreal even.' She rubbed her face as if to try and change the radio station, then stared at the floor. 'I'm not oblivious to the world.'

'I know that. You're also used to witnessing only the fun side of life.'

'Is this whole pattern of their behaviour normal for Jae and Stu?'

'No. It's the opposite. According to lecturers and other

students, they're good kids. They studied hard and got good grades. Jaed's got no priors. Stuart has a juvenile count for a minor traffic matter, but nothing like this. But I need you to understand how dangerous those men are, out there, in your van,' he said firmly.

'Now you're scaring me.' She hugged herself.

'Criminals who were once good people scare me too.'

'No way.' Her body trembled in a shockwave at the sincerity of his statement.

'I won't lie to you, and you need to be fully aware of the seriousness of the situation. You can't put glitter on a murder and call it a fairy tale, Emma. You need to be careful. They've been here at your premises and—'

'Will they return for the money if they run out? Will they bring the van back? Oh no, am I in danger?' Her clammy hands trembled and her shoulders tightened, it was hard to breathe.

'Hey, it'll be okay.' He wrapped his arms around her and she burrowed into his warm chest, inhaling his warm, exotic aroma. She'd never known such comfort like this before.

'We're doing everything we can to catch them. We're widening the search area to include National Parks and camping grounds. I'll also be doing my best to keep an eye on you to keep you safe.'

She arched an eyebrow at him. 'Is that Ryan the Detective speaking, or Ryan the civilian?'

'Both. I'm not on duty and it's not because of your bar either.' He then, ever so lightly, feathered his lips across hers.

Emma was surprised he was there. Surprised by his kiss.

She sat back and blinked at him.

'Sorry, I—' Ryan cleared his throat.

Whether it was the stress of the day, she forgot all rational thought, and focused on Ryan. 'Don't be.' Not when she wanted to wrap herself around him and forget her heart was ever alone. She doubted she'd survive the night without kissing him deeper and taking this ride as far as he'd allow it. Just this once.

Clutching his shirt, she reached up and kissed him. His delicious lips against hers, she traced his tongue that tasted of temptation. It filled her lungs, channelling into her blood, filtering to her heart where the heat spread. Fast. It was needy, hungry, and raw.

She wanted to trust, to fill this craving, and to overfill on this high. It was unintentional and irrational—but she didn't want to stop. Licking deeper into his mouth, she then bit his lip as her hungry fingers unbuttoned his shirt, scraping nails over his hot muscular chest. His skin tasted like music on her tongue, lapping down his neck, and lower she went. She wanted to be desired beyond all her worries and fears, filled with this need to feel his weight upon her.

He gripped her hand that wanted to have a conversation with the rest of his skin at the waist of his jeans. 'Emma?'

Emma licked her lips, swollen from his kiss, and prepared herself to do the most daring thing in her life. She was done being walked over, done being treated like staff. She knew what she wanted…

Him.

'You can stay, or you can go. But I'm done talking,' she said. Life would go on but it would never be the same after this. He would either bring on the symphony that would make the stars sing, or become another verse to her soul's sad songs of fantasies as another haunting tune that would leave her forever wondering.

* * *

He was in knots.

Why did he come back?

Because he couldn't stop thinking about her.

He shouldn't have come back. It was asking for trouble.

Ryan smoothed down her fine, soft hair the colour of butter, tucking it behind her ear to frame her beautiful face. The look of her large grey eyes reflected her inner fire. He wasn't a king, but the way she gazed at him, he felt like a god.

But this was sweet Emma. The one who panicked when he asked her out. The frightened Emma who'd sat scared in an interview room. The innocent Emma, who rode the back of his bike with the widest smile reflecting in his side mirrors. She saw the good in the world when he lived in a world where angels were destroyed by monsters.

Should he kiss her and be damned? Or should he walk away and be damned forever?

But when she licked her plump bottom lip with the tip of her pink tongue, it unbuttoned him, turning him on like a light switch.

His control disintegrated when his lips found hers. Tearing off his shirt, and dropping it to the ground as their kiss deepened. She wrapped her arms around his shoulders, her legs around his hips, and he carried her to the end of the bar.

His trembling fingers undid the buttons of her dress. Her breath on his hair, lips on her skin, his hands on her hips and the fuse was lit. Down her slender throat, nipping his teeth on her collarbone, he tasted her curves, and the swell of her breasts and lower, to lap up her luxury. His tongue lapped and lunged, his fingers stroked her as she writhed on the bar, until she screamed with no voice, but it was a god damned symphony.

She helped undo his jeans like it'd undone his soul. Chest to chest. Lips to lips. The ache to be inside her had him dancing on the dangerous edge of the wild.

Her nails scraped across his back, as her moan travelled from her chest to his like a stereo of desire. This was beyond the unlevelled madness of lust, where he was used to demons in dresses who were just another one-chapter wonder he chose to forget.

But she was different. She was a story to be read, to be savoured with each new layer discovered beneath her soft covers. To taste another reality beyond the emptiness, he slid into a place that felt like a future of tangled bedsheets and sunshine.

Her trusting eyes locked with his, trapping their hearts in a place where he could lose his soul. Holding her hips he buried himself deep. Her back arched. Her mouth opened. And he pushed past her vulnerability. Time didn't matter, just distance, and he held her closer to his chest. Ryan swallowed her moans while burying deeper with each thrust, filling her.

He wanted to go slow and savour, but she was like lightning, cracking wide all his conventions. Wrapping her hair around his wrist, her neck in his palm, it was the leverage he needed, and poured everything he had inside her.

He might be undone—but he most certainly wasn't done with her.

* * *

Emma woke up the next morning in bed, wrapped in Ryan's arms. His warm breath brushed against her shoulder and tickled down her arm. His chest against her back, breathing in sync with each other.

It took a moment to register this was real and she had a man. Asleep. In. Her. Bed!

Why was he still here?

She winced, pulling up the covers to her chin. Last night, she'd gone crazy, like her body had a mind of its own. Was it because of her self-imposed sexual repression that she was so demanding of the guy?

She'd lost count of the positions she'd shared with the man who was the god of lust.

But things changed in the light of day.

Emma started to creep out of bed when Ryan's arm tightened around her.

'Where are you going?' His voice, a deep sexy bass that carried through her body, stirring a heat inside her. Wrapped in his arms, he kissed her tingling skin, her lips, her nose, her lashes, then rested his forehead against hers. 'Are you okay?' he asked, gently stroking the side of her face. 'Emma?'

She swallowed to find her voice. 'I, um...' Her body had never reacted like this, so alive within this one pure moment the way his chartreuse eyes reached into her soul. 'To get up and readily get work for.' Was she even speaking English?

His chesty laugh vibrated against hers, it made her smile. 'Not yet you don't.' Stopping all her thoughts and all her embarrassment, he pressed his lips to hers. Mornings had never been so good.

Showered, dressed, and waiting for her kettle, Emma sat at her dining table. Ryan soon joined her, carrying his boots. He sat beside her to face the sky view and slid on his socks. 'You have glitter in your shower.'

'I know, it sneaks into the weirdest places. I swear there's these glitter gnomes that spread it around after midnight.'

He chuckled, slipping on his boots. 'Hasn't the kettle boiled yet?'

'It's been thirty minutes, so it shouldn't be long now.'

He grinned, shaking his head. 'How old is it?'

'Um, eight years.'

'No wonder it takes so long to boil. How come you haven't got a new one?'

'You'll think I'm silly.'

'No, I'm guessing it's a game for you.'

'How do you know that?'

'Is it?'

She shrugged.

'I'm surprised you don't have an Espresso machine.'

'Do you have one?'

'I'm in a room that fits a bed, bar fridge, and a ten-dollar kettle I picked up from the supermarket that's faster than that thing.' Ryan pointed to her decrepit monstrosity.

'I've never bought a kettle. It's on my list.'

'Where did you get that one then?'

'My father bought it for my sister as a wedding present. Helen didn't want it because it didn't go with her kitchen décor.' Emma had forgotten the kettle was a relic from her father. Especially when she'd been cherishing it as a gift he'd never bought for her. It was like intercepting hugs at the airport that weren't meant for her. Why?

'Where does your father live?'

'In New South Wales. Where's yours?' Emma didn't like talking about her father, when Ryan was a new playlist she wanted to hear.

'Townsville, still in the Army, and still with my mother.'

It cried, whined and bellowed to the world, and she grinned with her shoulders raised at the decrepit kettle's cry.

Ryan frowned over his shoulder to her kitchen where steam poured like a geyser in a volcano that rumbled on the bench. 'Sounds like a dying bird in some child's cartoon.'

'It does.' Emma flicked off the kettle and it sighed with relief. Was it ready to be retired?

'I'm assuming your parents are divorced?'

'Yes.' She poured the water into the coffee press, grabbed two mugs and put them on a carry tray. 'Do you have milk and sugar?'

'No thanks, black's good if you have none.'

'I may have a decrepit geriatric kettle, but I have milk I share with my cat.' She carried the tray and took her seat. She pushed the plunger and inhaled the deep rich roasted coffee aroma. It may take time to boil but it was so worth it when she had that cup in hand and a view of the skyline.

'I'm not used to having any around at the station and I don't keep any in the bar fridge in my room. The bonus is the pool and gym are right there.' Ryan sipped his coffee. 'This is good.'

'Are you one of those super fit gym junkies?'

'No. Why?'

'Well, you're...' He had the perfect six pack. She swallowed the heat rising in her chest. 'You're ripped.' Ryan should be the captain of international torso day, leading the gym-parade while she threw glitter from the sidelines.

'I run the obstacle course and do the gym after work to keep in shape, you?'

'God no, athletics, or any form of physical exercise and myself don't go together, it's a grapple with gravity. I'm good with my hands, if I don't have to walk at the same time.'

'I remember you being exceptionally athletic last night,' he mumbled over his mug.

'Oh-no.' She hid her face in her palms. The heat radiated through her fingers like a street light flashing through a swaying motel curtain. 'Sorry, it's been a while.'

'Don't apologise to me, I was having just as much fun. How long has it been?'

'Do I have to answer that?'

'That long, huh?' He grinned behind his cup.

'Over three years ago. I broke up with my ex-boyfriend, before I built this apartment.' She'd lived here, camping in the front office while they renovated.

'So that'd make me the only guy who's ever stayed over?'

Ryan peered around the room with shiny eyes and a growing grin.

'Yes, besides family and friends,' she mumbled behind her cup.

'I like that.'

'I'm no virgin.'

'You wouldn't be after last night or this morning.'

She gave him a shy smile and shrug.

'My last relationship was my ex-wife,' said Ryan, 'and I told you that story.'

And he was a man who liked his stories. Did she dare share hers?

Why not confess over coffee and protect herself now, instead of later. It'd either bore the guy or scare him away for good.

Emma put her coffee down on the table and started. 'I was with this guy, Frank. I don't remember how we met, or even the length of time we were together.' But she sure remembered how he treated her. 'Frank got caught performing the horizontal tango with the neighbour's wife.'

'Ouch, who caught them?'

'The neighbour's adult son and her husband. They gave Frank a touch-up and then they came and told me what happened. The thing was, it wasn't a one-off event—' She hesitated, toying with the handle of her coffee cup.

'They were having an affair?'

She then inhaled deeply and spilled her secret. 'A long affair that started way back when she was his high school teacher.'

'You're kidding?' Ryan sat back with a grimace.

'Shocking, huh? Frank treated her like a queen and I got treated like dirt. Victoria said Frank only liked me because of my bar, and Benjamin says Frank had mummy issues. And Helen and my mother said it was all my fault Frank left me.'

'They don't know, do they?'

'No. Only Victoria and Benjamin, and I can't believe I told you.' That time her self-esteem had been kicked to the lowest point of her life and it stayed there. 'Can I ask you something?'

'Sure.'

'Why me? You're a nice guy who's good looking, with this perfect body. You're like the complete package. Why are you even bothering with someone like me? Is it because of my stolen van saga?' She had to clear the air now, because she wasn't going to relive her past. Not anymore.

She knew her packaging was broken, when the man deserved nothing but perfection.

* * *

Her question made him realise her self-esteem had taken a severe beating. He reached across the table and again found the luxury of holding her hand. 'I'm not perfect, Emma. Far from it, and if that's what you think of me, please stop. But I do want to keep seeing you, if you want to?'

'Am I to expect you ignoring me for your work? Frank and my sister treated me like that. I don't want to be the dirty little secret you only visit after dark.'

'Hey?' He pulled his chair closer, his fingertips under her

chin to make her look at him. 'I did and I didn't ignore you yesterday. I couldn't.' He licked his lips and stared at the ceiling searching for the right words.

'It's your job. I get that.'

'I don't think you do. You see, I almost lost my job over my ex. I shouldn't have gone near you with the case still going and kept a professional distance. I spoke to David about it, who is my senior, and he said I should've been pulled off this case. But I don't want to.'

'Why?'

'It's personal. I might not have spoken to you much yesterday, Emma, but I never took my eyes off you. That's why I came back last night. I couldn't stop thinking about you when I left here.'

'In case those guys return?'

'That, and to be with you. Look, I had to be distant yesterday. I'm sorry if you thought I was ignoring you, but it had to be done. It's why David interviewed you and your friends with the other detectives, Mannis and Bircher, assisting him. It was so nothing tarnishes our investigations in any way. I'm also new to this promotion and this team. I don't want to muck it up when I've just made detective, and I finally have a work partner, who's a mentor I truly respect.'

'I get it.'

'Thank you for your understanding.' He could read it in her eyes that reflected the morning skyline.

'Are you being moved off this case thingy?'

'No. But there were some tough questions asked of me. Some of the guys I work with shared their advice and told me they'd met their spouses through the job. And I remember you that first day. You looked cute. Even if you were sitting in the gutter, drinking wine straight out of the bottle, with prawn muck all over you. It's something I'll never forget.'

'Hey, I felt terrible. I stank—'

'You looked gorgeous then and even better now.' He leaned over and kissed her, then glanced at his watch. 'I have to go, I don't want to be late for work. Talking about work, there's a phone guy coming out to set up a phone trace. I want to find out who's been making those prank calls.'

'The singing *Parte'* girls? Not my band? I was going to offer them a recording contract to sell it to the masses using that jingle for a future advertising campaign.'

'Really?'

'No.' Her laugh made him laugh, and she truly was like sunshine.

'Look, he's a trainee techie testing some new equipment. He needs the practise and I volunteered your situation. I know I should've asked first, but I'd like to put the wind up your *Parte'* band of groupies because they sound terrible. Call it one of the perks of the job when sleeping with a cop.' He kissed her cheek, nuzzling into her ear.

She squirmed but still kept smiling. 'Okay, you've convinced me.'

'For what? Agreeing to see me or the tech-guy? I really like talking to you, Emma. You're not technically part of my day job, and you see the good in the world.' He held his breath hoping for the right answers. Even if he was kind of breaking the rules to do it, he'd do it to keep her safe.

'Tech guy, okay. Us, can we...' But then she licked that plump lip of hers and again he was undone. He had to kiss her, imprinting her flavour to his memory.

'Okay, you can definitely come back,' she murmured gazing up at him with glassy low-lidded eyes.

'Good. So, can you let me out?'

'That I can do.'

He hoped by tapping her phone they'd lock in on where Jae and Stu were, if they rang again. Ryan was worried about the threat of those two men returning. Mostly he was worried for Emma's safety, and she meant more to him than his job.

SIXTEEN

Stu poked around the campfire coals while Jae sat back at their table sketching. The freshness of the cool morning air mingled with their fire's smoke, where dew dangled like diamonds off the tip of olive-leafed gum trees. Birds whistled, as the soft breeze carried light floral-earthy fragrances that shifted with the grasses and wildflowers. Jae had never known such peace.

The camp was small and had become a home this past week. They had a tent with a tarp stretched across the van for shade in an area filled with assorted camping equipment. They missed nothing. It had become a new way of living for Jae, one that gave him an insight into what his heart desired.

Stu sat on the chair opposite. 'Hey Jae, we should follow the creek upstream, there might be a waterfall up there?'

'Do you think so?' Jae closed his sketchbook, then slid his lead pencils into their tin.

'If not, there's bound to be somethin' to go swimmin' in.'

'Sounds like a plan.' Jae put the sketchpad into his daypack beside the rulers and his hardcover resource book that was like his personal branded-bible. No outside beliefs reached him here, except life, and today was another adventure. 'What do we need to go on a proper bushwalk?'

'A backpack each for drinks and food, and our boots. Not thongs this time.'

Last time they'd cut their feet going bushwalking. 'Do we take the first aid kit and rope? There's nothing wrong with being prepared, you know. Were you ever a boy scout?'

'Nah, you?'

Jae just cocked an eyebrow at his friend.

'Yeah, silly question, but you're gettin' there, mate.' Stu gave Jae a pat on the shoulder.

Jae was learning daily of life on the outside. 'I'm packing more water this time, instead of beer.' The idea of getting drunk all day had worn off soon after they'd arrived. They still drank at night around the campfire, staring at the stars, but it was different. The pressure from the city, surrounded by its sprawling suburbs was swapped for a calm natural wonderland that soothed him.

Uphill, an hour from their campsite, they followed the small wallaby track. Ducking under low-lying branches, wiping away cobwebs and flies, they focused on negotiating the rocky terrain. The fresh scents of eucalypts, bark, and the rich soils, mixed with crisp clear air. Tall feathery grass-heads waved amongst the wildflowers that added colour to the morning beauty of Jae's climb. It was a world he'd dreamed about and found. This is what he'd wanted to do for so long, now he was living it.

'Are you going to provide me with a lesson on bush-tucker?' Jae pointed to some strange berries hanging from the trees.

'I had this uncle who taught us. Been a long time,' said Stu as they plodded further upstream. They came to the edge of a massive sheer drop on one side of the hill. 'Check that out for a view.'

'Simply superb,' said Jae. They stood side by side in silence enjoying the natural splendour before them, filled with nothing but tree-covered hills. 'I have got to move to the country.'

'Yeah, beats being stuck in the city with all that noise pollution, streets, houses—'

'Rude people, road rage, and prejudiced banana-butts,' said Jae, pushing his glasses higher along his nose.

'Yeah, back to nature, huh? Like it's a clean slate.'

Jae sat on the rock and admired the view. 'You could get lost in all that country. It'd be the perfect place to hide secrets no one would find.'

'My culture has stories for certain trees, rocks, and even the river systems on their homelands.'

'Do you know any of them?'

'I'm forgetting them. But I don't want to. Should we go up further?'

'What, up that hill?'

'No, north. See my country, my people. They'll take care of us. I know my uncle will.'

'Isn't it hot up north?'

'Sure. But you'd get used to it.'

'My parents are from a hot climate. Desert, and rocks with a river.'

'Did you ever want to go there?'

'No. All I've heard of their country are horror stories of war where my parents' heritage has been destroyed. That's not my homeland. But, this…' Jae waved his arm across the view that stretched beyond the horizon. 'This is paradise. Although, I'm not climbing any higher up that hill.' He grinned over his shoulder where the creek's upstream curve disappeared into the bushland.

'But that's where the waterfall is.'

'I don't know, bush-tucker man, it seems the higher we climb the skinnier that creek is getting. I have a sneaky suspicion there's no waterfall up there, just a natural spring.'

'You think so?'

'I'm no expert but…'

'You might be right.' Stu squinted up at the sheer climb ahead. 'We can try again tomorrow, huh?'

'Great idea.'

'We'll come here for lunch now we know the climb. I think we've got some of 'em fancy hiking poles in the van from that camping store too. Will we have enough power now to not go and buy ice for our food?'

'I'm quite positive the solar panels are doing their thing for our fridges and lights. We're almost self-sufficient,' said Jae, proud of what he'd achieved.

'You'd know about solar-stuff to go with your sketches?' Stu led the way down the hill, following the winding skinny track that ran along the cliff side.

'I'm learning about it. But we may need more meat, unless you want to go hunting?'

'I hate eating roo. My mum used to burn the bugger out of it on the barbecue.' Stu's laughter echoed as the rubble and dried leaves crunched under their boots.

'Do you realise we're the only country in the world that kills its national animal emblem.' Jae carefully picked his way through the rocky terrain in his new hiking boots that fit better than any shoe he'd worn before. Even the pants did, with their deep cargo pockets.

'What, the kangaroo?'

'Yes, it's on the coat of arms along with the emu.'

'Have you ever tried emu?' Stu asked.

'No. But I'd try it. Have you?'

'No. What's the weirdest thing you've ever eaten?'

Jae paused to push up his glasses as perspiration trickled down his temple while his legs ached from the downhill hike. 'I'm still trying new foods so it's all weird to me—especially the hotdog. What about you?'

'My sister's cooking.' Stu laughed, stopping to face Jae on the thin track. 'This one-time Jess was learning how to cook while Mum was at work, I had no idea what she put in that pot, I don't think Jess did either. You should've seen it, this crock-pot filled with this brown mud that smelt like a septic tank.'

'Did you eat it?'

'We had to taste it or she'd smack us if we didn't. So there we were, all seated at the table staring at this steaming pile of muck, until my younger sister threw up all over the table right into the pot itself. Little Bindy saved us all.' Their laughter rang in the air, wiping their happy tears that mingled with their sweat, hiking toward the rocky creek bed.

Then Stu lost his footing and slipped. 'Shiiiiit!' He cried out as the path crumbled beneath his boots and he slid downhill towards the creek as rocks and dirt followed, stirring up a dust storm.

'*Stu?*' Jae rushed to the steep side. He gripped onto the branches of a spindly sapling and leaned over the edge.

Stu rolled helplessly among the other tumbling rocks, unable to get a grip on anything, until he was flung against a thick tree trunk and held on, staring face down into the deep gully. 'JAE?'

'*Hold on, Stu. I'm coming.*' Jae dumped his pack, tied his rope to a tree and began the downhill climb, sending smaller stones tumbling ahead of him.

The tree creaked beneath Stu like straining leather and it shuddered, groaning in protest as he slowly slid down the trunk. 'JAE.'

'I'm coming.' Jae's palms stung from rope burn as he wound down the hill toward the man who was his brother.

There was the sound of a thousand whip-cracks as the tree's trunk snapped in half like a matchstick. The ground ripped open, exposing roots, and the entire tree gave away, Stu hurtled through the air, his screams disappearing into the thick vegetation that was soon drowned out by the rumble of falling rubble.

'STU!' Jae scampered down the path of destruction. He wound down the hill, with more rocks falling under each step. He couldn't spot Stu anywhere.

Face slick with sweat and dirt, his palms full of splinters, Jae slid his way down the side of the hill. At the bottom, beside the creek bed they'd been following, Jae found him.

'Stu?' Jae paused for a second.

Stu lay on his back, with eyes staring up at the sky. Rich red blood spread around his head like a halo across the rock.

'No, Stu. *No.*' Jae scrambled over the rocks, grazing knees and shins, desperate to get to his best friend. 'Get up, Stu.' He clambered over the cold, unforgiving boulder that Stu lay across like a sacrifice on his stone altar where Jae's shadow covered the shine in his friend's eyes.

'Stu?'

Nothing. No smile. No laughter. No breathing. As the cheeky glimmer in his friend's eyes died, so too did the rustle of the breeze as the small gully that surrounded them became silent.

Jae wept, clutching his friend to his chest as his howls of grief echoed.

What was once his paradise had now become his hell.

SEVENTEEN

In the *Parte'* shed, Emma unpacked her mother's car, putting the boxes to one side. She glanced at her answering machine resting on the bench and smiled, there were no messages.

Her stolen van had disappeared, and there were no robberies or reported sightings for almost a fortnight. Even with Stu and Jae's parents pleading for the boys to surrender, they never came forward.

The media had moved on to other matters and the van was no longer headline news. Even though Ryan and David had been in helicopters searching for the van, they found nothing. Still on the case that had come to a silent halt, they had other cases to deal with.

Emma flicked on her stereo, cracked herself a beer from her bar, and fed her silent companion, Mister. Tonight was the second time in two weeks she'd been home alone. She didn't want to admit she missed Ryan's company, but she also liked her own space.

She approached her workbench to pack away the boxes onto the shelf, and to tinker her night away. It's what she was used to, being home alone, yet she had no idea what to do about Ryan. Was he with her because of who she was, or because of this deep need to do his job?

Her friends approved of Ryan, which was rare. She'd even copped a lecture from Victoria to not judge Ryan by her past.

But it was hard not to.

Whenever she saw the guy it was hard to breathe. But when he smiled at her, she wanted to perform an air-guitar solo while throwing glitter and high kicks in her own private cabaret. It scared her. The guy was almost perfect—and she was just Emma.

'Hello, Emma?' Called out a short, skinny young man, standing in the middle of the wide-open double doorway of her shed.

'Hey, you gave me a fright.' Emma slapped a palm to her chest. 'Can I help you?' She glanced at the clock on the wall. It was just after seven. Stars shone between a few clouds above the neighbour's roof all closed up for the night. Did she forget to lock her gate?

He removed his cap that he slid into his backpack and brushed fingers through his black hair. He then pushed his round-rimmed spectacles higher up his nose and took a few hesitant steps toward her. 'I'm Jae, remember me? The guy who—' He winced, hugging the bag against his chest. 'I'm the one who took your van.'

Emma gasped and stepped backwards 'Wh— wh—what are you doing here?'

'I didn't mean to frighten you. I'm not here to hurt you, Emma. I swear it.' He dropped his pack and raised his palms as if in surrender.

'Why are you here?' Her back pressed against her work table, she couldn't go any further. 'How did you get in here? Did

I forget to lock the gate?'

'The gate's quite locked, I assure you. I came to tell you I've bought your van back. When I saw the lights on, I climbed onto the van's roof and jumped the fence.'

'Why?'

'To tell you I'd brought your van back. Hey, nice bar.' His eyebrows lifted. 'Amazing. Would it be improper of me to get a beer? Please? I'll gladly pay.'

'Sure.' The words just came out. Emma never said no to anyone asking for a drink at her bar—except her sister, Helen.

'Do you want one while I'm here?' Jae stood at the beer fridge peering through the glass door. 'You have quite the selection. Are you one of those beer sommeliers? There's another word for it…'

'Cicerone.' She bit on her tongue to stop speaking. How did he know about beer tasters, along with his old-fashioned speech not normally heard from someone so young?

'That's it. Are you?'

'No.' Although her friends thought she should be, with the many varieties she had to offer. And she did compare Ryan's hair-colouring to toasted malts of the Indian Pale Ale through to the hearty Imperial Stout when she first met him.

'Are you sure you wouldn't mind if I had a beer?'

Emma shook her head. The beer fridge opened and Jae leaned inside, distracted. Did she dare risk grappling with gravity and run for the first time in almost two decades? Or would she kiss concrete?

But there was no way she could climb her own fence. And if she did manage to climb, she had three strings of barbed wire on top she'd never get past.

She stared at her gate keys that hung on their hook near the wide-open side of her shed.

If she managed to run, make the fence, unlock the gate, where the hell would she go? All the other sheds on this street were locked up like hers. The street was deserted. Mr Brunswick, her neighbour on the corner, was partially deaf at the best of times, and was no doubt sleeping off his beer consumption and day in the sun.

She was home alone, trapped inside her sanctuary—*oh shit.*

Emma slapped her hand over her racing heart. 'I can't breathe.' She gasped for air, unable to swallow. Her lips trembled as bad as her knees, scared she was going to pee all over the floor.

The fridge door closed, and she yelped like a puppy, flinching, as sweat broke across her skin.

'Hey Emma, calm down. I won't hurt you. Promise.' Jae placed an imported beer and another bottle Emma had been drinking, on the workbench. 'Where do you want me to put my money for the beverages?'

'N-n-no charge.' Was another automatic reply.

'Why not?' He twisted open the bottle's top and took a mouthful, watching her through his glasses as he drank.

'They're gifts. No one pays for a drink at my bar. I might get them to clean up or take out the rubbish.' She took a deep breath. Why couldn't she just shut-up?

'So how come you've got all this then?' Jae sipped his beer and the light glinted on the metal handgun tucked into the belt of his jeans.

'You're not going to shoot me, are you?' Emma whimpered, then she blinked again. *Was that glitter on his gun?*

'No. Emma, please take a seat before you faint.' Jae showed her to a stool as if he was the maître-d' of a restaurant and not her gun-carrying van-thief.

She hit her stool hard before she fell.

'Here, drink this. It might calm you down some.' Jae put the cold bottle in her hand. 'Cheers,' he said with a grin, and sat on the stool near the corner within arm's reach.

Emma's mind rattled at a thousand miles an hour. What should she do? A—run; B—die of sheer terror; or C—drink?

She blinked at the bottle in her hand. Raised it to her lips and drank, mouthful after mouthful, after mouthful. It hurt to swallow past the bubbles in her chest. But it was cold, wet and alcoholic, and she drank until it was dry.

'Augh.' She slammed the empty bottle onto the table like a blue-singlet-wearing brickie at a tradesman's bar. Patted her chest that was battling to contain its whirlpool of bubbles, while her stomach rolled, unsure if she was going to throw up or burp?

'I've never seen a woman do that before. I'm impressed.' Jae grinned at her.

'I'm scared and I could do with another one.' She could drink to forget. Again, as if on autopilot, she went to her bar. The empty beer bottle clinked inside her recycling bin and she snatched another one from the fridge's icy interior. If she drank without thinking, it should stop her death-by-terror. She hoped?

With a deep breath, she faced her unexpected visitor. 'Jae, is it?'

'Yes. Cool cat.' Jae pointed to the feline in his cat-gym.

'That's Mister.' Who was calmly spying on them from his all-seeing perch. 'Where's your mate, Stu? Should we get him a beer too?'

Jae's shoulders hunched over. Cradling the beer in his lap, his fingernails picked at the corner of the label. His eyes went glassy as he licked his lips and said with a shaky voice, 'Stu died.'

'Oh no, I'm so sorry, Jae.' She reached for the box of tissues and put them in front of Jae as he grabbed one.

'We were camping and, well...' Jae pinched the bridge of his nose. His glasses pushed up into his hair. He took deep, shaky, wet breaths, as tears squeezed past shut eyelids. 'Stu fell. He, um, smashed the back of his head on the rocks, and died.'

'I'm so sorry,' Emma said in soothing tones. Her throat ached to say the right words as her hand hovered to pat the guy. But she didn't. She just sat there cradling her beer in two hands while he wept. She was trained to remain silent and listen, only this time she was too terrified to say anything.

Jae snatched a handful of tissues and wiped away his tears and blew his nose. Again, he snatched more tissues only this time he cleaned his glasses. 'Anyway...' He inhaled and his skinny chest rose as his shrunken shoulders straightened. Glasses cleaned, he put them back on and held his beer tight in hand. 'I buried him under a pile of rocks. He was too heavy for me to carry.' Jae frowned as the tears again threatened to fall like the condensation trickling down the sides of his beer bottle. 'I returned to our campsite and drank myself stupid for a bit, then decided to bring your van back.'

'Why?'

'It's what Stu would've wanted. On the night we met you, Stu and I agreed that when we'd finished with the van, we'd bring it back, and we've finished with it.' He took a large mouthful of his beer as if to wash down his emotions. He then thumped his beer back onto the table.

Emma trembled, biting her lip as the table shuddered.

'Unfortunately, the ignition lock's broken, and so is the lock on the driver's door,' Jae said. 'Other than that, once it's had a good clean and a service, your van will be as good as ever. We never scratched it, nothing.'

The silver mobile, resting on the table, beeped its alert of an incoming text message. They both stopped to stare at it.

Was she quick enough to snatch it up and scream for help?

'Is that your phone?' Jae reached for her smartphone.

'Yes.' She sighed; all hope lost. What she'd give for Ryan to swoop in, she'd kiss his feet. 'I don't know how to use it, I had a quick lesson, although, I suspect it's faulty.'

'Looks fancy.'

'It's new to the market. My friend is doing the advertising for it and she gets demonstration models to try out. She gave it to me the other week because my niece drowned my old phone in a rowboat on the river.' Why was she talking so much to a complete stranger? She was used to listening and not speaking, especially with strangers—but not one with a handgun.

'Did you get upset with your niece?'

'No, it was an accident,' replied Emma, even grinning a little. She couldn't help it. Was the beer she'd downed in seconds finally kicking in?

'You've received a text message.'

'Can you open it? Seriously, I can't. I've got the instruction manual upstairs and planned to study it tomorrow.'

Jae pushed a few buttons and held out the phone. 'There, it's a message from Ryan. Is that your boyfriend?'

'I guess so, we've only been dating a few weeks.' Should she mention Ryan was also a gun-carrying detective?

To stop her dribble, she read the text message aloud, 'Hi, how was work? Hope you didn't work too hard and I hope you locked the front gate.' She smiled at the phone. Ryan was so perfect, doing his best to protect her. 'I locked the front gate, didn't I?' She tried to turn it off, pressing the buttons and gave up, dropping the silly thing on the table.

Jae's lips curled into a grin. 'Yes, the gate is still very much locked. I had to jump over it using the roof of your van.'

'Good. No, that's not good, Jae. You jumped my fence, and I've been here for five years and no one's jumped my fence. Didn't the neighbour's dogs bark at you?'

'No.' He chuckled.

'They probably recognised my van,' Emma mumbled, trying to calm herself down.

Jae rummaged in his pack and pulled out a packet of cigarettes. 'May I smoke in your shed?'

'I'll get you an ashtray.' While at the bar, as a habit, she grabbed another two beers. If she just treated this situation as a casual drink with a client she could survive. Right?

'So, you're not married?' Jae asked, lighting his cigarette.

'No, don't believe in marriage. And I don't do weddings if that's your next question.' She put the beer and ashtray down in front of her uninvited guest.

'Thank you.' He slid the ashtray to the other side, expelling the smoke away from her. 'Why not?'

'Why not, what?'

'Marriage and weddings.'

'That's personal, don't you think? I don't know you. You've jumped my fence. Stole my van. And you've got a gun on you.' Her voice rose as her throat got tighter and her knees trembled. She couldn't walk if she tried. Not now.

'Calm down, Emma. I'm not here to hurt you,' Jae said calmly, taking a drag of his coffin-nail as if they were sharing coffee in a street side café.

'I'm not used to this kind of thing.' She could adapt, it was her nature to adapt to her clients ever changing needs. She had to.

Emma took a deep breath and blurted out the first thing that came to mind in the midst of her terror. 'Have you got a girlfriend?'

'No. Until a few weeks ago, I'd never kissed a girl.'

'Really?' A few weeks ago, she'd never kissed anyone as handsome as Ryan who broke her three-year drought.

Jae pushed up his glasses. 'I'm short, skinny, and look like a nerdy foreigner. Not the kind women go for. No one bothered to notice me or even talk to me.'

'I can relate.'

'Why do you say that? You're a pretty lady with a boyfriend.'

Emma pointed to her silent phone. 'Ryan's gorgeous, with this buffed body that should be modelling men's gym-wear.'

Even better naked. 'Aaand he's a nice guy. He's this complete package of looks, brains, generosity, kind-heartedness, with this spontaneity for adventure. He's like this grand prize of the international lotto for lovers.'

Jae chuckled as he wiped the red tip of his cigarette on the edge of the glass ashtray. 'And?'

'Well, my superpower is to blend in, so he's way out of my league. Plain fact.' And took a mouthful of her beer to shut herself up.

'Not true.'

'It is true. I'm just plain old, boring Emma, who works behind the scenes of the glamorous parties. I'm the one who blends into the background or on the sidelines. I still pinch myself to check if it's real that someone like Ryan is even interested in me—and I can't believe I just shared all that crap with a complete stranger like you.' She hid her face in her palms.

Why hide when she had nowhere to go.

Jae smiled. 'I won't hold it against you.'

'You'll have to excuse me, I'm nervous because you've jumped my fence, and you have that handgun that's staring at me. Is that glitter on the barrel bit?' Why couldn't she shut up!

Jae pulled out the handgun from his belt. 'Your van had glitter in it, it gets into everything.'

'I know. But how did it get on a gun?'

'Beats me.' He brushed the glitter off then tucked it back into his belt and pulled his t-shirt over the top. 'How's that? Now it's no longer staring at you, will that make you more comfortable?'

'You're hiding it under your shirt, Jae. I know it's still

there.'

'Out of sight, out of mind.' He stabbed his cigarette into the ashtray. Pushed it away and picked up his beer and asked, 'So what does this Ryan do for a living?'

Biting her bottom lip she tried to work her way around a tricky question. 'Ryan works for the State Government. Don't ask me his official title because I couldn't tell you the name of his department. But he looks exceptionally sexy-smart in his suit and tie. He has a desk in this large open-plan office that he shares with his other colleagues, who all look busy talking on their phones, staring at computer screens. There's this pretty young receptionist who suffers leaning-neck-disorder every time Ryan walks past.' She leaned over to demonstrate and started to lose her balance. 'Oh-no.'

Jae caught her arm, keeping her upright. 'Careful, you almost fell.'

'Thanks. Sorry. Gravity has its moments.' She sat securely back on her seat, knowing it was now impossible for her to run. Besides, she'd tripped so regularly in her lifetime she was over being embarrassed. 'Where was I' —*rambling*.

'So, he's a suit, a professional?'

'Ryan's no executive, I guess he's working his way up the food chain within his department.' She had to change the conversation away from Ryan and his job. 'I hear you've been busy with my van, partying with the ladies?'

Jae grinned wide as colour brushed his cheeks, pushing his glasses along his nose. 'We had mattresses in the back.'

Her face screwed up. 'You had sex in the back of my van?'

'Ah-huh.' Jae's grin widened as he sat taller with skinny

chest out and chin up.

'I've never had sex in my van. It's been christened, huh?' She arched an eyebrow at Jae who sat there and grinned like a kid. 'What was it, the good girls wanting to play with the bad-boy-syndrome or something?'

'I guess so, it's never happened to me or Stu before.' His smile faltered as his shoulders deflated. 'These girls we met at the beach approached us. They recognised the van from the news and asked for a drink and ride and—'

Emma held up her palm cutting him off. 'I don't want to know. That's my van, Jae. I'll never be able to look at the back of my van the same after this. I hope you got rid of that mattress.' She even smiled, hoping to put him at ease, and herself.

'I emptied the van back at our campsite. It's amazing how much crap we accumulated in almost three weeks.'

She couldn't hide anymore, so Emma sat straighter, smoothed down her dress and faced her fear head on. 'What are you going to do now?'

Would Jae let her live?

Would she get to see Ryan, just one more time?

* * *

Jae shrugged, frowning at Emma's question. 'I haven't thought that far, except to return your van.' It was the only thought he could hold onto in his thick grey world of misery. It was as if he was wearing blinders that blocked him from admiring anything that once was so beautiful to him.

'You do realise you're in a heap of trouble,' said Emma.

'The police are looking for you and my van?'

'Always wanted to be famous. And it'll be just as easy for us to be forgotten again.' His smile was as weak as his half shoulder shrug, resting his elbows on the table. 'Stu and I were talking about going north before he…' He hesitated as the grief gripped his heart. It hurt to breathe. He clutched his beer and drank back his tears.

'Do you want me to call Stu's family to tell them where they can find him, so they can give him a proper burial?'

Jae looked at Emma with her blue-grey eyes, much too big for her oval face. But he also saw her empathy. 'You'd do that?'

Emma nodded, tucking her hair behind her ear. It was the same colour as the beach sand where he'd watched his first sunset and sunrise stretch across the ocean.

'Would you want Stu buried or would he like it where he is, out there? If you tell me where he is, his family could say their goodbyes and maybe put a plaque out there as a place for you to go back?'

'I won't go back. I'm done living in the past.' The past only held his pain. He sniffed, wiping his nose with the back of his hand and sat straighter to light another cigarette. 'You're right,' he said, inhaling on his cancer-stick. 'Stu deserves to have a proper funeral. He'd like his mother to visit him. The easiest way to find him is if you head for Mecket's point, the scenic spot. Have you heard of the place?'

'I have. Ryan took me for lunch there not long ago, it was my first motorbike ride. It's not going to be my last is it, Jae?'

'No. I've never been on a motorbike.'

'It's amazing. Totally recommend it. I mean, I don't ride,

but as a passenger it was mega-cool.'

'Nice.' Would he get that chance? Did Stu ever ride a bike?

Jae dragged heavily on the cigarette, it seared his throat. 'Well, you head for Mecket's, then you go ten k's past the turn-off where there's a fire track the rangers use on the left. You then follow that for miles until you hit the creek. Go upstream and that's where you'll find our camping spot. Nice and secluded with plenty of shade. It had a great view of this valley where we could watch the birds and the odd helicopter in the distance. There were brumbies, kangaroos, wombats, and everything out there, but no people. Just us.'

'Did you have fun?'

'I'd never left the city limits unless it was a school trip. I loved it. Stu did too.' Jae stared at his cut fingers, with his dirty, torn nails. The place had been paradise for both of them, but not anymore. Where was his paradise now?

Jae pushed up his glasses and faced Emma who was patiently waiting for him to speak. 'If you follow the creek upstream from our campsite for about an hour, you'll find a heap of large boulders in the bend. I made Stu a cross and tied his favourite cap to it. He loved that hat. He liked your music too. So, um, yeah, that's where he's resting.' Jae stabbed the butt out, tempted to light up another. 'Do you want one? Help yourself.' He didn't care about lung cancer, didn't care he was making himself sick in the stomach, or burning his throat with the nicotine that was giving him heartburn. He just didn't care.

Yet, he used to.

'I don't smoke. It's a disgusting habit—but you're making me nervous, Jae, with that pistol under your shirt, and the way you jumped my fence.'

'Still hung up on the fence thing, huh?' He grinned at her. Jae knew he was invading her space. But she seemed a nice lady, and right now he needed someone to be nice.

'You could've seriously hurt yourself on that barbed wire,' said Emma.

Strange for someone he'd just met to show so much compassion, for Stu, and now him. 'One of those barbs got me.' He showed her the scratches on the back of his upper arm. He'd never broken into a place before.

Sure, he'd done other bad crap that was the opposite of his life of always being good. Always being polite and proper.

But being obedient got him nowhere. If anything, it broke his soul.

He just wanted a change, which was the biggest risk — daring to be different and believing in himself. It was the scariest and bravest thing he'd ever done. Out of everything, looking at himself was harder than anything else he'd faced this past few days alone.

Jae didn't believe he was bad. He'd never believed Stu had been bad either. They both had their separate demons, where Stu had been sexually abused by one of his mother's boyfriends and had to get out. Jae had his own demons he danced with. Yet, as best mates, brothers, they'd shared their stories, tears, and their secrets around the campfire where the stars were their silent witnesses.

This gesture of returning the van, Stu would've approved of too.

'The reason I jumped your fence was because I wanted to

tell you I'd brought your van back. I swear I'm not here to hurt you, Emma. I've never hit a woman. It's wrong. Stu and I scared the crap out of Stu's mother's boyfriend the other week, he'd been abusing Stu's mother.' Stu called it a *payback* for what had happened to him, another new term he'd learned in such a short time. 'This guy, Bob, was so bad, the other kids would hide from him in the cupboards. He was a big guy, he reminded me of a clothed sumo wrestler behind the steering wheel of his truck. It was by pure chance we spotted him too, and we did this U-turn, and I shot at his truck while Stu gave him the warning to stop hitting his mother.'

'Do you know you killed him?'

Jae frowned. 'No, I didn't. I'd aimed for the side mirror, I missed and hit the windscreen. I've got a lousy aim. Did that Bob have a heart attack behind the wheel?'

'According to the news he died from a bullet to the side of his head.'

Jae pushed up his glasses so hard they hit his eyebrows. 'No, I couldn't have? I didn't mean to. We'd only meant to scare him to stop abusing Stu's mother.' *Holy crap.* What would Stu say to that? 'H-H-Has any man hit you?'

Her eyes widened as her back straightened in fear. She was still pale and visibly shaky, but this was a whole new layer she'd added to her fear.

'Someone did, didn't they?'

'Yeah.' Emma gave the slightest nod, looking down at her hands in her lap.

'Why?'

She shrugged her reply.

'Emma, don't be ashamed. I bet it wasn't your fault, right?'

'You're right. My ex used to—' She lunged for his cigarette packet that rested between them as her fingers trembled. She almost pulled out half the packet for her one and held it up.

'I'll do it.' Jae lit it up for her.

'Ugh.' She coughed, frowning with tongue out, looking at the smouldering smoke in her hand like a piece of chalk. 'That tastes terrible.'

'First one does. I've only just learned the habit, found it calms my nerves a bit. Don't know why or how.' He didn't enjoy them, taking a deep drink of his beer to wash away its aftertaste.

She sucked at the end of the smoke in a short puff and blew out an even smaller puff. 'My friend Victoria smokes. She says it settles her down and she suffers shocking nerves. It's her crutch.' Emma inspected the smouldering stick she twirled in her fingertips.

'How often did this ex hit you?'

She shrugged, sucking on the filter's tip, she winced through the smoke. 'The last time my ex hurt me, he was so angry he gave me a backhander right across my face. It knocked me off my feet. I hurt my back landing on a stack of boxes here in the shed and wore the bruises for a week. I've told no one that. Not even my best friends.'

'Arsehole. Why did he do that?'

'I'd moved into this shed, ages before anyone knew I was living here. You could say I was hiding from him. He was the first person I'd ever banned from my bar and shed. Swear he liked my bar more than me.'

'Have to admit it's an impressive bar. I haven't been in any bars, except the uni-bar.' Jae admired the mirrored walls and neon lights, with its 50's retro style. 'So, what else did they say about me and Stu in the news?'

'Um, the armed robberies. Can't remember them all but you did a few.'

'I can't remember them all either.' Jae chuckled. 'We never had a plan, just did, living in the moment.'

'Jae, you seem a nice young man, what happened? Weren't you in university?'

Was he still nice? 'I was studying law, that's how I met Stu. We were in the same dorm together and I got a job tutoring. Stu was hopeless, yet smart on paper, he'd rather sleep and eat than study. I made him study with me and go to classes. I'd take notes while he slept in class, and yet, he got better grades than me.' His chest ached, missing Stu.

'Did you see your parents on TV pleading for you to give yourself up?'

'No way? My mother on television?'

Emma nodded.

His chest tightened more as did his throat while he sniffed back the tears. 'How did my mother look?'

'She was upset. Both of your parents spoke, just your brother.'

'My mother doesn't speak English.' His father would never speak his second son's name again. 'I should call her sometime.' But would his mother listen? No, she'd wail as if he was a ghost.

'You could tell your mother was worried about you.'

'My mother worries about everyone. It's all she did, worry.' Worried more about upsetting his father. Jae frowned, clutching his beer tighter. 'I studied law because of my father.'

'Did you enjoy it?'

'No, I hated it.' Swallowing the hatred burning his chest.

'Why do it?'

'Because of my family. You wouldn't understand.' Few did.

'Try me? Can't be any worse than my family.'

'Well, I'm from a Syrian family, so close to the Iraq border they could be classed as both. Me, I was born here and we're Muslims, of the strict kind. We're restricted with food choices and there's no smoking, no alcohol, no music.' He pointed to the speakers. 'We loved your music. You've got an amazing collection. Is that just for parties?'

'Kind of. Music is meant for moving, for dancing.'

'For road trips.'

'Exactly.'

For the past few days, the van's music played non-stop as if it sang to his soul while he lay in the back of the van staring at the ceiling. It was the only thing that brought him comfort. 'Did you set up that stereo in the *Parte'* van for parties?'

'No. That was purely for me, like here. I like my music. It's like this lesson in geography, moving everywhere while I'm sitting still, working countless hours at this bench.' She patted the table as if it was her altar.

'Have you travelled a lot?'

'Oh, yeah, some days I try the view from that side of the table all the way to my couch.' They mirrored each other's grin across the table.

She put her smoke on the side of the ashtray they shared, crossed her hands in front and leaned lower to look in his eyes. 'And? Go on, you were telling me your story.'

Wow, undivided attention. How rare. Jae only got that from his mother when his father and brother weren't home, and recently from Stu.

Jae took in a deep shaky breath, and with a nod he said, 'I'm not looking for any sympathy, but you could say I got picked on a lot.' Understatement. It was a daily ritual, like changing his underwear and brushing his teeth.

'I've been there, almost every day at school,' Emma said, raising her hand as if in class.

'You? No way. Not that I'm calling you a liar, but I can't picture it.' He pictured Emma coming from a white-middle-class suburban house with white picket fences and a two-car garage.

'It's true. I was a kid who had no sense of balance or any form of coordination. I'd fall over my own feet all the time, still do. But back then, I'd go home every day in tears and show my mother my new set of bruises and scratches. While she bandaged me up she'd feed me her famous butter cookies. So then, not only was I warring with gravity, I got fat too.'

'I copped it for being Muslim. For my skin. For being short. For being geeky and naive to the world beyond my father's borders. Take your pick.'

'It doesn't matter what colour, creed, religion or shoe size you are, kids can be so cruel,' announced Emma.

'Until a few weeks ago I was still in school. At Uni they weren't as outright prejudiced as high school. But people on the street, or when I walk into a shop, it's the way they'd look at me. They'd judge me without even knowing me, as if I offended them by breathing.'

'People forget we're all people, who all have to eat, drink, and sleep. It'd be such a nice world if no one judged each other for what clothes they wore or what car we drove. *No way*—I just gave a speech! The girl who drives a van and hangs out in a shed gave a speech. I should've stood on some soapbox with a megaphone getting people to vote for me.' They both laughed.

'You're right, though. I was on my way back to campus, when these two guys in this gold ute started abusing me. I'd stalled the *Parte'* van and was trying to restart it and get out of the way. But instead, he's shouting at me, even ripping open the door, and grabbed my shirt. I knew I was about to kiss his fists. That's when I grabbed the gun and I shot up his fancy gold ute that was his personal trophy. I didn't kill them, did I? I'd never shot at anything until then.'

'I don't think so. That ute was damaged, and the guy was upset.'

'He was a rugby player for the university team, him and his mate, the passenger. I remembered them from this job I took to clean the rugby change-rooms and deliver water to the benches. That pair tripped me up and poured ice water all over me on my first day. I never went back. Butt-wipes.' He frowned, shifting in his seat, gripping his beer tighter. 'So, when I collected Stu, we tore up the rugby oval to get back at them.'

'I've never done doughnuts in my van. Or skids.'

'I'm not a pro either. I had some scary moments in those small carparks with the length of the van, but I never scratched it.' He was proud of that. 'But then we found this place to sleep for a few hours and this other guy started banging on the van. You know, he never once asked me to move the van. Just screamed all this abusive language at me, calling me names, and banging away on the van like it was a drum.'

'My poor van!'

'I agree, it showed no respect. I told him all he had to do was ask me to move the van, I wouldn't have shot him like I did. Did he live?'

'The bread delivery guy?'

'We smelt bread, and he was in a small truck.'

'He lived.'

'Good. Stu wanted him to. I made sure he had his phone to call for help. I felt like an idiot afterwards, losing my temper with the guy, but he woke me up screaming in my face. You were the only one who spoke to us nicely. It's like no one's got any manners anymore—except you.' Jae reached for another cigarette. Could he stomach it?

'I have to ask, Jae, what made you…' Emma paused as if to search for the right word, '…borrow my van?'

He forced cigarette smoke through his nostrils, with lips drawn tight. Funny thing was, the van felt like his too. But it wasn't.

Nothing belonged to him anymore. He had nothing. He had no one.

Yet it still hurt to say the name, 'My father—' He hesitated, licking his lips. 'For the first time in my life, we had an argument. He was a surgeon, but his qualifications aren't recognised in this country and he's more of a nursing sister. But he still practices in the community. His office is at the front of the house, so he's always home. My brother is doing his residency at the nearby hospital and making my parents prouder every minute of the day.' That's all he heard, *why couldn't he be like his big obedient brother?* 'I didn't have the grades to be a doctor, never wanted to be one. My father was disappointed and decided I would then do law, and I hated that too.'

'What did you want to do?'

'Architecture.' Jae reached for his backpack and pulled out his sketchbook. 'I want to create eco-friendly houses, specifically designed for harsh environments. Stu and I were talking about going up north to his uncle's place, where I could design homes for remote indigenous communities, suitable to their cultural needs.'

'Wow, that's amazing.'

'This is what I worked on while we were camping.' Jae flicked the covers of his sketchbook and held it out to her. 'I'd met this gentleman,' he said, pulling out the worn-edged hardcover textbook. 'Glen Marcotte. He's my hero, the best architect in not only Australia but worldwide. He creates ecological and socially responsible homes. He's a visionary. A genius who's won prizes for his structures that are the equivalent to the Pulitzer and the Nobel.'

'Where did you meet him?'

Jae smiled with his heart wide open as if filled with light and that greyness in his brain started to clear. 'In the city museum. We were there for this law lecture and I went into the wrong room. I ended up watching Mr Marcotte's presentation on Eco-friendly homes, promoting his Architecture Masterclass.

We had a coffee and from there it was amazing. I had four weeks to put in my application. I'd always liked architecture in high school, making model bridges, thinking I'd get into engineering. So, I thought, hey why not, and submitted my drawings for remote indigenous housing.'

'And what happened?'

'I didn't get in. It's a masterclass for qualified architects. But I got a once in a lifetime offer.'

'For what?'

'He offered me a job to work as a waiter, bartender, baggage carrier, you name it, as an underpaid assistant. But I'd be there while the masterclass was operating and could listen to all of the lectures if I wanted. He said he liked my drawings. He said I had talent and recommended I use the time there to listen and learn, because he was right, it'd be too advanced for me. But all I had to do was come up with the airfare.'

'Sounds great.'

'I know, I'd never been so passionate about anything before.'

'You sound it, and these houses look great.'

'All solar, with water collection inbuilt, it's almost self-sufficient within a remote environment. Perfect for places in the Northern Territory. Mr Marcotte said my structures were ground-breaking. It was like that calling you get where those people go into the priesthood. I'd found it with a brilliant opportunity. I tried to transfer all my legal courses to architectural studies and catch up on the semester, and the University was okay with that too. I'd spoken to the lecturers and got the booklists, so I started doing my research from the library, I lived there more than in my room waiting for my father's okay to transfer.'

'So what did your parents say?'

The smile died and his heart squeezed cold in the blink of an eye. All his inner happiness shutdown. 'My father refused. Told me if I didn't become a lawyer, I would disgrace the family. He said no one had been an architect in the family before and refused to listen.'

'That's harsh.'

'That's my father. Before this, I'd never said anything or dared go against his word, but I couldn't let this go. We argued and then he hit me for daring to speak back to him. But I had to convince him. They'd never listened to me before and so I kept going and he hit me again.'

Jae leaned back in his chair and examined his ripped dirty nails that were so jagged and coarse, just like he felt on the inside. Unclean. 'My mother came rushing in. But she got in his way getting me up off the floor and he hit my mother, pushing her to the floor so he could hit me more.'

'Your father beat you and your mother?' Emma gasped, covering her mouth with her hand. 'That's so wrong.'

'I know, I saw red for what he'd done to my mother and I punched him. For the first time in my life I stood up to him. I don't know where it came from. I got bullied at school daily, when I was allowed to attend school, then I got picked on at home for not being good enough, I've always complied. But not with this.' He tapped his sketches on the table. 'Not when I knew in my heart what was right for me.' He fisted at his chest, where his heart pounded loudly in his skinny chest.

Emma flinched with rigid shoulders.

'Sorry,' he mumbled, trying to exhale the hatred from inside. 'I may have let him hit me for being true to myself, but never would I allow him to hit my mother.'

'You should be proud for standing up for your mother and I'm sure she was too.'

'You'd think so.' He shrugged. 'When I helped my mother off the floor, she kept telling me I had to go.'

'Why?'

'She said I'd done a bad thing in hitting my father. It showed I had no respect for family. My father told me I was no longer his son. No longer a part of his family. I was a nobody, and that they'd grieve for me. No more university, nothing.'

'I'm so sorry.'

'Me too. I returned to my dorm to pack. Instead, I told Stu. I'd never drunk before, but I did that night, even smoked. Somehow, we ended up at this party at the Marina where I crashed on this fancy yacht. That's where I found this handgun with a stack of bullets, when I'd been searching for painkillers. I walked through the car park looking for a public phone box to call Stu to come get me. That's when I saw the *Parte'* van and it sang to me.' He cleared his throat and shuffled in his seat; it wasn't his van. 'Sorry.' Again, he shrugged. *Did Emma use that money to get another van?*

'Were you going to use it to get to campus?' Emma asked.

'Yeah, just a short trip. I'd only planned to use your van to get back to the dorms, when those guys in the gold ute abused me. That's how it all began. Something snapped inside of me. I'd had enough of being called names, for offending people because of my appearance, or the way I spoke. Because we were home-schooled to learn English as a second-language, I don't know the common terms. Stu was teaching me. Before that, I was always getting picked on because I'm easy prey being the smaller guy stuck in this life sentence of living my father's life plan. For what?'

'So, what happened then?'

'I remember little after that. Just snippets. I was off my head on a two-week binge, eating and drinking everything my family never allowed me to have. I didn't care anymore. My family didn't want to know me. All I had left was Stu. You were the only person who spoke to us like a human being during that time.' He scooped up his beer and picked at the corner of the bottle's label.

With Stu, Jae had had a plan. Now he had no idea what to do. But at least he'd brought the van back. The van that had shown him how to live.

'What about your dad, he ever hit your mum?' Jae asked. It'd been days without speaking to another soul. Facing the woman he'd hurt by stealing her van, how could he have been so cruel?

Yet, how could he move forward when he'd lost all sense of direction.

* * *

'Mine? No, my father never hit my mum. Although my mum punched out my dad's new wife at my sister's wedding.' For the first time Emma grinned at the memory.

'You're kidding?'

'No.'

'And?'

Emma sighed. It's not like she had a choice.

'Your father had an affair—'

'*Affairsss. The arsehole.* Lots and lots of affairs. When he left us, all his ex-lovers came looking for him. It was horrible. I'd answer the door to these women looking for my father, and they were nice ladies too. I couldn't understand how my dad could do that to us. And then I got picked on at school over it, so I was glad we moved.' She rubbed her palm over her face as if trying to be rid of the memory.

'Where is he now?'

'Interstate. Got a transfer with the bank and divorced my mum. Didn't see him again until my sister's wedding, which was the last wedding I ever attended.' She held out her cigarette, her nerves swapped for anger that still burned. 'This has gone out.'

'Allow me.' Jae leaned over flicking the lighter and relit it for her. 'Aren't you, like, one of those wedding planners?'

'Used to be. Swore I'd never do them again.'

'Tell me. Who am I going to tell? I've confessed to you.' He raised his skinny arms in the air to the empty shed.

'Huh, you have. I have this company policy that what's said in this shed, stays in this shed.'

'I like that. So, go on, tell me the story.'

She inhaled the cigarette and took another sip of her beer. 'It all starts with my big sister, the bitch. And that's being nice. Helen got engaged to be married to the best brother-in-law on the planet, and I wasn't allowed to be near the wedding. It hurt.'

Emma thought it was her one and only chance of actually personally knowing the wedding party. To maybe even be considered as a bridesmaid.

She sat up straighter and wiped the tip of her nose. She had Victoria's proposal to be the Maid of Honour. And it was a place of honour.

She'd be proud—if she wasn't so scared.

'Why not? I was an attendant for my brother's wedding,' Jae said. 'Did your sister tell you why?'

'Oh yeah. Helen told me straight to my face I was fat. Told me I'd fall over and embarrass her because I was clumsy, and I didn't fit into the aesthetics of her wedding. She was right.' Emma tapped the edge of her cigarette on the ashtray.

'That's not right.'

'I blend, I never attend or stay to the party's end.' It was her motto. 'At the time I was working for a wedding planner, so of course, they wanted me to talk Julie into doing Helen's wedding. Julie's the best in the country, so why not? I'd use her too, if I believed in marriage.'

'Did this Julie do it?'

'No, she's booked out years in advance. Julie told me to do it and offered to advise me throughout the process. It was a golden opportunity for me. If I pulled this wedding off, I'd make my name in the industry, and I put everything into it. But I also saw it as an opportunity to re-connect with my family, especially my sister.'

'Did you re-connect with them?'

'Are you kidding? I was just the staff as far as my sister was concerned, who turned into the hugest Bridezilla ever. I even warned William he might want to reconsider marrying her.'

'You didn't.'

'Oh, yeah. I completely broke the wedding planner's code on that one.'

'There's a wedding-planner's code?'

'It's unwritten, but it's there. You're paid to ensure the show carries on, even if you can predict the bridal couple's divorce date post-honeymoon. We're coordinators, putting all of these elements together for this one timed event. Weddings are also this huge balancing act to contain this fierce intensity of crackling emotions. The pressure was the worst because the bride was my sister. Funny thing was, outside my immediate little family, very few even knew I was the bride's sister, even the bridesmaids.'

'You're kidding?'

'Nope, I was known as the wedding planner's assistant. My sister and mother didn't even give me a seat at the family table. Their excuse was I'd be too busy working, so okay I allowed that one. But I wasn't even included in the family photos, and I'd spent a fortune on my outfit that day. It was the last time I bothered to dress to impress. In fact, that whole wedding completely sucked.' She puffed on the dragon that irritated her sinuses.

'How did the wedding go?'

'It was perfect. The ceremony, the dinner, the first dance, everything went smoothly. Then at the final part of the reception…' She stabbed the filthy cigarette into the ashtray with a need to wash her hands clean.

'Yesss?' Urged Jae.

'According to my mother, she'd overheard my father's new wife, who's an ex-car-saleslady—huh, no wonder I hate car yards!' It was like the double doors of the darkest dungeon were ripped wide open to let the light rid the room of all its shadows. Emma didn't have a caryard-phobia at all. She hated the car-sales-woman who'd stolen her father.

No way. The money she'd lost and the deals she could've made doing party planning for caryards.

Jae waved his hand in front of her. 'Can we get back to the wedding story, please?'

'Oh, um, where was I?' Emma drank her beer to rid that nicotine taste.

'What did this other woman say that was horrible about your mother?'

'She said my father left his wife who was an old hag. A woman who didn't like sex, too busy baking biscuits like she was living back in the 1950s.' Was that why her mother changed overnight into a sex-loving cougar and never baked those butter biscuits again? No way, that one night had changed both mother and daughter, she'd never realised until now.

'That's rude.'

'My father was to blame for bringing that homewrecker to that wedding. She was never invited. But it got worse. The woman was an idiot, raving in the loo, and she had no idea my mother was in one of the cubicles. So, on the way back from the ladies she was crossing the empty dance floor to their table when my mother came up from behind and rugby-tackled this woman across the floor.'

'You're kidding.' Jae snorted a series of snickers as if trying to contain himself while being polite at the same time.

'Oh yeah, it was a full-on bitches' bar-room-bikers-brawl in the middle of over a hundred seated guests. It was a smack down in the centre of the grand ballroom, beneath the crystal chandelier. All in front of these hob-knobs of the finance sector and highbrow society that my sister married into.' *Was that why Helen had to play the Perfect-Princess all the time?* The pressure must be enormous, considering they didn't come from money, and had the worst wedding of the century.

Jae chuckled. 'Sorry for laughing.'

'Don't be.'

'What did you do?'

'I tried to break it up,' said Emma. 'It was my job as the wedding planner to keep everything calm and on schedule. We're there to keep the focus on the wedding party at all times, to make the day special for them. We're meant to control any situations and coordinate this huge team like a stage show production.'

'And did you?'

'Up until then, it was pure perfection. Then it became a catastrophe.'

Jae cupped his beer in two hands and leaned closer on the edge of his seat. 'What happened when you stepped in?'

'My mother swung at the other woman. She ducked and my mother punched me so hard she broke my nose. I bled everywhere. All over my sister's white bridal gown. Blood flew over the wedding cake, women fled for their lives into the foyer in fear of blood stains on their outfits. Someone pulled the fire alarm to evacuate. William tried to hold back his blushing bride, who was throwing handfuls of her bloodied cake at me, screaming at me for ruining her wedding. Mum was screeching at me for allowing the homewrecker inside the reception. Even Dad shouted at me for ruining Helen's wedding, and then he shouted at Mum for punching his new wife, who was speed-dialling the cops to have Mum charged with assault. Finally, the fire brigade burst into the reception with the police who pulled us all apart.'

'Did your mother get arrested?'

'No. Charges were never laid. The police separated everyone, and along with the fire brigade they took away the best parts of the cake. The Hotel's general manager shut down the reception and guests were sent home. My sister got on the plane for her honeymoon. My mother got blind in the bar downstairs and went home with some random guy, and I sat at the hospital on my own.'

Jae frowned. 'No one went with you?'

'No.' It was the loneliest she'd ever felt. 'The wedding planner dropped me off, after advising me weddings may be a tricky balancing act at the best of time, and to try not getting emotionally involved in family events again. Especially my family. My professional reputation as a wedding planner was ruined, and so was my outfit I'd bled all over. I had two black eyes, a broken nose that was puffed up like an overcooked hot-dog. I had to wear this plaster to keep it straight for weeks. It was terrible. That's where I met my ex.' Emma frowned, blinking at the memory. It was incredible how one catastrophic event just kept dishing out everlasting consequences.

'How?' Jae asked, pushing up his glasses.

'My ex, Frank, was in the ER getting stitches in his hand from a work incident. Besides the medical staff, Frank was the only person who'd bothered to talk to me that day. He dropped me home from the hospital, and that same night I officially moved into my friend's place. Victoria was away interstate and I was house-sitting anyway. My mother and sister didn't speak to me until Helen's third wedding anniversary came around. Which, hey, no surprise, I'd just bought this shed as the party planner and they wanted me to cater for it.'

'Did you?'

'Wish I'd said no. But it was William who talked me into it. My fault too, my brother-in-law was the only businessman I trusted for free advice and saw him about buying this place. It wasn't his fault he'd married into a family of bitches, where my newly created superpower was not only to blend, but I'd earn the tag of embarrassing family member.' Emma exhaled the horrible cigarette smoke as if to blow past the many shades of sadness that were just another smokescreen on the scars she wore. 'I'm getting light headed from this.' She gagged at the taste of it, it was like licking tar off the road and her forehead was hot, or was that just nerves?

'I've just learned the habit,' said Jae. 'So, is that why you don't do weddings?'

'Yep. I never did another wedding after that one. I swore to myself I never wanted to deal with overly emotional brides and mother and father-of-the-brides again. I prefer parties. They're much simpler and more fun, free from all this emotional stress. I've even got it in the contract for every function that all I do is set up and leave before the first guest arrives because I rarely attend and I never stay to the end.'

'So you never get made to clean up anyone's mess?'

'Exactly. Especially with my family's functions.'

'Do you get on with them now?'

'Yeah. Mum's happy holidaying with her toy boy lover in South America. My sister, meh.' Emma shrugged. 'Helen only stepped inside this place a few weeks ago for the first time. And I can't believe you jumped my fence.'

'Are we back to the fence thing again?' Jae grinned with his head tilted.

'I can't believe I'm telling you all this,' she exclaimed in disbelief.

Jae inhaled deep, lowered his head and said, 'I'm very sorry I stole your van.'

'How come you knew how to steal it? I mean, you don't strike me as the type who has the skills to steal one? No offence there.' She didn't dare offend the young guy with the gun under his shirt.

'Stu bought this dump of a car. It was so bad, the windows never wound up, and the seats were wrecked from the weather. But it was cheap to run and came with six months registration on it. We drove that thing everywhere, even though the exhaust system was barely hanging on. We never had a key for the thing, except this anti-immobiliser gadget we got off E-bay for a few dollars. It switches off car alarms. That's how I learned, by hotwiring it daily.' Jae pointed at her mum's car parked in the shed. 'I can't picture you cruising around in a van—that sports car suits you more.'

'Me, no way. That car's so low I'm less than an inch off the road. I've had fun with it though. But I was always one for being practical. Driving the van never bothered me, it was part of my work. Besides, no one gave me a second look when I'd rock up in it.' It was all part of her superpower to blend.

'Yeah, I can relate.'

'Do you think your father will forgive you?' Should she forgive hers? Did she suffer with daddy issues? Is that why she never trusted another man? The Frank fiasco didn't help either.

With elbow on the table, Jae rested his chin on his hand and patted his heart with the other. 'My parents won't forgive me, they'll grieve like I've already died. Like I grieve for Stu, for a home, for something more than this nothing in my chest.'

'THIS IS THE POLICE. WE HAVE YOU SURROUNDED. PUT YOUR HANDS UP AND SURRENDER, JAED ZAFAR.' An amplified male voice bellowed from outside the shed and they were doused in blinding lights.

They both jumped from their seats and the cat ran for cover at the bright lights.

'Did you call the police?' Jae asked her over his shoulder, his hand shielding his eyes from the lights.

'How? I've been here with you the whole time.' Emma raised her trembling hands to shade her eyes as her legs wobbled with fear.

'How did they know I was even here? If the van had a tracker on it, they would've found us sooner.' Jae licked his lips as sweat broke out across his skin. His wide eyes darted around the shed to the wrought iron stairs, to the front, closed. The door to the back also closed. Would he take the stairs and find her apartment?

'How did they know I was here? We never saw one police officer,' said Jae, 'not one police car, nothing, the entire time we drove around in that van. Stu was right, hiding in plain sight did beat the law of averages.'

'I don't know, Jae, maybe they saw the van out the front.' Emma took a shaky step back from Jae. She had no idea how the police got here, but at least they were here. Thank God.

'THIS IS THE POLICE. WE HAVE YOU SURROUNDED. PUT YOUR HANDS UP.'

'What are you doing?' Jae asked Emma.

'I'm doing what they said.' Her whole body shook with nerves, holding up heavy arms.

'What do I do?' Jae patted his chest as his wide eyes darted around the room searching for an escape. 'They'll shoot me. I deserve it for shooting those people. I'm already dead to my family. My best friend's dead.'

'Jae, no. You can work this out.'

'THIS IS THE POLICE WE HAVE YOU SURROUNDED, PUT YOUR HANDS UP.'

Red and blue lights flashed everywhere like disco lights across her wall, while heavily armed police officers aimed their guns at Jae.

'Who are these people? They're not the normal cops. These guys have heavy artillery. Unbelievable. They've got snipers!'

'What did you say?' Hope rose so fast in her chest she couldn't breathe. The love of her life told her he used to be a sniper. Was her heart's hero here? *Wait*—when did Ryan become the love of her life?

'Shiiit.' Jae stared at his chest, alive with red laser dots all aimed at his chest.

Emma's eyes widened; it took the last shred of courage inside to stare at her own chest that was free from red laser dots. Then more floodlights came on and they were bathed in blinding hot white light.

* * *

Ryan lay on the roof of the neighbour's shed, the voices of the other officers in his earpiece, but he didn't hear. With his finger on the trigger, he knew this position so well. Hell, his father taught Ryan as a kid when they'd go hunting together. As an adult it came naturally. The hours lying in the gritty mud, or in the tropical summer sun on searing beach sand. Dodging mozzies in monsoonal jungles, or on rooftops congested with car exhaust and the icy winds of winter. All while watching, waiting for something to happen, to protect someone he'd never met, just so they could smile and wave at the cameras for votes.

All those years of training were what he was counting on to save what his heart only worked for—Emma.

'Come on baby, move.' He muttered, watching her through his scope.

'I've got a clear shot,' came the call over the earpiece.

Jaed's chest was alive with red dots standing in the open doorway of the brightly lit shed. They'd used every spotlight inside the Taskforce's suburban assault vehicle. All those times he'd driven around to look busy between training, now was the real deal, with a new set of Taskies Ryan didn't know.

Did he trust them enough?

For the first time, Ryan took charge. He told them what to do, how to do it, and had them spread along the perimeter blocking all exits, with all weapons aimed inside. More men breached the fence to line-up along the shed's side. The street was cordoned off, and ambulances waited nearby.

Sure, David might be the ranking officer in charge, but Ryan was the more experienced in this situation—and they both knew it. And he would not risk the only thing he realised he truly cared about.

'Not yet,' Ryan said through gritted teeth over the headset. 'Emma's still too close.' Ryan could take the guy, but the rounds he had in his rifle would shred steel. Unfortunately, *his* Emma stood directly behind Jaed.

She was frightened like a frozen baby wallaby under spotlights. Her fear made Ryan grind his molars, swallowing the sour taste at the back of his throat. He inhaled the familiar scent of gun oil and polished steel of his weapon that he could strip down and rebuild in less than a minute. His cold fingers restrained to not squeeze that trigger until absolutely certain, because one wrong move and they might hit her.

'That Jaed's got no gun in his hand,' said David beside him on the roof, wearing his bulletproof vest with the radio in hand. 'Give the kid a moment. He hasn't harmed her,' ordered David over the mic. 'She'll be okay, Ryan.'

Not even half an hour ago Ryan wanted to punch David in the mouth for daring to get in his way.

'The arsehole shouldn't even be there.' Ryan's blood ran

cold, it mixed with hate and fear. It was a potent combination for a man with his finger on the trigger. Ryan had never killed a man. But he'd shot plenty, trained to injure as the proficient pet for the AFP.

But this time he wanted the threat annihilated.

This was Emma. *His* Emma, in danger, and he'd never known true fear for anyone, not even for his ex-wife. Not until he'd spotted that *Parte'* van parked in Emma's driveway.

It was David who'd held him back and made him wait for the Taskies when Ryan had wanted to storm the place. In his other jobs in remote regions where he had no backup, he would have. But he'd followed orders, and that's when he stepped in and co-ordinated it all because he knew the layout of this shed well. That was Emma's home. He knew how to control the neighbour's rottweilers that were chewing up the backseat of their sedan. He had the best position, right over the fence line and could jump from here and be inside that shed in the blink of an eye. Yet, it took everything inside him to not storm the place.

But Emma had remained calm, and because she did, so would he.

Watching through the rifle's scope the only woman he cared about, his guts churned with the guilt of failure bearing down on him. He'd failed to do his job. Failed to protect the one he truly loved. But he was damned sure going to do everything he could to save her.

'Move, baby, please move.' For once he hoped her clumsy grappling-thing she did with gravity took hold. If she moved, and if that kid grabbed his weapon, Ryan would take that shot. And to hell with the consequences.

* * *

'THIS IS THE POLICE. WE HAVE YOU SURROUNDED. PUT YOUR HANDS UP AND SURRENDER, JAED ZAFAR.' Came the booming voice again.

The lights were so blinding it hurt. Emma winced and turned away and there she saw her hope and let gravity do its best. She dived for the shadows of the bar to hide.

'Emma?' Jae called out. *'Emma, where are you?'*

She couldn't help herself, she had to peek from behind the bar.

'STOP OR WE'LL SHOOT.'

Emma froze.

A line of policemen dressed in black bulletproof vests and helmets stood just beyond her large open doorway. They aimed their long automatic guns at Jae's chest that was alive with laser lights giving his skin a neon glow.

'I know what to do. I'll meet you in paradise, Stu,' Jae shouted to the air. He reached for his pistol and before he squeezed the trigger, gunfire exploded. It reverberated in the shed as Jae's body shook from bullets that shred his skinny chest.

Emma screamed, crawling backwards behind the bar until she couldn't crawl anymore and curled into herself.

'EMMA?' Ryan, called out. 'EMMA!' He ran behind the counter and found her huddled under the sinks, her arms shielding her head, trembling.

Ryan put down a massive black gun he'd been carrying and crouched before her, reaching for her hands. 'Emma, baby, it's okay. It's over.' He pulled her into his arms. 'He didn't hurt you?'

'Ryan?' She gazed at him, confused. 'How are you here?'

'You're not hurt, are you?'

'No. Jae didn't touch me.'

'Thank god.' He wrapped his arms around her, holding her tighter as she inhaled his familiar scent.

'How did you know? Why? H-how did you get in here? Is my gate still locked?'

'You called me.' Ryan helped her to her feet.

'I did?' She tapped her ringing ear. 'No, I didn't call you. I got your text message and Jae helped me open it to read it. I put the phone down on the table over there.' On shaky legs, she walked toward her table for her phone. It sat beside the ashtray still smouldering with Jae's cigarette and their half-drunk beers.

'Yes, you did. When I sent you that text message you must have pressed the dial button, and you rang me. We've been listening to you the entire time.' Ryan passed her the phone. 'See, it's still on.'

'We? That'll cost me a fortune on my next bill.' And pressed end. A phone call lasting over an hour. Had it really been that fast, when it felt like a week had been stretched into a minute? 'Dodgy phone.'

'It saved your life.'

'You heard everything?'

'I thought you knew? You warned us about his gun that he had hidden under his shirt, how he'd jumped your fence, and you got him to confess as to why he did all those crimes. Because you were so calm, it kept me calm, and I was able to plan the attack to get you out. You're a hero.'

'I did? I am?' Yet, Jae was the bad guy, who didn't seem like a bad guy, but a lost young man.

Her ears still rung from the gunfire. Police were everywhere inside her shed. All heavily armed like Ryan who was carrying one lethal looking long gun in his hand. 'You came to my rescue?'

'As soon as I realised what was happening, David and I drove straight over here. I wanted to jump the fence straight away, but David and the rest of the men held me back.' He hugged her again, whispering with his deep, silky tones that soothed her. 'You really scared me.'

'I was scared myself. I wanted you here, I kept wishing for you to be here. I'm so glad you're here. I missed you.' She clung to him, the adrenaline had her legs trembling like jelly.

'Woah, Emma, stay with me. Don't go into shock. Look at me, baby.' He held her chin to face him. 'It's over, you're safe now. I'm not going to let anything happen to you. He'll never bother you or anyone again.'

'He's dead, isn't he?'

'Let's get you upstairs, away from all these people who'll be cleaning this up for you, okay?' Ryan escorted Emma up her wrought iron stairs to her apartment.

From the landing Emma saw all as if she had box seats to oversee a nightclub's costume party she'd planned. There were officers in different styles of police uniforms busily mingling. Blue and red flashing lights spun around her shed's walls like a disco. Sirens rang like music, and the guest of honour in the centre of it all was Jae, laying on the concrete floor staring at her from the middle of a growing pool of blood. Was it time to leave—she'd never stayed to the end of a party before?

'He's dead, isn't he?' She'd never seen a dead body before.

Ryan stepped in front of her and blocked her view. 'Hey, Emma. I bought you a present today.'

'You did? Why? It's not my birthday.' Was she sleepwalking and this was all some bad dream?

'I bought you a kettle.'

'Really?' She blinked up at Ryan until he came into focus. The fluttering glitter parade in her tummy was only slight, fighting against the numbness of her body. 'Did you really buy me a kettle?'

'I did.' His grin defrosted her a little more.

'Wow, that's the best present ever. Where is it?'

'In the car and it boils in under three minutes' Ryan opened her apartment's door. 'I think you'll like it and it'll look good in your kitchen.'

She shared a meek smile.

'I'll get someone to bring it up.'

'You do realise, I'll have to reschedule my whole morning routine for the new kettle.'

'You're a flexible and adaptable lady, I'm sure you'll adjust quickly. It's one of the many things I love about you, Emma.'

'Huh?' Did Ryan just say the L word?

With an arm around her shoulders, he led her inside and shut out the world behind them. She'd never stayed at any parties because she wanted to avoid the mess that was always left at the end.

EIGHTEEN

The rumble of the beefy engine surrounded him as Ryan steered his bike down the familiar road. He nodded at the neighbour on the corner, Mr Brunswick, seated under his caravan's annexe with a blue cattle dog at his feet.

He rode down to the end of the cul-de-sac that was all quiet now. So different from a week ago when the *Parte'* van had come home and the place had been surrounded by the police.

The night of Emma's phone call, and the sight of the *Parte'* van in her driveway, had twisted Ryan's stomach into knots. It was the night pure fear had run like ice through his veins. A true fear, not for himself, but for Emma. A fear he never wanted to experience again.

But it was also the first time he'd taken charge, proving to himself he was fit for this job, and how much he truly cared about Emma.

Ryan steered past the wide double gates. The red carpet lay before the fancy front door with potted palms on either side below the hooded awning. So normal.

The wide side-door of the shed stood open and the four red cars were parked under the trees in the driveway. *Ah-huh, the Glitter Parade was here.*

Ryan rode his Harley down the side of the shed. The

neighbour's super tame rottweilers wagged their tails as they followed him along the fence line. He turned the bike around and parked just inside the open doors, facing the driveway for a quick exit. He switched the bike off and there was instant quiet. Ryan removed his helmet, then grabbed the black leather saddle bags off the back.

At the centre table sat Victoria with an unlit cigarette in hand, beside her were Benjamin and Helen. There were no jugs of Bloody Marys, no neon lights lit over the bar, no glitter, and no music pumping. 'Is Emma upstairs?' His eyes followed the wrought iron staircase to her roof-top apartment.

'Where else,' said Benjamin.

'Did Emma help set-up today?' Ryan asked the bouncing assistant, who had the most well-developed calves Ryan had ever seen on a guy who wasn't a bulked-up body builder. Benjamin said his springy step and over developed calves were from his days as a cabaret-dancing, Tina Turner impersonator.

'No. Helen helped me,' replied Benjamin. 'Took twice as long, guess that's why the boss-lady sent us out earlier.'

Ryan frowned. Emma hadn't left since the shooting.

It'd taken her ages just to go downstairs.

He'd made sure there was no evidence left. Even enlisting their corner neighbour, Mr Brunswick to help him, using his gurneys to clean the entire shed floor. His lady didn't need any reminders. 'Has Emma got any functions on for the next few days?'

'Why?' Asked Helen, sitting tall with chin raised.

He'd had little to do with Emma's sister and didn't know if he wanted to. Ryan hitched the black leather bag higher up his shoulder and said, 'I thought I might kidnap Emma for a few days.' He didn't need their permission, but their approval made life easier.

'We were just planning on ways to get her out of the shed, to hopefully break this rut she's in. Emma's never been like this,' said Benjamin, resting his chin on his hand with elbow leaning on the table that was clear of any creativity.

'Do you blame Emma? Held hostage in her own shed,' said Helen in disgust.

'We know this, Helen. Why, what have you got in mind, Ryan?' Victoria asked. 'And why would you want to kidnap Emma, considering she was a hostage?'

'Can you do that, kidnap?' Benjamin asked.

'Figure of speech. I'm a cop, not a crook.' Ryan had to admire their protectiveness over Emma. He was the same. 'Benjamin, does Emma have many functions on for the rest of the week?'

'No.'

'I thought you'd be so busy,' Helen said to Benjamin, 'you have all those bookings for the next month?'

'Emma's been so busy being busy, she's so well prepared we're ahead for the next two months of party preparations. They're all in boxes on the shelf to load and set-up, even with checklists and plans all set.'

'The babe knows what she's doing. She is the best in the biz, and even emailed me ideas for my wedding.' Victoria sucked on her unlit cigarette and exhaled.

'Does that mean Emma's wedding planning again?' Helen asked.

'For friends only,' said Benjamin with raised chin.

'At least Emma's finally agreed to be in my wedding as my right-hand babe,' said Victoria.

'I can't wait. I get to assist Emma who'll assist you. She's also said she'll help me too. Did you start Emma's pre-wedding checklist quiz? I started it with Simon last night for our wedding, it opened up a whole new dialogue for us,' said Benjamin. 'I guess I could use this spare time to research. All I have left is the minimal admin duties of phones, email, plant watering and mail collection, until the set-ups on the weekend.'

'Good. Then you can feed the cat while we're away.' Ryan knew Emma hadn't been sleeping, hiding behind her work. So now she had no excuse for what he wanted to do.

'Mister ignores me.' Benjamin sighed, peeking over his shoulder at the empty perch where Mister usually watched all.

Was it because the cat was deaf, when all three at that table were impossible to ignore? But Ryan did, jogging up the stairs. But they'd been there for Emma like he wanted to be there for her now.

Ryan knocked on the apartment door and walked inside.

'Hello?' The kitchen was empty except for his shiny kettle standing on the bench next to the coffee plunger. It was one of the best things he'd ever done, giving her that kettle was a gift they both enjoyed.

It was also the most amount of money he'd ever spent on a kettle in his life, but there was no more thirty-minute-waits for the perfect cup.

But Emma wasn't admiring her view through the treetops at the table while sipping her morning coffee. She wasn't on any of the comfy couches to watch a movie, nor reading in the perfect spot for a library upstairs. There were no vinyls playing to dance to while they cooked dinner side-by-side in the kitchen. All precious images of past scenes they'd shared before that damned van came back. Now nothing.

That left one area. Ryan walked to the large bedroom and knocked, pushing the door open. It was dark and cool and there she was, seated on her king-sized bed working on her laptop, just like he'd left her this morning. But she was dressed, coffee cup on the bedside table, curtains closed, and the cat, Mister, on the bed. 'Hi.'

'Hi, was that your bike downstairs?'

'Yeah. What are you doing?'

Her big slate-blue eyes were dull with none of that shine that used to reflect the sky, and there no smile. He hadn't seen her full smile, not since the van came home.

'I'm surfing the net for some ideas,' Emma said. 'Is it your day off?'

'Yes, and for the next two days, so I'm taking you out. I want you to pack this bag for yourself for the night. It's all the room you have, so pack light.' He dropped the saddle bag onto the bed. 'Hey, Mister.' He didn't mind the cat that came up for a scratch on the bed. 'Tough day at the office, mate.' The way the grey cat yawned and purred amongst the soft doona was soothing. They'd both been worried that they'd lost the cat from the gunfire. But being deaf, he came home to his perch on the shelf the next day, crying loudly for his dinner. Emma had shed happy tears at the sight of him.

'Why do I need to pack light?'

'Because we're going out.' He walked over to her chest of drawers.

'But I've got—'

'Benjamin says he's got your functions covered. If you won't pack, I will. Underwear first, so I can check out your collection.' With his back to her, he grinned and opened a top drawer.

'Hey.' Emma jumped off her bed and pushed the drawer shut. 'That's personal.'

'Have you got red lace G-strings in there?'

'Never you mind.' She stared up at him and colour brushed across her cheeks. It was an improvement to her pale complexion.

'Pack, get dressed, please. Boots again are a requirement.' Pointing to her socked feet.

'Um, my coat's dirty, so I can't go.'

'Don't need it, because I bought you a better one.' He pulled a small black leather jacket from his saddle bag and hoped he'd done the right thing.

'Wow, it's nice.' She held the leather jacket like it was priceless, the same way she did with the kettle he'd given her. Emma was practical and liked surprises, and she'd certainly been a surprise to him.

'It's a safety jacket designed for riders, like mine. I've never bought clothes for a woman before, but it's adjustable.' Should he take her lingerie shopping for his birthday? *Hell yeah.*

'It's unusual these holes?'

'That's a special pocket for your phone, where the headphones go through here to your helmet. Or, if you care to share, in our new helmets, there's a digital amp Bluetooth audio system I'm keen to try out.'

'Really?' Her eyes sparkled. He saw it.

It wasn't the full spark, but it gave him hope he was on the right track. 'Didn't you tell me that music was made to move? And I like your playlist or we can use mine, but it's nowhere near as good as yours.' Her collection was endless, she had a wall full of vinyls and her phone, tablet, and PC were all networked to one never ending stream of music.

But she hadn't played anything since that night.

'Now, where are your boots? There.' Inside her huge closet that was half empty he grabbed her boots. He'd never seen a woman's closet so barren before and liked that about Emma. She wore what fit to suit her day. No fuss. 'You've got ten minutes or I'll pack for you.'

He dropped her dress boots at her feet. Maybe he should get her a proper pair of boots for the bike for Christmas?

'What if I say no?'

'I'm not taking a no on this, Emma. I'm quite prepared to throw you over my shoulder, take you downstairs and handcuff you to the bike. You're going.'

'But—'

'No buts. Pack now. I'll let the cat out.' Ryan was determined to get her out of this place, to find that spark in her eyes, and wasn't going to let her talk her way out of it. Not today.

Ryan let Mister out onto the landing where the cat dashed across to the massive shelving system. He was safe there.

So was Emma, where he watched her pack and change, then led her by the hand down the stairs to the bike so she wouldn't trip. He wasn't giving her any chance of running away from him and his bike.

'Oh sweetie, I love that jacket, where'd you get it?' Called out Benjamin.

'Ryan got it for me. Did I thank you for the jacket?' Emma asked Ryan as he strapped the saddle bags to the back of his bike.

'Don't need to. Wearing it is thank you enough for me. You look good in it.' He was proud he'd chosen well, and proud of the blush brushing her cheeks.

'Where are you going?' Helen asked.

'No idea, Ryan won't tell me.'

'And I won't until you get there.' Ryan helped Emma put on her new helmet, set her music up, and with a roar of the engine they headed out on his mission to find Emma's smile.

* * *

Emma rode behind Ryan as he steered his Harley along the road. She stared blankly through her sunglasses, where everything was a blur, with the music silent in her ears.

No matter how hard she tried to shake it off, she couldn't stop thinking about what happened to Jae. Jae had said he was sorry. Said he wouldn't hurt her and had explained his reasons while returning her van.

But to throw himself at the police like that?

What would've happened if she hadn't accidentally called Ryan that night? Would Jae have kept on drinking with her, turning his anger against her?

But to go out like that and give up on life so young, when

there was so much more life to live for. Life was a present to be cherished, a gift you just didn't return or check out, it was more.

As the final thought rattled inside her, Emma sat taller and took in the scenery that passed her. It'd been nothing but buildings and congested traffic when they'd started this journey.

Now, it was lush open fields and valleys of trees. A few clouds floated like cotton candy in the blue sky. Ahead of her, the black road rolled out like liquorice disappearing into the sloping hills. It was like a cinematic curtain revealing moment, where the *Movie of Life* began.

There were no other cars, no trucks, and no streetlights. It was as if they were the only two people on the road.

She inhaled the clean air whipping past her like she was flying. The music sang in her ears, while she wrapped her arms around Ryan's waist giving him a gentle squeeze. She'd been lost in some crazy world. And, yet again, Ryan had shown her the ordinary could be extraordinary, and its beauty trickled back into her world.

And for the first time in a week…

Emma smiled.

Ryan steered his Harley down a lane that went through the centre of the forest. Enormous fir trees lined the road where she had to crane her neck back to find the blue sky. It opened to a clearing and there stood an impressive rustic two storey lodge.

But Ryan kept riding further down the road from the lodge. She peered over his shoulder and gasped.

He stopped just beyond a clearing, in a dirt carpark area. Turning the bike off, he held her arm as Emma got off as elegantly as she could, still feeling the engine's vibrations and the adrenaline rush of the ride. But it was the scenery that took her breath away. It was like standing in the middle of a postcard. It was perfect.

Fallen leaves and rich earthy soil softened the steps beneath her boots. She stopped on the edge of a large clear blue lake and lifted her chin to the slight breeze, carrying a vibrant crispness that brushed against her cheeks. The water was like soft glass, reflecting the sun and sky, edged by a silent forest nestled in the hills, cocooning this secret wonderland.

'Are you okay?' Ryan asked from behind her.

'This is awesome!' Her voice echoed across the water, the natural acoustics repeating her words, listening to her own laughter.

Ryan's laugh behind her made her smile more. He'd been by her side this entire week, making sure she was never alone, yet giving her the space needed.

And he'd bought her a kettle.

She didn't want to hold on to the past and had happily retired the old one. For good.

'Thank you, Ryan. For this, and for being there.' Life was a gift of discovery, the more you opened the packaging the greater the surprise inside. Like the man himself.

Ryan helped her remove her helmet and set it on his bike. 'My pleasure. We'll be staying up at the lodge for the night, but I wanted to show you the lake first. They've got rowboats and we can go fishing or just float on the water if you want. We might keep your phone on dry land, huh?'

'I'd like that, I've never been fishing. Have you ever brought anyone here before?'

'No, just you. I used to come up here when I had a problem I needed to sort out. Hanging out here helped put things into perspective for me in the past, I'm hoping it might do the same for you.'

'You are such an amazing person. I still can't believe you'd bother with someone like me.'

His frown flickered and he stepped closer taking her hand in his. With the other hand, he held her chin and gave her that sexy steely stare of his. 'Listen please, Emma, I've told you before I'm not perfect. You have to stop—'

But she stepped back, pushing on his chest. 'I have to ask, how much of that conversation did you hear, the one between me and Jae?'

He grinned at her. 'All of it.'

She hid her hot face in her palm and turned away, but he wouldn't let go of her other hand. 'Who else listened in?'

'A few. I told you, I recorded it for David and I to work out how best to get you out of there. You were giving us vital clues while calmly carrying on a conversation. So please, don't take it personally, okay? It's evidence, and it's locked away now. It's safe. And okay, I'll admit it, I've listened to that phone conversation a few times now.'

'Why?' Emma bit on her bottom lip and wanted to go drown herself in the lake. She'd revealed secrets she'd told no one, except to a guy with a gun. He'd confessed, she'd confessed.

It broke her company policy of *what was said in her shed—stayed in the shed* because her conversation of secrets had been broadcast to the police.

'When I first heard you on the phone live, I didn't take it

all in. I was more worried about you. I just wanted to jump that fence to get to you, but David and the others held me back. So yes, I listened to that tape again.'

'What did you hear?'

'You were scared, nervous, and yet you showed an amazing amount of empathy for that guy. You saw the good in him like you see the world with open compassion towards other human beings. Jae had issues, but they're not your burden to carry.'

She rubbed the heel of her palm over her heavy heart.

'Now the investigation is over, do you want the van dropped off at the shed?'

'No.' She shook her head and gazed at the lake's pristine waters. 'I'd like to take it to a detailer to clean it up and get rid of the logo, then sell it at the auctions.'

'Good idea. With that van's stereo system alone, you'll get a good price.'

'I hope so. I'd like to combine the money from the sale and the insurance claim to buy something else. With your help?' She shrugged. 'I don't want to hold on to it, it's got too many bad memories.' Like the old kettle she no longer needed—it was a gift that wasn't meant for her. It was time to move past all those things that held her back.

'I don't mind looking at cars with you, and keeping you safe from car salesmen. Feel free to use my ute at any time.'

'Thank you, that's very generous of you.' Ryan was so giving, but was she deserving? 'Why did you listen to that conversation so many times?'

'It gave me an insight into the person you are and what

you've experienced in your past that made you who you are today.'

'I said stuff about you. I think bingo was mentioned?' She winced.

His grin flashed wide. 'I'm the grand prize in the International lotto for lovers.'

'*Oh man.*' Again, she hid her face in her hands.

'Hey?' Ryan gently turned Emma around to face him. 'That conversation allowed me to learn a lot about who you are. I didn't do that to judge you, or to use that against you, but to learn how I could love you more. When I was listening to your conversation live, I didn't truly hear because I was gripped with this true fear I'd never known before.'

'You weren't the only one.'

'I know, I heard it, and I was frightened to death of losing you. It made me realise how much I love you, Emma. You have so many amazing qualities that the more I learn, the more I love about you. I'm in love with you.'

'Why? How?'

'It's true.'

Emma opened her mouth to speak, but he put his fingers over her lips to stop her.

'You are the most incredibly courageous woman I've ever met. You taught me how the smallest can be the biggest and the softest is the strongest person, which is you.'

Her eyes widened at his words, but did she have the courage to truly hear what he was saying?

'Whether it's too soon and you want to tell me to back off or something or slow down, I'm okay with that. But I am not going anywhere, Emma, you have to believe that, because I want to spend the rest of my life with you.'

'You mean that, don't you?'

'What do you think?' Ryan grinned at her, but the way he focused on her, she was his entire world.

How dare she say no to that?

Ryan was the good that came out of the bad from this whole situation. She'd met him when she was at her worst, with her van stolen, sitting in a carpark gutter with a seaside million-dollar view. Now here she was, still no van, in another car park, but with a parked Harley that shone in the sun beside a magnificent water view worth more than all the money she had.

It'd been worth it, just for this one true moment.

'I should warn you, there may be glitter found in the most unusual places, due to an interesting and unpredictable journey, you know? Adaptability and flexibility is a requirement.'

'It's been like that since I met you, and I'm not after perfection, only the perfect girl who's perfectly real for me.' He smiled at her, and she couldn't stop smiling at the fact he loved her.

Wow, someone said they loved her, and she believed he'd never take her scars for granted.

She realised, then and there, that the way to mend her past hurts was by truly living in today. And in those few words she understood that beautiful truth.

'And there it is.'

'What is?' Emma asked him.

'That smile of yours, with that cheeky shine in your eyes I saw that first time we met. It means you're back.'

'Did I go anywhere?' Emma shared a smile that didn't want to hide. 'Is this where you kiss me?'

'Only after you've admitted how you feel about me?'

'Nah, I might leave you hanging—'

Ryan kissed her, stopping all thoughts except one…

Him.

And his kiss.

Which was a kiss that was the lip dance of the divine slow dance, taking her breath away.

Giddy and punch-drunk, she sighed against his chest with her arms around his neck. The magnificent water view was the background as she gazed up at the God of Lust, her Detective Adonis who was that extra layer to her personal brand of happiness. She said with all her heart, 'I love you too.'

His smile was better than sunshine.

'I love you too, Emma. Now, I want another kiss.'

'Me too.' This time she was prepared and wrapped her arms around his strong shoulders. There was no pomp or ceremony, no crowds, no balloons, no confetti bombs or fireworks. But there was glitter from the sky reflecting sunshine across the water. The birds sang, and the leaves rustled with the breeze that was the music that accompanied her heart's song. It was the most perfect party for two, filled with the purest of emotion. Accepting his invitation, she planned to party with him well beyond…

the end.

Avoiding the
PITY PARTY

MEL A ROWE

ONE

Her STOMACH SPIRALLED like a stone sliding off the cliff's edge. 'Can I do this?' Deanne Harrison clenched sweaty palms as she peeked through the door's gap to spy on her seated guests, divided by a red carpeted aisle. Light streamed through stained-glass windows that haloed the groom standing beside his groomsmen adjusting their suits.

And they all waited for her.

Piped organ music began, and Deanne scooted to the side of the curtain just as the doors opened. 'You can do this, Lou.' She urged the first bridesmaid, who scowled at her. 'Please?'

'*Fine.*' With a death grip on her delicate floral arrangement that contrasted against her bulging bodybuilder's frame, Lou started down the aisle. Her strapless cocktail gown complimented her bleached hair spiked to near dagger points. In her mannish gait, she hobble-plodded on heels, glaring at the groom, then lurched towards the sidelines to wait and watch for the rest of the bridal party's arrival.

'Can't believe we're doing this,' muttered the petite Jane, as the next bridesmaid to walk down the aisle. With each step, Jane choked the stems of her bouquet, while her rogue ringlets sprung-free in their rebellion against the attempted intricate up-do that Deanne knew Jane had tried so hard to achieve. At the end of the aisle, Jane stopped beside Lou, scowled sideways at the groom for all to see, and then forced a smile to the waiting guests as another one of her curls escaped from its clutches.

The matron of honour, the statuesque Clare, made her appearance, with her thin-lipped grimace and red-rimmed eyes she glared at the groom from the start of the aisle.

'Clare, it'll be fine,' said Deanne, urging her friend on.

'I hope so.' Clare raised her chin, her complexion pale against her midnight hair slicked into an elegant French twist. She glided gracefully with her long-styled stride down the walkway to stand beside the other bridesmaids. There she faced the crowd, sniffed back tears, and with pursed lips she waited.

At the doorway, the father of the bride, Reg, tugged at his collar, brushed fingers through his grey receding hairline, pushed his glasses up his nose and puffed out ruddy cheeks. He sucked in his potbelly, rolled his shoulders, swallowed, and then held out his bent elbow. 'You ready to do this, luv?'

Deanne nodded beneath the fragile, snow-laced veil. Reflecting against the sun streaming through the windows, the delicate diamantes detailed within her gown sparkled tiny rainbows.

'Yeah?' She swallowed an oversized lump and tried to shake the tremored tension in her hands. 'Let's do this.' She wrapped her arm around her Dad's extended elbow, re-gripped her bouquet of lilies, and counted. 'One, two, and three ...' And they stepped in time to the music, hoping her gown's small train would trail perfectly behind them.

Reg nodded to the gathered guests as they headed down the aisle and at the end of the red-carpet, he unveiled the intended bride.

Deanne couldn't fool her father when the worry in his eyes mirrored her own.

'Um?' Reg's brow crinkled as his shoulders slumped. He blinked back tears as his teeth clamped on his quivering bottom lip.

Deanne squeezed his hand. 'It'll be okay, Dad.'

'You sure?'

'I know what I'm doing.' She hoped.

'Okay.' Reg kissed his baby girl on the cheek and replaced her veil back over her face. He took his seat in the front row beside his sniffling mother, Nan, where they gripped hands and prepared to watch in teary silence.

The groom, Darren, in his tailored suit, turned on his movie-star smile that spread across his spray-tanned features. He swept a hand through his blond hair, and he winked at the crowd where his bright blue contact lenses caught the light. He stepped in alongside his wife-to-be and they stood before the Minister and the service began.

The service was well underway when the Minister called out, 'Should anyone object to this union, speak now or forever hold your peace?'

Darren twitched his shoulders, his palms clasped tightly in front, as beads of sweat trickled down the sides of his face. He licked his lips and stared at the carpet.

Time dragged.

Outside birds twittered. Traffic shuffled. Children's laughter carried across from the park.

Inside, gowns rustled, paper programmes fanned faces,

but no one spoke.

The Minister's chest rose high as he inhaled to continue.

Darren exhaled as his stature relaxed.

'STOP.' Deanne flung her veil free as her words reverberated off the walls.

'What?' Darren asked.

Deanne turned and met his gaze. 'Did you sleep with my cousin, Katrina?'

Find the rest of the story
at your favourite online bookstore...

Did you like the story?

If so, *your opinion* matters to me!

I'd love to read your review on

GOODREADS & BOOKBUB.

Or share a cover of this book on social media so I can see
how far this story has travelled!

Please add **#Escape2HEA** for me to find you.

With much gratitude,

Mel.

ACKNOWLEDGEMENTS

Thank you!

Thank you to the Uni-Crew who shared their experiences of life within their changing multi-cultural world, you guys are the real heroes.

Thank you to the amazing *Handbrake* for not disowning me, and to my sister for her support. I'm okay with the knowledge that neither of you have ever read a word I've written, so I'm putting this right here in case you do dare to indulge.

Thank you to my online writer friends who've helped me so much in my word journey. In particular my sparkling gems, Suzie Frewin, Shona Ford, Renee Conoulty, and Claire Louisa Holderness—I can't thank you ladies enough!

Thank you for reading *Unplanned Party* that is a story that addresses a lot of today issues, the good and the bad. Perhaps we should take the time to celebrate the small moments in life where today is a present. And on that note, I thank you, again, for daring to take that chance in reading this novel.

Until next time,

Mel A. Rowe

MelAROWE.com

About the Author

Australian Bestselling Author, Mel A ROWE, creates escapes for you to enjoy from the comfort of home.

Delivered with a dash of drama, witty humour and quirky family units, Mel is known for reinventing romantic versions of *home*, taking her common characters on uncommon journeys that lead from boardrooms to billabongs as they try to find their own HAPPILY EVER AFTER.

Living in Northern Australia, Mel enjoys random outback road trips, fumbling with her camera, annoying her family with her bad singing, and making new friends in the middle of nowhere— except for water buffalos. She's been chased by a few.

Feel free to contact Mel as her word journey continues at...

MelAROWE.com

Winter's Walk

The Football Whisperer

Avoiding the Pity Party

Unplanned Party

The Australian Bestselling

ELSIE CREEK SERIES:

The ART of DUST

DIAMOND in the DUST

CAKED in DUST

XMAS DUST

Visit MelAROWE.com for more

www.ingramcontent.com/pod-product-compliance
Lightning Source LLC
Chambersburg PA
CBHW050134120726
47903CB00002B/354